LIGHT OF REQUIEM

LIGHT OF REQUIEM

SONG OF DRAGONS, BOOK THREE

DANIEL ARENSON

Copyright © 2011 by Daniel Arenson

ISBN: 978-0-9878864-1-5

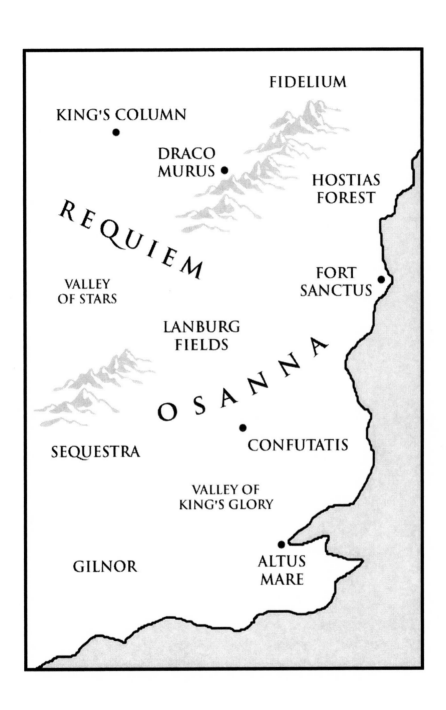

FOREWORD

Light of Requiem is the third volume of *Song of Dragons*, a series of fantasy novels inspired by Mozart's Requiem.

The first volume, *Blood of Requiem*, introduced us to the Vir Requis, an ancient race of men who can turn into dragons. *Tears of Requiem*, the second volume, continued their story.

This third novel assumes you've already read the first two. If you haven't, you'll probably still get the gist of things... though I do recommend reading *Blood* and *Tears* first.

With this introduction out of the way, I welcome you back into a world of blood, steel, and dragonfire.

TEETH

The three boys swaggered down the streets, arms pumping, eyes daring beggars, urchins, and other survivors to stare back. The dragons had left this city; so had the nightshades. In the ruins after the war, new lords arose. The Rot Gang ruled now.

"Slim pickings today," said Arms. The wiry, toothless boy was seventeen. He crossed the arms he was named for--arms long and hairy as an ape's. "We've been searching this cesspool all morning. These streets are clean."

Teeth glowered at him. "Shut your mouth, Arms," he said. With a long, loud noise like a saw, he hawked and spat. The glob landed at Arms's feet and bubbled.

Arms glowered back, spat too, and muttered.

The third Rot Gang boy--a gangly youth named Legs-- watched and smirked. Drool dripped from his heavy lips. He towered seven feet tall, most of his height in his stilt-like legs. He was dumb, even dumber than Arms, and useless in a fight. Teeth kept him around because, well, Legs made him look normal. *So what if my teeth are pointed like an animal's? Around Legs, nobody notices.*

"You like that, freak?" Teeth asked him. "You like me yelling at old Arms here?"

Legs guffawed, drooled, and scratched his head. He had a proper name, though Teeth didn't know it. He didn't care. Freaks didn't deserve proper names.

"Yeah I like Arms angry, I do," said Legs. "Makes me laugh, his little eyes, all buggy like so." He brayed laughter.

Arms turned red. His eyes did bulge when angry. He trundled toward Legs and punched his face. The lanky boy screamed. Tears welled up in his eyes. He swiped at Arms, but the wiry youth dodged the blow.

Teeth spat again. "Useless in a fight, you freak," he said to Legs. "I don't know why I keep you around. Come on, break it up! You want to eat tonight? Let's keep looking. You too, Arms. There are bodies left in this city. We'll find them. And if we can't, we'll make our own."

Legs was crying and Arms muttering. Teeth snarled, pushed them forward, and the Rot Gang kept moving down the street. Blood dripped from Legs's nose, leaving a trail of red dots.

Confutatis lay in ruins. Fallen bricks, shattered statues, and broken arrows covered the city. The nightshades had done their work well; the dragons had finished it. You could go days without seeing a soldier, priest, or guard, but you always saw urchins. They huddled behind smashed statues, inside makeshift hovels, or simply under tattered blankets. When they saw the Rot Gang, they cowered and hid. Teeth smirked as he swaggered by the poor souls. On the first week after the dragons, when survivors were claiming their pockets of ruin, many children had challenged him, adults too. His sharpened teeth had bitten, severing fingers, ears, noses. One boy, he remembered, had tried to steal a chicken from him; Teeth had bashed his head with a rock, again and again, until he saw brains spill. The memory boiled his blood and stirred his loins. He missed killing.

Legs guffawed and pointed. "Hey boss, look here, you see them, little ones, hey." He snickered and wiped his nose, smearing blood and mucus across his face.

Teeth stared. He saw them. A gaggle of urchins--little girls, eight or nine years old by the look of them. They hid behind a fallen statue of Dies Irae. One cradled a dog in her arms. When they saw the Rot Gang, the girls froze. Then they began to flee.

"Catch them," Teeth commanded.

Arms and Legs took off, the former lumbering like an ape, the latter quick as a horse. Teeth stood and watched. Three girls disappeared into a maze of fallen columns. Arms hit one girl with a rock, knocking her down. Legs grabbed the girl with the dog.

"Bring her here," Teeth said.

The girl was kicking and screaming, but Legs held her tight. Arms approached with his own catch. He held his girl in his arms; she was unconscious, maybe dead.

"Let go, help, help!" The girl in Legs's grasp was panting, face red. Her dog shivered in her grasp.

Teeth stepped forward. He snatched the dog from the girl. He clutched it by the neck, squeezed, and held it out.

"You want your dog back, you little whore?" he said. His blood boiled. A smile twisted his lips. The mutt was squirming and squealing, but powerless to escape.

The girl nodded. "Give him back. Let go!"

Teeth slammed the dog against the ground. It whimpered. Teeth kicked it hard, and it flew toward Arms. The apelike boy laughed and kicked it back, and blood splattered the cobblestones.

"Kick dog!" Legs said. "Kick dog, I want to play it."

The girl screamed and wept as they played. Finally Teeth grew bored. The dog was no longer squealing, and the game was no longer fun.

"Enough," he said. "We've come seeking bodies, not whiny little whores. Legs, let her go."

The gangly boy dropped the girl. Her knees hit the cobblestones, and her skin tore, but she seemed not to notice. She raced forward, lifted her dead dog, and cradled it.

Teeth laughed. "You idiot. The damn thing's dead. What kind of freak wants a dead dog for a pet?" He scratched his chin. "I wonder if Irae would pay for a dead dog."

Arms shook his head. "Nah. No way. You know Blood Wolves?"

Teeth glared at him. "You know I do. You know I hate Blood Wolves. You calling me an idiot, Arms? If that's what you're doing, I'll play some Kick Arms and have a nice body to sell."

Legs laughed, spraying saliva. "Kick Arms, Kick Arms, I like to play it."

Arms picked his nose. "I ain't calling you nothing. Cool it, Teeth. But Blood Wolves, you see, they've been bringing dead dogs, and horses, and whatnot. I hear the soldiers speak of it. Even brought a whole dead griffin, they did, Sun God knows how they dragged it. Worth coppers at best, the dogs. A griffin might fetch gold, maybe, but not dogs and horses and all that rubbish. He needs limbs most, human limbs. Heads too. Men, you know. With brains and whatnot. That's how you make mimics, not dogs." He snatched the dead dog from the girl and tossed it. It flew over a pile of bricks, and the girl ran weeping to find it.

Teeth knew that Arms was right. Sometimes he saw mimics with animal parts--a horse's hoof here, a dog's head there--but they were rare. Human bodies were what the Rot Gang specialized in, but pickings *were* slim lately, other gangs were growing, and their pockets were light. Teeth knew it was a matter of time before they'd have to stop hunting bodies... and start making bodies.

But who *could* he kill? The urchins were too small, mere children with frail limbs; Dies Irae wouldn't pay much for them. And it seemed everybody else in this city had joined larger gangs, arming themselves with daggers, clubs, even swords. *And I only have one knife, an apelike oaf, and a skinny giant who'd piss himself in a fight sooner than kill a man.*

"All right, let's go, north quarter today. Lots of ruins there. Bodies underneath them, rotting maybe, but they'll still fetch some coin, good bronze too."

They continued through the winding streets, passing by fallen forts, crushed hovels, and cracked statues of Dies Irae. Old blood stained the cobblestones. Nightshades' ash and dragons' fire had blackened the ruins. Teeth remembered the battle, not a moon ago. The five dragons had swooped upon the city, blowing fire. Benedictus the Black had led them, and he led griffins too. Nightshades had fought them, and Teeth had never seen so much fire and blood; it rained from the sky. The next day, as men lay rotting in the streets, Teeth had begun to collect.

Finally they reached the smaller, northern quarters, where there were barely streets anymore, merely piles of bricks and wood.

"Dig," Teeth barked at the other boys.

They climbed onto the piles of debris and began rummaging. Wind moaned around them, smelling of rot. Teeth cursed as he worked. If there were no bodies left in the city, there was no money either. He'd have to escape into the countryside like so many others.

I could become an outlaw... live in the forests, hunt travellers, grab plump peasant girls when I can find them. That didn't sound too bad, but Teeth knew little about the forest; he had spent his life on these streets.

I could join the Earthen too, if they're real, he thought. Folks whispered about the Earthen sometimes--wild Earth God followers who lived in caves. Some said they were building weapons, preparing for a strike against Dies Irae, the man who had toppled their temples and banned their faith. But Teeth didn't care much for gods or holy wars, no more than he cared for the wilderness. *This city is a cesspool, but it's all I know.*

The smell of decay hit his nostrils with a burst, so strong he nearly fell over. Teeth spat, dizzy. He pulled aside two bricks and saw a rotting head. He pulled it up by the hair; it came loose from its body. The head was pulsing with maggots, so bloated it looked like a leather sack. Teeth tossed it aside in disgust, and it burst.

"Bah! These bodies are useless now." He clenched his fists. "They're too old, too swollen, no good for anyone anymore. How would Irae sew these together? You just look at them, and they fall apart. Nothing left of them but rot."

Behind him, Arms brayed a laugh. "I tolds you, Teeth. I tolds you. We need to bring animals, dogs and whatnot, and those little girls maybe, they have teeth that can bite."

Teeth growled. He marched across the pile of bricks and grabbed Arms's collar. "Dogs? Little girls? I want silver, Arms. Gold if we can get it. Not copper pennies. I'm not a beggar like the Blood Wolves."

Arms stared, eyes burning. "I should join the Blood Wolves, I should. Look at you. This is your gang? A group of freaks. You with your dog teeth, and Legs with those stilts of his. It's pathetic, it is."

Legs guffawed and drooled. "Dog teeth, dog teeth! I like to see them."

Teeth growled, drew a knife from his belt, and held it at Arms's throat. Arms stiffened and his eyes shot daggers.

"You don't like it here?" Teeth hissed. His stomach churned and rage nearly blinded him. His hands shook and his heart pounded. "You want to join the Blood Wolves?"

Arms snarled, the knife at his neck.

"Yes," he hissed.

Teeth swiped the knife across his throat. Blood spurted. For an instant, Arms seemed not to notice. He merely stared, eyes narrowed. Then he grabbed his throat, trying in vain to stop the blood. He fell to his knees, and suddenly he was weeping, and trying to speak, trying to breathe, but he could do neither.

Teeth stared down at him. "There's your blood, Arms. Blood's what you wanted. Blood's what you got. And I got my body. A body with nice long arms."

He could have given Arms a better death. He could have finished the job--stabbed him in the heart, or bashed in his head. But Teeth wanted to watch. He stood over the thrashing boy until

Arms merely twitched, stared up with pleading eyes, then gurgled and lay limp. For several moments he merely whimpered and his eyelids fluttered. And then Teeth had his body for the day.

The wind moaned as Teeth and Legs carried the body through the rubble. It cut through Teeth's clothes and pierced his skin. The blood was sticky on his fingers. The sun was setting when they saw Flammis Palace ahead. Two of its towers had collapsed, and several walls had crumbled. It wasn't much better off than the rest of the city, but Dies Irae still ruled there. His banners, white and gold, thudded atop the remaining towers. His guards covered the standing walls, bows in hand.

Teeth and Legs approached the front gates. The bricks were blackened from fire, and the doors were charred. The dragons had breathed most of their fire here when storming the palace. Guards stood at the gateway, clad in plate armor, swords in hand. Their skin looked sallow, and sacks hung beneath their bloodshot eyes. There wasn't much food in Confutatis anymore, and folk whispered that some of the guards had taken to eating the bodies. The stench of rot hung heavy here.

"New body for the Commander," Teeth told the guards. "Fresh, this one."

Legs nodded, holding Arms's other end. "Fresh, fresh! We like them that way. Yes sir we do."

The guards grunted. "All right, boys. Looks better than your last catch. In you go."

Teeth tugged the body, moving past the broken doors. Legs followed. They stepped into a hallway, its northern wall fallen. Bloodstains covered the floor and ash coated the ceiling. One column was smashed and stained red. Teeth knew the way. Hoisting the body, he turned left into a stairwell. The stairs wound into shadows. Torches lined the walls, but most were unlit. Teeth and Legs delved into the dungeons of Flammis Palace, the stairway leading them down and down into the cold and darkness. The palace was twice as deep as it was tall, and Teeth climbed down to its deepest chambers.

Screams, creaks, and squeals echoed through the tunnels. A man laughed. A saw grinded. Screeches rose and fell.

Teeth and Legs walked down a hallway, its floor sticky with blood, and entered a towering chamber. Torches lined the walls, flickering against rows of tables. Body parts covered the tabletops. Rows of legs covered one table, arms another, heads a third. A pile of torsos rotted in the corner. Uncarved bodies hung on walls and filled wheelbarrows.

Dies Irae stood at the back of the room.

Teeth froze. On previous visits, he had met underlings, not the Commander himself. He had not expected to meet Dies Irae here. Once emperor of a mighty realm, Dies Irae now ruled a wasteland of desolation, death, and disease. His skin was grey. Blood stained his clothes. He stood by a table, hunched over a rotten torso. Sleeves rolled back, he was gutting it.

Teeth cleared his throat, blinked, and tried to quell the shake that found his knees.

"Commander," he said. "We brought you a body. A fresh one, my lord."

Legs brayed. "Fresh, fresh, that's how we like them, yes sir we do."

Dies Irae looked up from his work. His one eye blazed blue. A patch covered his other eye. Teeth knew the story. Benedictus the weredragon had taken that eye from him, as he had taken Dies Irae's left arm; a steel arm grew there now, its fist a spiked mace head.

"A fresh one?" Dies Irae asked. His voice was hoarse. Wrinkles creased his brow. "Yes. Yes, very fresh."

Teeth and Legs placed the body on a table. Teeth stifled a cough, struggling not to gag from the chamber's stench. Maggots were crawling on some of the bodies. Worms filled others.

"A fresh body, and look at its arms," Teeth said. "Look at how long they are, my lord. Long and strong, like an ape's. This one's worth two silver coins, one per arm at least, my lord. A good body. Strong and fresh."

Dies Irae examined the dead body, furrowed his brow, and touched those long arms. He smiled, his lips twisting like worms. "Yes. Yes, strong. Fresh."

Teeth didn't like this. He wanted to leave. On previous visits, underlings would examine his finds, mutter, and pay. But Dies Irae seemed... too quiet, lost in his own world. Teeth noticed that specks of blood covered the man's lips. He shivered. Had Dies Irae been eating the bodies?

"My lord?" he said. There were bite marks on the body, he saw. Now Teeth definitely wanted to flee. "My lord, two silvers would be our price, if it please you. We'll find you more bodies. We're the Rot Gang."

Dies Irae walked around the table and approached him. He was tall, Teeth saw. Not as tall as Legs, maybe, but heavier, all muscle and grit. Dies Irae stared at him with his good eye.

"Those are good teeth you have there," he said. He licked his lips, smearing blood across them. "Sharp. I bet they can just... *bite* into somebody." He snapped his own teeth, as if to demonstrate. "I could use teeth like that."

Beside them, Legs guffawed. "Dog teeth, dog teeth, I like to see them. Yes sir I do."

Dies Irae turned to face him, as if seeing Legs for the first time. "Well, young man, aren't you a tall one. Look at those legs you've got there. I bet they could just...." Dies Irae stamped his feet. "*Run!* Run like the wind, I bet they can."

Legs brayed. "They run, Legs they call me, yes sir they do."

This was all wrong. Teeth found that he no longer cared about the coins.

"My lord, if you'll excuse us, we'll be on our way," he said. He turned to face the doorway.

A mimic stood there. Not a dead body, but an animated thing, patched together, sewn from the strongest parts. A creature with worms for hair, claws on its fingers, and death in its eyes. It blocked the doorway, grinning. Insects bustled in its mouth, and its eyes blazed red.

"They are strong," Dies Irae said. "They are made from the best. The best parts. I build them myself."

He swung his mace at Legs.

It hit the boy's head, crushing it.

As Legs collapsed, Teeth ran to the wall and grabbed a torch. He held it before him as a weapon.

"Don't touch me, old man!" he warned, waving the torch.

Dies Irae's lips curled back; Teeth couldn't decide if it was a snarl or a grin.

"But I *will* touch you," he said. "I will make you stronger. I will give you the right parts."

Teeth lashed his torch.

Dies Irae sidestepped.

The mace swung.

Pain exploded against Teeth's chest. The mace swung and again hit his chest. His ribs snapped. He couldn't breathe. Blood filled his mouth.

He fell to his knees. The last thing he saw was Dies Irae grinning, and the mace swung again.

Light exploded. Blood and pain flowed across him... and faded. He knew nothing more.

GLORIAE

She flew over snowy trees, a golden dragon in the wind, when her magic died and she turned human.

Gloriae yelped. The forest rushed up toward her. She tumbled. The firewood she had collected fell around her. She uselessly flapped her arms as if she still had wings. Wind howled. Gloriae gritted her teeth and tried to become a dragon again. Nothing happened. Her magic was gone.

Pain exploded.

She crashed into a snowy treetop. Branches cracked. They snapped against her breastplate, tore her leggings, and lacerated her arms. For a moment she hung between two branches, and then they too snapped. She fell ten feet, and her helmet hit another branch. White light flooded her. The pain was so intense, she couldn't even scream.

With a crack, more branches splintered, and Gloriae hit the forest floor.

She lay in the snow, moaning. Everything hurt. She dared not move, fearing the pain of broken bones.

Thank the stars for my armor, she thought. *Without my helmet and breastplate, I'd be jackal food.*

She moaned and took slow breaths. *What happened?* How could her magic fail? For thousands of years, the children of Requiem could become dragons at will, could breathe fire and soar over forest and mountain.

Gloriae pushed herself onto her elbows. Her head spun, and she blinked several times, trying to bring the world back into focus.

That was when she heard the growl.

Wolves, she thought. She leaped to her feet, which made her head spin more wildly. She drew Per Ignem, her sword of northern steel, and looked around. If she could not breathe fire, she could still swing her blade.

She heard the growl again. It came from somewhere between the trees ahead. It was no wolf, Gloriae realized. This growl was too deep, too... twisted, wrong, cruel. She had never heard anything like it, and despite herself, she shuddered. A stench filled the forest, like rotting bodies and sewage, so heavy Gloriae nearly gagged.

She wanted to call out, to ask "Who's there?", but forced herself to remain silent. Whatever creature growled ahead, it might not have seen her yet.

Slim chance, she thought. Anyone around would have seen her fall from the sky, but Gloriae was a warrior, and stealth was beaten into her like the folds in her blade. She narrowed her eyes. Her body still ached and the world still spun, but Gloriae could still kill if she had to.

The growl rose again, and a second growl sounded at her right, this one closer. Gloriae spun around, sword raised, and finally saw the creatures.

One stepped out to her right, one from ahead, and one from her left. She knew them at once.

Mimics.

"Damn it," Gloriae whispered.

For a moment, terror froze her.

They walked toward her, rotting, rustling with maggots. Dies Irae had sewn them together from body parts, mixing and matching. One had the torso of a woman, bare breasted and gutted, flies breeding in the cavity of its stomach. One of its legs was the bent, hairy leg of a man, while its arms were tiny, the arms of babies. Another mimic had the torso of a man, but the legs of a goat, and arms that ended with blades instead of hands. The third had two torsos of children sewn one atop the other, and its four hands held knives. Each was different, but each had long blond hair. Each stared with baleful blue eyes.

Each looked like her.

"Hello, mother," they whispered as one. "Hello, first Gloriae. Your father sends his regards."

Their voices--twisting, screeching imitations of her own-- snapped Gloriae out of her paralysis. She screamed and charged.

Per Ignem swung, slicing through one mimic's neck. Its head, stitched on, fell and rolled. Black blood splashed the snow. Its body, headless, lashed at Gloriae with claws.

Gloriae stepped back and stabbed a mimic to her left. She ducked, dodging another mimic's blades. The headless creature reached out its claws. Gloriae leaped forward, drove her helmet into its chest, and swung her blade, slicing another.

Claws grabbed her shoulder, bending her steel armor as if it were mere leather. Gloriae screamed, spun, and kicked. She hit the mimic's leg, snapping it. She brought down her sword. Black blood flew. The other mimics attacked.

As she jumped, dodged, and swung her blade, Gloriae remembered. The one time she had seen mimics before, she had tried to shift into a dragon, but could not. *Their magic undoes my own.*

The severed mimic's head bit her boot, and Gloriae screamed and kicked it. A severed arm grabbed her leg, cutting her with fingernails like blades. She stabbed it, freed herself, and turned to run.

She could not kill these beasts with steel, she knew. She remembered. *Fire kills them.*

As she ran, she heard them following, grunting like rutting beasts. Gloriae reached into her leather pack and grabbed her tinderbox.

Fingers grabbed her legs, and she fell. Her face hit the snow. The tinderbox flew from her hand.

Gloriae flipped onto her back, shouted, and kicked. Her boots knocked back a mimic's head. Its mouth opened to scream, spilling maggots. She kicked again and its head caved in, spraying centipedes and blood onto Gloriae's face.

Her tinderbox lay three feet away in the snow. Gloriae scurried for it.

A second mimic kicked the tinderbox aside, then walked toward her, grinning. Her sword had split its torso in half, from shoulder to navel, but still it moved, each half of its body swaying. Gloriae drove forward, swung her blade, and halved the mimic's head like a grapefruit, ear to ear. Only its jaw remained, and it squealed. Its claws sliced her shoulder, but Gloriae ignored the pain. She leaped five feet, landed by her tinderbox, and grabbed it.

Mimics screeched behind, lurching toward her.

Gloriae opened the tinderbox, gritted her teeth, and began rubbing flint against steel. *Light, damn you, light!*

A mimic grabbed her helmet and pulled her to her feet. It snarled, and drool sprayed from its mouth, green and thick with small white worms.

Gloriae frantically slashed flint on steel.

The mimic leaned in to bite.

Her tinderbox crackled with fire.

Gloriae drove it forward, shattering it against the mimic's face. The tinder spilled onto the creature, and its hair caught fire. It blazed.

She leaped back, watching the mimic burn. Cockroaches screeched and fled from it. The mimic tried to run toward her, but stumbled and fell.

The other mimics lunged at her.

Gloriae kicked the burning mimic's arm. It came loose and burned in the snow. She grabbed the arm, as if it were a torch, and swung it. The mimics cried like slaughtered pigs. Gloriae swung the arm into one's head, and its hair--blond locks like her own--caught fire. Soon its whole head burned.

One mimic remained. Gloriae stared at it, and though her wounds ached, she managed a small, crooked smile.

"Let's play," she said.

She swung her sword in one hand, the burning arm in the other. She dealt steel and fire. Black blood and maggots flew. Body parts fell, burned, screamed, and twisted.

"Gloriae," the last mimic hissed, a mere head with spilling brains, its body burning five feet away. "Gloriae, your father wants your head, and your arms, and your guts, and your--"

Gloriae stabbed it through the face, burned it, and watched it die. The stench of rotting meat and burning grease filled the forest.

She tossed the burning arm aside, disgusted. She breathed deeply, sword still in hand, blood covering her.

Mimics. Stars.

Gloriae looked around for more, and when none arrived, she examined her wounds. A finger had punched a hole through her armor, cutting her under her shoulder blade. More cuts ran along her calf. The fall onto the treetops had covered her with scratches and bumps; tomorrow bruises would cover her.

"Damn you, Irae," she whispered, staring at the burning bodies. She had killed three mimics a moon ago in the dungeons under Flammis Palace. She had never imagined Dies Irae would create more. How many mimics crawled the world now? Were more heading here, into the northwest, toward Requiem?

She had to warn the others.

She had to fly.

When she stepped far enough from the dead mimics, she found her magic. Wings sprouted from her back, scales covered her, and soon she roared as a golden dragon. She flew, crashed through the treetops, and found the sky.

She looked around, and in the distance, she saw trees sway and creak. She narrowed her eyes. Figures moved between those trees, many of them. Soon they moved into a clearing, black and red under the sun, and then disappeared into more trees.

Mimics. A hundred or more--an army of perverted humanity created by the man she had called Father. And they were heading home, to Requiem.

Gloriae cursed and flew.

KYRIE ELEISON

Kyrie was on guard duty, and he was freezing.

Snow fell, flurried in the wind, and covered his world. Kyrie saw no end to the horrible stuff. A blue dragon, he perched atop an orphaned archway, the walls around it long fallen. Below the mountaintop where the archway stood, ruins spread into the horizons: toppled walls and smashed columns and burned trees, the snow covering them all. Winter had come to the ruins of Requiem.

Kyrie shivered and wrapped his wings around him, but found no warmth.

"Stars, I hate guard duty," he muttered and spat. Snow covered him, and he shook it off, but more soon coated him.

He looked north to a valley between a cliff and mountain. Boulders rose from it like teeth, and a frozen river snaked through it. Benedictus was buried there--Kyrie's king, mentor, and brother-in-arms.

"I miss you, old friend," Kyrie whispered. "I wish you could have lived to see this, to see us back in Requiem." A lump filled his throat. "Our home still lies in ruins, but we're back, Benedictus. We've defeated the griffins, and we've defeated the nightshades, and we'll rebuild our home. The home you died to give us."

His eyes stung, and Kyrie shook his head, swallowed, and looked away. Thinking about Benedictus was too painful. *I'm the only male left. I must be strong. I'll be like him.*

Kyrie turned and looked down from his perch. A courtyard covered the mountaintop below him. Once a fortress had stood here, and warriors of Requiem had manned it. Draco Murus, they had called this place; the center of Requiem's military might. It had withstood Dies Irae's griffins longer than any other fort... but it had fallen too. Today only this archway still stood, a hundred feet tall. The rest of Draco Murus lay shattered across the mountain, buried in snow. The skeletons of a thousand Vir Requis lay buried there too.

A hole gaped open in the courtyard, and smoke rose from it. Kyrie smelled sausages and baking bread. He licked his lips. If the fortress had collapsed in the war, its dungeons were still sturdy, a network of cellars and tunnels. Lacrimosa and Agnus Dei huddled there now, Kyrie knew. They'd be warm and cozy by the fire, while he shivered here.

"Where are you, Gloriae?" he muttered. She had flown seeking firewood hours ago. Once she returned, she would guard, and Lacrimosa would fly for firewood. Then he, Kyrie, could enjoy a precious few hours in the cellars, alone with Agnus Dei.

For the first time all morning, Kyrie felt warm. He lived for those moments with Agnus Dei. He could already imagine it. While Lacrimosa and Gloriae were away, he'd hold her by the fire, warm under blankets. They'd whisper of losing Benedictus, and rebuilding Requiem, and of their love. They'd comfort each other with kisses and caresses, then undress with trembling fingers. He'd smell her hair, embrace her, and kiss her lips. She'd kiss him back eagerly, seeking healing from pain, fire to melt the world's ice. Her fingers would dig into his back, and her breasts would press against his chest, and--

With a roar, a golden dragon emerged from the clouds, flying toward him.

His dream shattered, and Kyrie started.

Gloriae panted. She all but crashed into the courtyard.

"Gloriae!" Kyrie said. "No firewood? No game? What happened?"

She looked at him, eyes fearful. Blood stained her scales.

"Gloriae, are you--?"

"Mimics," she panted. "I killed three. More are on the way."

Kyrie froze. Terror stabbed his gut, colder than the snow and wind. He remembered.

"Stars," he whispered. His heart pounded.

He leaped off the archway, landed by Gloriae, and shifted into human form. Gloriae shifted too and stood before him as a human girl. Snow filled her blond curls, her leggings were torn, and her breastplate was dented. Blood dripped from her calf and shoulder, and scratches covered her arms. Her cheeks were pink.

"They're not ten leagues away," she said. "A hundred of them, maybe more. They'll be here by nightfall."

Kyrie swallowed. His chest felt tight. He had seen mimics only once, the day Benedictus had died. They still haunted his nightmares.

He grabbed Gloriae's wrist. "Come. Underground."

They crossed the courtyard and reached a makeshift trapdoor they'd built of branches and rope. Kyrie pulled the door open, revealing a staircase leading underground. He raced downstairs, nearly slipping on the damp stone, and emerged into a cellar full of firewood, jugs of ale, and sacks of flour and lentils. He hurried into a tunnel, ran past more cellars, and entered a chamber with a crackling fireplace.

Lacrimosa, Queen of Requiem, sat there upon a fleece. The firelight danced against her pale cheeks and turned her fair hair red. Agnus Dei was stirring the fireplace with a poker. She turned toward them, her mane of black curls bouncing, her eyes wide.

"Gloriae!" Agnus Dei said. "You're hurt."

Lacrimosa rose to her feet. "What happened?"

Still panting, Gloriae sat by the fireplace. Lacrimosa sat beside her, removed the girl's armor, and began tending to her wounds. Agnus Dei sat at Gloriae's other side, smoothed her hair, and looked at her with worried eyes.

"What happened, Gloriae?" she asked.

They all listened as Gloriae spoke of meeting three mimics outside Requiem, of losing the ability to shift, of seeing many more mimics travelling west. Kyrie and Agnus Dei cursed and muttered throughout the story, but Lacrimosa only listened silently, face blank.

Once Gloriae had finished her tale and her wounds were bandaged, Lacrimosa stood up. Kyrie approached her and stared into her lavender eyes.

"Lacrimosa," he said, "we must flee. Requiem is no longer safe. I've fought griffins and nightshades a hundred times, and mimics only once, but it's that last battle that haunts me most. Let's run. Now."

Lacrimosa took a deep breath and tightened her lips. She stared into the fireplace. The twins sat by the hearth, holding each other, looking at their mother. For a long time, Lacrimosa said nothing. They all waited.

Finally Lacrimosa spoke. "What would he have done?" she said, gazing at the crackling flames. "That's what I always ask myself. I miss him so much. He'd know what to do." She took a shuddering breath. "But we must continue without him." She turned to stare at Kyrie, her eyes large and haunted. "He died for Requiem. He would want to stay and fight."

At that moment, Kyrie felt such love and pain for Lacrimosa, that he wanted to embrace her. But no; she was Queen of Requiem, and she needed no embraces from him, but strength and courage.

"I'd fight for you anywhere," he said. "But... we've always fought as dragons. We can't shift around mimics. Are you sure, Lacrimosa? There are other places to hide, places safer than Requiem's ruins."

Agnus Dei chewed her lip. She opened her mouth, shut it, clenched her fists, and finally spoke. "I want to fight! I do. I've never run from a fight. Ever! But... Mother, I'm scared." Her eyes dampened. "I was never afraid of a fight before, not against all the griffins and nightshades in the world. But I'm scared now. I... if something happened to you too, Mother, I...."

Suddenly Agnus Dei was crying. Gloriae embraced her and patted her hair, and Kyrie held her hands.

Lacrimosa squared her shoulders. The firelight danced against her face. "I might die in this fight, Agnus Dei. I might join Father in our starlit halls. I can't promise you that we'll all live. But no place is safe anymore. We've been running and hiding for over a decade, and Dies Irae sends his creatures to all corners of the world. Where more can we run? We promised Father that we'll rebuild Requiem. We promised it to him when we buried him. We cannot run forever." She gestured to a doorway, beyond which lay their armory. "We knew Irae would attack. We've stored bows and arrows, blades, and armor. We don't have much, but we've prepared."

Kyrie shook his head. "Lacrimosa, I want to fight too, but... we have only four bows, only a hundred arrows. We have only a few pieces of armor, and only Gloriae has a breastplate. We're not armed well enough. To beat two or three mimics, yes. But a hundred? We never expected that many."

Lacrimosa took a deep breath. Her eyes stared at nothing, reflective, as though staring at a memory of her husband. "We'll build more weapons." She gestured at piles of firewood that filled the chamber. "We'll build javelins and arrows and torches. We can't shift around mimics, but we can still fight them. Dies Irae is weakened now. It's time to make a stand. We will tell him: You cannot keep hunting us. Requiem is reborn, and we will defend her."

Gloriae rose to her feet and drew her sword. "Yes," she said. Ice filled her green eyes, and her cheeks flushed. "Yes. We fight. We kill. We bring fire to our enemies. I'm ready."

Agnus Dei stood up too, looked at Kyrie with uncertain eyes, then at her mother. She bit her lip, gazed to the fire, and whispered something so quietly, Kyrie could not hear. He thought he heard her say "Father". Then she clenched her fists and nodded.

"Yes," she said. Her dark eyes burned. "Yes, I'll fight too. I'm a fighter. It will be a day of flame."

Kyrie looked at the others, one by one. He loved them all, Kyrie thought; even Gloriae. He loved them so much that his chest ached. *The last Vir Requis. I will defend them. I will fight for them, and if I must, I will die for them.*

"A day of flame," he repeated. "Let us make torches, and let us make arrows of fire."

AGNUS DEI

As she worked, she couldn't stop her fingers from shaking. Piles of firewood, kindling, and jars of oil filled the underground cellars. They had been collecting it for weeks from beyond Requiem's borders, enough to last all winter, to warm their bones and cook their food. As Agnus Dei carried log after log outside, she couldn't help but shiver. She had never imagined they'd use this wood for war... to kill mimics.

Mimics. Even in the chill of winter, sweat washed her. She hated mimics. She had seen them only once, but still woke most nights, out of breath and sweaty, memories of their rot and worms filling her mind.

"I miss you, Dada," she whispered as she carried four logs upstairs, out of the cellar, and into the snowy courtyard. A pile of branches, twigs, and logs rose there, ten feet tall.

Mother stood by the wood, frowning toward the east. The wind filled her hair and fluttered her old, tattered dress. Her eyes seemed dead; no fear, pain, or mourning filled them. Agnus Dei wanted to hug her, but something held her back. She was not only her mother now, but Queen Lacrimosa of Requiem. Ruler of these ruins. Widow.

A lump filled Agnus Dei's throat.

"Here, Mother," she said and added her logs to the pile. Her sister Gloriae stepped out from the cellars behind her, also carrying wood. Finally Kyrie emerged and added more wood to the pile.

Mother seemed not to notice. She kept staring into the snowy horizons, as if imagining the mimics that approached.

"Mother," Agnus Dei whispered. Gingerly, she touched her shoulder. "We've brought the last wood from the cellars. What now?"

Mother turned to face her, and Agnus Dei realized she'd been wrong. Mother's eyes were not dead. Pain saturated them, but steel lived there too, a strength that held the mourning at bay like a breakwater holding back the waves. The passing clouds reflected in those lavender eyes. For a long moment Lacrimosa was silent, and when she spoke, her voice was soft and cold as the snow.

"You will build spears, Agnus Dei. Spears with tips of kindling, to burn mimics."

Agnus Dei nodded. She lifted a long, narrow branch from the pile. Her knuckles turned white around it. "This one will do. I will kill mimics with it."

Mother turned to Gloriae. "And you, daughter. Take our hundred arrows, and wrap their tips with kindling, and soak them with oil. Then make more arrows from straight, strong sticks; they won't have blades or fletching, but they'll still fly and burn."

Gloriae nodded. Her lips were tight, her fists clenched at her sides. The wind fluttered her golden locks and pinched her cheeks pink.

"Yes," she said. "I'm ready for fire. I'm ready to kill."

Mother then turned to Kyrie. "And you, Kyrie, will help me. We'll build a ring of fire around the fort. When the mimics arrive, it'll shield us."

Kyrie nodded. "I'm good at building fires. We'll soak the wood in oil, and crack it, and stuff kindling into it. When the mimics arrive, it'll catch fire quickly and burn high." He touched Mother's shoulder. "We'll be safe, Lacrimosa. I promise you. I... I'm no great warrior like Benedictus, but...." He swallowed and squared his shoulders. "I'll do all I can to protect you and your daughters."

Agnus Dei smiled sadly. She was better than the pup in a fight, and Gloriae was too, but she knew what he was doing, and she loved him for it. She approached Kyrie, embraced him, and kissed his cheek. He held her, his gloves sticky with sap.

"I love you, pup," she whispered, her head against his shoulder.

Another pair of arms held her, and Agnus Dei saw that Gloriae joined the embrace. For a moment the three stood, warm in their embrace as the wind blew. Then they broke apart.

"We prepare for fire and for war," Agnus Dei said.

She began collecting the long, straight branches from the pile. She placed them in a corner of the courtyard, in the shadow of the archway. *They'll make good spears,* she thought. *Not strong spears like those of soldiers, carved from the heart of boles and tipped with steel, but they'll do.* Gloriae was collecting the smaller sticks and placing them at the courtyard's other end. Kyrie and Lacrimosa were collecting logs, crooked branches, and any pieces the twins could not use; they began arranging them in a ring around the courtyard.

As she worked, Agnus Dei kept scanning the horizon for the mimics. From here upon the mountaintop, she could see leagues of ruins. The land was dead.

When will the mimics arrive? The wind howled, and Agnus Dei shivered. The sun was setting, and it was getting colder. The clouds thickened.

When evening fell, a ring of wood and kindling surrounded the fort's courtyard, soaked in oil. Torches stood in the ground in an inner ring, two feet apart; wherever mimics attacked, the Vir Requis could grab one to swing. Piles of javelins tipped with oiled brushwood lay around the courtyard for easy access. Each Vir Requis wore a steel helmet, greaves, and vambraces. Gloriae wore her breastplate too. They each held a bow, and their quivers held arrows tipped with oiled straw.

"We're ready for battle," Agnus Dei said, surveying the scene. Splinters, sap, and oil covered her gloves.

Kyrie raised an eyebrow. "Ready? No. This is not what I'd call ready. If we had a hundred men, I wouldn't call us ready. But it's as ready as we'll be this night."

Snow began to fall again, and Agnus Dei cursed.

"Will the wood light when wet?" she asked.

Kyrie frowned. "We soaked it with oil. I hope so." But his eyes didn't look hopeful, and his fists tightened.

The sun sent a last flicker of red light, then sank behind the horizon. The wind screamed, and Agnus Dei shivered. She clutched Kyrie's hand.

"I'm scared," she whispered. "Where are they?"

Gloriae and Lacrimosa came to stand by them. They held their bows.

"Do not light fires yet," Lacrimosa whispered. "We don't want a beacon for mimics to see."

Agnus Dei held Kyrie's hand so tightly, he grunted, but she would not let go. She kept scanning the valleys around them, but saw nothing in the darkness. The wind pierced her cloak. She wanted to shift into a dragon, to blow fire, to rush into battle, but dared not. Her magic would fail once those creatures arrived. Agnus Dei gritted her teeth.

"I wish they'd show up already," she said, struggling not to scream out challenges to them. "I hate the waiting. I hate the dark. I want a fight. I want--"

A howl rose in the distance.

Agnus Dei squeezed Kyrie's hand.

For a moment nobody spoke.

"A jackal?" Agnus Dei finally whispered.

A second howl answered the first, distant but loud, gurgling and rising to a squeal.

"That's no jackal," Gloriae said. She hefted her tinderbox. "It's them."

Agnus Dei scanned the night, but saw only shadows. "I can't see them!"

"Quiet," Gloriae said, voice like silk. "Do not speak."

The wind moaned, and another howl sounded. Agnus Dei snarled. Her fingers trembled, and her heart thrashed. Suddenly she wanted to flee, to shift into a dragon and fly for leagues, to disappear into the west.

Stay strong, she told herself. *For my family, and for Kyrie.*

"Come on," she whispered and growled. "Come on, you bastards. Show yourselves."

Grunts sounded in the distance, and squeals, and thumping feet. A creature screamed, a chilling sound like a slaughtered animal. A rumble answered it, and a shrill cry like a dying cat.

"Weredragons!" rose a cry, high-pitched and inhuman. "We smell them. Yes, brothers. We smell them ahead. We will suck the marrow from their bones."

Agnus Dei released Kyrie's hand and reached into her pack. She clutched the tinderbox she kept there. Strangely, her fingers no longer trembled, and her heart steadied. Now was not the time for terror. Now was the time for battle, for fire, for blood.

"Be brave, Kyrie," she whispered, speaking to herself more than to him. "Be brave for the memory of Father."

The howls grew closer, and a stench hit Agnus Dei's nostrils, a stench of bodies. Countless feet thumped up the mountainsides. Screams curdled her blood.

"Weredragons! We smell them, brothers. We smell sweet blood and marrow. Ahead! On the mountaintop!"

Agnus Dei opened her tinderbox. She placed its flint against firesteel, prepared to strike a spark.

A night of fire. I will be brave, Father. For your memory. I will fight well.

A light flickered--Gloriae lighting her own tinderbox, and soon an arrow blazed in her bow.

Agnus Dei sparked flint against steel, drew an arrow from her quiver, and lit it. She nocked, drew her bowstring, and aimed.

"They have fire, brothers! Fire ahead. They seek to burn us! Feed upon them. Make them as we are!" The squeals and screams filled the darkness.

A third light flickered; Kyrie igniting the ring of fire. It burst into flame around them, a towering wall of light and smoke and heat. Lacrimosa was hurrying from torch to torch, lighting them too--hand-to-hand weapons, should the creatures breach their defenses.

Agnus Dei could see the mimics now, and she couldn't help it. She screamed.

A hundred scurried up the mountainside like cockroaches. They were creatures of rot, worms, maggots, bones and stitches. Blood covered their teeth. Their eyes blazed, and their claws reached toward them. Their leader bore two swords. When it held them out, Agnus Dei saw that its arms were seven feet long; each was sewn together from three normal arms, like a string of sausages.

"Weredragons!" this mimic cried, voice guttural and thundering. It brandished its swords. "I will feast upon your entrails."

Another voice rose, commanding and deep, and Agnus Dei realized it was Mother.

"Burn them!" she cried and fired a flaming arrow. "Burn them dead."

Her arrow pierced the night, a comet of fire, and slammed into a mimic's chest. The creature screamed and fell.

First blood spilled. The mimics screamed and charged.

MEMORIA

Memoria had never gotten used to living in an ice palace.

Even after all these years, she remembered and missed her house in Requiem. She remembered walking upon mosaic floors, stepping over dolphins and elks and dragons, and how the colorful stones tickled her bare feet. She remembered the rafters of her attic, where she'd hide and read books. In her mind, she still saw the balcony over the vineyard, where she'd paint the sunsets. Most of all, she remembered the southern warmth, how she'd lie in the garden and soak up the sun, hear the birds, and watch the dragonflies.

Here there were no birds or dragonflies, no gardens or trees, no warmth. She lived in a palace now, but it was built of ice. The floor, the ceiling, the columns that rose two hundred feet tall; nothing but ice, cold and glimmering and cruel to her southern bones. She could see the sun through the ceiling, blurred and small, but even it seemed cold, like the glimmer of icicles.

She walked across Whale Hall, her slippers silent. Few elders came to Whale Hall anymore; it was an ancient place where ice crystals rose like a whale's ribs. It had become her sanctuary, her place of prayer. At the edge of the hall the ceiling was thin, and sunlight fell like raining fireflies. Memoria knelt in the sunbeams, the ice hard against her knees, and closed her eyes. She wrapped her seal furs around her, this raiment of exile, and whispered to her stars.

"If you're up there, Kyrie, know that I love you. If you watch over me from Draco's stars, hear my words." She hugged herself, and her eyes stung. "I love you forever, little brother. I miss you every day."

She heard footfalls behind her, opened her eyes, and turned to see her second brother. Terra was walking toward her, clad as always in his old armor. Frost coated the filigreed plates, his horned helmet, and the silver scabbard of his sword. He wore a walrus moustache in the style of the bellators, Requiem's noble warriors; he was the last of their order, but still clung to their symbols. A fur cloak draped over his shoulders, a single piece of the north over his steel garb of southern glory.

"Sister, I worry for you." He sighed. "You spend hours here, speaking to him every day. I miss our brother too. I loved him. But... Memoria, how do you know that he hears?"

Memoria stood up and glared at him. Terra was tall and broad, and she was short and slim, but she glared at him nonetheless. His hair was fair like hers, but already white kissed his temples. His eyes were brown like hers, but sadder, she thought; weary eyes that had seen too much. He was two years her senior, thirty this winter, but looked forty. Youth's hope and grace had left him. She remembered him a dozen years ago, always laughing, bronzed from working in their vineyard. She had not heard him laugh since.

Not since our baby brother left us, she thought. *Not since Kyrie died at Lanburg Fields. My sweet, small Kyrie, the light of our family... forever extinguished, forever a hole inside us.*

"Kyrie's spirit shines among the Draco stars," she said softly. "I know he can hear me. So I speak to him, and I will speak to him every day. You should too, Terra." Tears stung her eyes. "Kyrie needs your prayers too."

Terra sighed again. His hands closed around hers, gloved in leather, warm despite the cold around them. "Sister, I was a knight of Requiem. I devoted my life to helping the living. I know nothing of the dead." He squeezed her hands. "Today the living need us. The icelings are hungry. We must fly. We must hunt."

They walked down the hall between its columns of whorled ice. They stepped between two crystals, then walked through chambers that rose three hundred feet tall. Crystals glimmered around them, larger than dragons. Through towering windows, like windows in a cathedral, Memoria saw a thousand more palaces. They spread for a league across the iceberg, built of ice and snow, glistening like stars. Most of those palaces were abandoned now, she knew, only ghosts left to haunt their halls. Only two hundred icelings lived today, but their ancestors' palaces still stood, their ice never melting, their beauty never fading.

These remaining icelings glided around Memoria between the columns. Their sealskin robes swayed, and their hair was white as snow, even the hair of the children. Their eyes were azure, like clear pools under the sun, and they bore whalebone staffs crowned with their birth crystals.

Memoria wore furs now too--her woollen clothes from Requiem had gone threadbare years ago--but she bore no staff like the icelings. Like her brother, she wore a sword of Requiem at her hip, a glimmering shard of steel she had named Luna Nova.

Why do we still wear these swords? Memoria thought, as she thought every day. *We swung them in Requiem's tunnels, in darkness too narrow for dragonfire. But they couldn't hold back the enemy. They couldn't save our parents... and they couldn't save Kyrie.* So many times, Memoria had wanted to toss her sword into the ocean, watch it sink forever from her memory, but she could not. She was still a soldier, even after all these years, even as Requiem lay in ruin. She still had a soldier's pride.

"Sky friends!"

The words echoed across the hall. Memoria looked up to see Amberus, the Elder of Elders, walking toward them. His flowing robes hid his feet; he seemed to float. His beard was so long, it trailed five feet behind him like a wake. A necklace of icicles hung around his neck, and he held a staff crowned with a garnet the size of a man's heart.

"May your hunt today bring you much fortune," he said, "better than the days before it." His bony fingers tightened around his staff. He looked around at the other icelings, who moved silently between the frozen chambers. "They do not run or laugh, not even the children. They are hungry. They are thin."

Memoria bowed her head. "We will fly far today, Amberus. We will fly close to the Jet Mountains, but we dare not fly beyond them."

The elder's eyes darkened. "If the giants keep eating, we must abandon the Ice City."

Memoria's eyes widened. She gasped. "Abandon it? But Amberus, the icelings have lived here for a million years, since the dawn of ice. How could you abandon it?"

Amberus swept his arms around him, his bracelets of icicles clinking. "We have already abandoned it, sky child. Countless icelings once lived here. Two hundred remain, their bellies tight. I will let no more starve. The day will come, and we will have to leave, to move north, to the very feet of the Jet Mountains where seals still gather. We cannot let the giants eat so many. Their appetite is greater than that of snow craving clouds."

Terra placed a hand on the elder's shoulder. "Do not move north, Amberus. The giants hunger for more than seal flesh. You know how many icelings they've killed for sport. You cannot fight them."

The old iceling shook his head. The icicles strewn through his beard chinked. "No. But you can. When you take the sky spirit forms, you are mighty warriors."

Memoria took a deep breath. "May it never come to that. Let us fly on one more hunt. The giants would not eat all the seals, or they too would starve. There are more. We'll find them." She turned to her brother. "Come, Terra, we fly."

Even here, a thousand leagues north from her home, the Draco stars blessed her. Memoria drew her magic, the magic of Requiem. Scales flowed across her body, green like the forests of her home, glimmering in the morning light. Wings grew from her back. Claws, white as bone, grew from her fingertips and toes. She flapped her wings, took flight as a dragon, and flew between ice columns into the sky.

Terra shifted too. Soon he was flying beside her, a bronze dragon with white horns, his scales frosted. They flew north, leaving the Ice City, gliding over sheets of ice and snow toward the cruel Jet Mountains that marked the end of the world.

Memoria breathed deeply, relishing the wind. True, it was too cold here in exile, at the northern fringe of the world. And true, she missed seeing forests and rivers below her, not endless leagues of white. But at least she still had flying. To spread wings, feel fire tickle her nostrils, dive and swoop and be free... this was happiness to her.

"Do you remember how we'd fly with the herds?" she called to Terra. He flew at her side, gazing forward with those brown, weary eyes. "Do you remember how we'd sing as we flew over Requiem?"

He did not answer. She knew he remembered, but Terra preferred to forget. *Let him seek solace in the ice,* she thought. *My solace remains in the whispers of warm, southern past.*

They flew for a long time, over gleaming sheets of ice, dunes of snow, and boulders that rose grey and black like ancient goblins turned to stone. The world was white, grey, and black.

Her green scales, and Terra's bronze ones, were the only colors for leagues.

At noon, the Jet Mountains appeared on the horizon, great walls of black stone, ice, and snow. *The home of giants.* Memoria had never seen a giant, but she had seen their footprints, three toed and six feet long. She had seen the blood, bones, and offal they left behind after killing those icelings who ventured beyond the Ice City. And she saw them in her nightmares, shadows always at the corners of her eyes.

"Memoria, look," Terra said. He gestured ahead to a sheet of ice behind a ridge of boulders.

She looked, and her heart leaped.

"Seals!" she said.

A dozen of them, fat and lazy on the ice! This was rare. This time of year, seals normally swam under the ice, and Memoria had expected long hours of searching for their breathing holes. To find a dozen on the surface.... She laughed. If she caught them all, they would feed the icelings for days. Their fur would make warm blankets and clothes; their bones would be carved into blades, buttons, and needles; their sinew would make thread; their teeth would make necklaces and bracelets. This was a treasure.

She dived toward them, reaching out her claws, her heart racing for the hunt. Flames flickered between her teeth. Terra dived beside her, his claws extended.

The seals weren't fleeing.

Memoria frowned. They weren't moving at all.

Something's wrong.

She landed, claws digging into the ice. Terra landed beside her.

"They're dead," Memoria said. She nudged one with her claws. "But there's no blood, and they're gutted. Who would do such a thing? Kill seals, and place them on the ice, and...."

She froze.

Terra finished for her. "Bait," he said. "Whoever did this was laying out bait."

Memoria looked wildly from side to side, seeking giants. *They must have done this.*

"I see nobody," she whispered. She sucked in her breath, prepared to blow fire at any enemy who might appear, but she saw nothing for leagues; nothing but plains of ice.

Terra frowned. "I hear something. Listen."

She listened, and she heard it--a low rumble beneath her feet. The ice creaked. Memoria opened her mouth to speak... and her magic vanished.

She gasped. Her wings pulled back into her. Her scales disappeared. Suddenly she stood on the ice as a human. Terra's magic vanished too, leaving him human and looking just as confused. He tightened his jaw, drew his sword, and stared from side to side.

"What happened?" Memoria whispered. She had never heard of Vir Requis losing their magic. She too drew her sword. The ice shook wildly now, and a shriek sounded from below it.

"Let's get out of here," Terra said. "Go!"

But before Memoria could move, a hole burst open in the ice, and three creatures emerged from underwater.

Memoria screamed.

They were dead bodies, bloated and pale. But no; they were not mere bodies, but creations, sewn together from bits and pieces. She saw the stitches holding their limbs and heads to their torsos. Even in the cold, they stank so powerfully that Memoria gagged. The creatures squealed like walruses. Blood stained their teeth. Their fingers ended with the claws of bears, and those claws swiped at Memoria.

She leaped back and lashed her sword.

Memoria had been a soldier once. She could still fight, even in human form. Her blade severed the creature's hand, but it kept charging. It barrelled into her, snapping its teeth. Its claws slashed her shoulder.

Memoria fell onto the ice. She kicked one creature's head. Its neck snapped back, and worms spilled from its mouth.

"Agnus Dei," it hissed at her. "Dies Irae wants you, Agnus Dei. He sent me to you."

What is it talking about? Memoria drove her sword's grip into its face, crushing its nose and knocking out its teeth. She scrambled to her feet, swung her blade, and sliced off its head.

She turned to Terra, and saw him swinging his sword, battling two more creatures. His eyes were narrowed, his jaw tight; he was the bellator again, a knight of Requiem. He had shattered one creature's face, but it was still trying to bite. Memoria ran and slammed her sword into its head. Blood and maggoty brains spilled, but the creature only laughed.

Pain blazed on her calf. Memoria looked down, and saw the head she had severed. It was biting her. She screamed, kicked it off, and hacked at it. The head cackled. She stabbed again and again, breaking the head into a jaw, teeth, bits of skull, but still the head moved and gurgled and laughed. Memoria kicked the pieces into the hole in the ice, and they sank. The rest of the body kept creeping toward her. Memoria screamed, stabbed it, and kicked it into the hole. It floundered, and its fingers grabbed the rim of ice. She sliced them off and kicked them underwater.

Terra was swinging his sword, keeping the other two creatures at bay. His mouth was a grim line under his moustache. Frost covered his blade; it glinted like a shard of ice.

"Kyrie Eleison," the creatures hissed at him. "We come to kill you, Kyrie Eleison. Our lord, Dies Irae, commands that you die."

Memoria growled. How did these creatures know her dead brother's name? How dared they utter it? Memoria shouted, her heart racing, her head spinning. She leaped to her brother's defense. Their blades swung together. A severed arm leaped from the ice, clutched her shoulder, and scratched deep. Memoria ripped it off and tossed it underwater.

Terra was wounded too, she saw. Grooves ran down his armor, revealing bloody flesh. *What kind of creatures can claw through steel?* Still he fought, eyes narrowed, until the creatures were cut and crushed like butchered seals. The fingers, feet, heads, and other pieces kept writhing and trying to attack. Memoria and Terra kicked and stabbed, tossing them into the hole in the ice, where they sank.

Memoria kicked the last finger underwater, then leaned over, struggling for breath. Blood covered the ice. The stench of rot made her gag.

Kyrie.

She looked at Terra. Blood dripped from his wound. He stared back, silent.

Kyrie Eleison.

Tears stung Memoria's eyes.

"They... they spoke of Kyrie," she whispered and trembled. The memories flooded back, so powerful that her head spun, and for a moment she was back in Requiem, back in the war that had flooded her home.

"Kyrie!" she had cried, weeping, a youth who had seen too much fire and death. "Kyrie, where are you?"

The bodies had spread below her, thousands of them, covering Lanburg Fields. Where was her brother? Where was Kyrie?

"Kyrie!" Terra had cried too, searching the bodies with her, until they found the remains of a burned child, and wept over it, and buried it, and fled... fled here to exile, to endless ice, to endless memories.

Kyrie Eleison, the rotting demon had said.

Kyrie. My baby brother. The light of our family.

"What were those things?" she whispered, eyes stinging. She stared at the hole the creatures had emerged from. Her wounds ached and bled, but she ignored them. "Why did they speak of Kyrie?"

Terra's breath frosted before him. He stared darkly at the blood upon the ice. "They must be Dies Irae's new pets, something even worse than griffins. These creatures were built to kill Vir Requis. That's why we couldn't shift around them."

Memoria hugged herself. A chill washed over her, as if she'd swallowed too much snow. "So the war still rages. He's still hunting dragons."

Terra lowered his head and clenched his fists. Icicles were forming on his moustache. His voice was strained. "It's still going on. We've been hiding for eleven years, and the war still rages. And now it's here. He found us, Memoria. Dies Irae found us."

She shook her head, her heart racing, and she could barely see. *Could it be? After these years... is it possible?*

"The creatures were seeking Vir Requis, yes," she whispered. "But not you or me. They called me Agnus Dei. Does that name sound familiar?"

He stared at her. "Of course. Agnus Dei was our princess. I met her several times--a young girl with a mane of black curls. She gave me a favor, a single bluebell, before the battle of Draco Murus."

Memoria nodded. "You see, Terra? These creatures were seeking Requiem's survivors. We're not the only ones." Tears filled her eyes. Something halfway between sob and laughter fled her lips. "Others lived and fled into hiding too, Terra. The princess Agnus Dei did... and so did our brother."

KYRIE ELEISON

The mimics charged uphill, howling.

The Vir Requis fired their arrows. Shards of flame shot through the night. Screeches rose from the mimics, and two fell burning.

"Keep shooting!" Lacrimosa cried, an unnecessary command; they were all already nocking new arrows. Four more flaming arrows flew, and more mimics fell.

"Burn, that's right!" Kyrie shouted, excitement pounding through him. His fingers shook and his heart thrashed. The smoke stung his eyes and lungs, and the flames drenched him with sweat. He loaded a third arrow. This was no dragonfire, but it would do, he thought. He could still burn and kill these creatures.

A swarm of mimics reached the ring of fire that surrounded the ruins of Draco Murus. They tried to cross, but leaped back and hissed. The Vir Requis fired arrows through the flames, and the mimics screeched.

"Break the fire," howled their leader, the towering mimic with arms sewn together like strings of sausages. "Into the flames. Scatter them."

As Kyrie kept firing arrows, his stomach knotted. Mimics plunged into the ring of fire, tossing logs left and right. They burned, screamed, and fell. Others replaced them.

"Kill them, those ones!" Kyrie shouted and shot a arrow. He hit one mimic who was scattering the burning logs. His arrow entered its head, and it fell.

"Stack more logs, quick!" Lacrimosa shouted. She ran toward the broken ring of fire. Three mimics were stepping through it, grinning and drooling. They swiped their claws at Lacrimosa.

Kyrie ran, dropped his bow, and grabbed a torch. He swung it and clubbed one mimic's head. It screamed and lashed claws. Kyrie leaped back and swung his torch again, and the mimic burned. Bugs screamed and died inside it.

The twins leaped forward, thrusting burning javelins. Claw marks ran down Agnus Dei's thigh.

"Seal the ring of fire, stop them from entering!" Lacrimosa shouted, face flushed, hair damp with sweat. They all began tossing burning logs into the breach, and soon new flames crackled, showering sparks.

Screams rose behind them, and Kyrie spun around to see mimics breaching the ring twenty feet away.

"Over there!" he shouted. He grabbed a javelin, dipped its tip into the flames, and tossed it. The burning missile flew and sank into a mimic's chest. It screamed and fell.

The twins charged, screaming and swinging torches. They clubbed and burned mimics, who fell before them. Kyrie and Lacrimosa tossed flaming logs onto the new breach, sealing it.

The Vir Requis looked from side to side, panting and coughing. Smoke and sparks covered them. The mimics were now attacking a third location in the flaming ring.

"Shoot them down!" Lacrimosa shouted, voice hoarse. They grabbed their fallen bows, loaded more arrows, and shot. Mimics fell and rolled down the mountainside, blazing. The stench of smoke and rot filled the night.

"Look!" Kyrie shouted. He pointed across the courtyard to the western side of Draco Murus. "They're over there too, more mimics. Lacrimosa, with me! We'll guard the west."

Leaving the twins to defend the eastern mountainside, Kyrie ran with Lacrimosa across the ruins. The ring of fire was thinner here; they had expected the bulk of the attack from the east, whence the mimics had travelled. And yet a dozen of the creatures were attacking the flames here. Their eyes blazed, and their grins oozed drool thick with worms.

Lungs burning, Kyrie shot more arrows, hitting the creatures, but more kept coming. His stomach curdled. They were low on arrows; he had only five left in his quiver. He shot one more, but missed and cursed.

"Girls, you all right?" he shouted while nocking another arrow.

Agnus Dei shouted from across the courtyard. "They're breaching two places. They're pouring in!"

Kyrie cursed, coughed, and spat. His eyes burned with the smoke; he could barely see. He shot an arrow, hit a mimic, and spun around. He loaded another arrow and saw two mimics charging across the courtyard. He shot, hit one, but the other reached him before he could reload. Its claws swiped, and Kyrie leaped back. It jumped onto him and bit his shoulder.

Kyrie screamed, wrestled it off, and reached for a flaming log. Fire scorched his hand, and he shouted but managed to swing the burning stick. It hit the mimic's face.

Kyrie jumped to his feet. His hand throbbed. Mimics were breaching the flaming ring beside him; Lacrimosa was swinging a torch, holding them back. Kyrie nocked an arrow, fired, and hit the mimic closest to her. He grabbed another arrow, fired again, hit another mimic. When he reached into his quiver for more, he found it empty.

"Great," he muttered. He dropped his bow and grabbed two torches, one in each hand.

"Kyrie!" Gloriae shouted from somewhere across the courtyard. "Kyrie, we need you! Twenty mimics broke in."

Kyrie looked at Lacrimosa. She stood at the breached ring, swinging her torch, holding back four rotting bodies.

"Go to them!" the queen shouted. "I'll hold these ones back. Help the girls!"

Kyrie cursed. He didn't want to abandon Lacrimosa, but the twins needed him. His hand throbbing, dread twisting his gut, Kyrie ran east across the courtyard. The twins were fighting back to back, swinging torches and thrusting javelins. Blood dripped down Agnus Dei's thigh and Gloriae's left arm. A score of mimics surrounded them.

Swinging his torches, Kyrie leaped into the battle. He clubbed one mimic's head, then another. The creatures howled and burned. One swung a sword. The blade whooshed, and Kyrie ducked. The blow glanced off his helmet and rang in his ears, dazing him. Kyrie managed to thrust his torch, striking the mimic's chest. It fell back, and Kyrie chased it, swung his torch, and burned it until it fell.

Two more mimics slammed into him, and Kyrie hit the cobblestones. The breath was knocked out of him, and claws slashed his chest. Pain blazed, and he couldn't breathe. All he could see was darkness and fire. Teeth bit his arm.

No. Don't die now. Not yet. Benedictus would not give up so easily. Kyrie couldn't allow himself to do any less. He shoved

himself to his feet, though the world spun, and lashed his torches.
Sparks flew in curtains. Kyrie screamed, and the mimics fell back.

Blood trickled down his chest, and the night blurred. He
didn't know how long he fought. Dimly, he was aware of the
twins tossing flaming javelins, pushing mimics back. He saw
Lacrimosa swinging a torch in each hand. Deformed, stitched
bodies burned and fell around him.

It seemed ages before the mimics stopped charging. Kyrie
lowered his torches, panting, ready to collapse. Piles of burning
bodies rose around him, raising black smoke. The stench was so
heavy, Kyrie could barely breathe.

He looked around. The twins stood side by side, covered in
ash, blood, and mimic drool. Lacrimosa approached them, helmet
dented and clothes charred, fire-tipped javelins in her hands. The
Vir Requis moved to stand back to back, looking around
cautiously.

"Are they all dead?" Agnus Dei said, voice hoarse.

Kyrie narrowed his eyes. The fires still crackled and
shadows danced; it was hard to see. But no mimics stirred. Their
bodies burned, unmoving, across the ruins and mountainsides.

"They're all dead," Kyrie said. "We--"

A howl shook the ruins.

A figure stepped through the orphaned archway, seven feet
tall. It unfurled its arms; each was grotesquely long, sewn together
from three normal arms. It held a sword in each hand. It grinned
at them, baring wolf fangs.

"Not all dead," the chief mimic said and approached them,
brandishing its blades.

Agnus Dei charged forward first, swinging her torch and
screaming.

The mimic swung one link of arms, hit her helmet with its
blade, and knocked her down.

"Agnus Dei!" Kyrie screamed and ran toward the mimic.
Gloriae and Lacrimosa ran with him, swinging their torches.

The mimic's arms shot out. Kyrie ducked, and an arm
swung over his head. Gloriae screamed. The mimic laughed.
Lacrimosa ran and drove her torch forward, but the mimic's blade
halved it. The top half, still aflame, landed at Kyrie's feet.

He kicked it, and it hit the mimic. Kyrie held his breath...
but the creature didn't catch fire. Instead it lumbered toward him,
swinging its blades.

Kyrie leaped back and raised his arms, protecting his face. A
blade hit his vambrace and sparked.

"Agnus Dei!" he shouted. She was struggling to rise,
blinking. Kyrie grabbed her and hoisted her up.

"Careful, Kyrie!" she shouted and pulled him back. The
mimic was laughing, and its blades swung inches from Kyrie's
face.

A scream of rage tore the air. Gloriae was charging, a lit
javelin in hand. She drove the javelin into the mimic's back. The
tip burst from its chest, still burning.

Kyrie gasped. Would it finally die?

No. Its torso did not catch fire. It turned to stare at Gloriae
and laughed. Drool dripped down its chin. Maggots covered the
javelin that thrust out from its chest.

"Gloriae," it said, voice guttural. Worms squirmed between
its teeth. "Your father seeks you."

It swung its blades at her.

Gloriae ducked, drew her sword with a hiss, and parried.
She swung her blade and severed one of the creature's arms.

Kyrie's heart leaped. He charged forward with his torch.
Agnus Dei and Lacrimosa ran too, screaming and waving torches.

The severed arm squirmed toward them, leaped from the
ground, and slammed against their chests.

Lacrimosa fell and knocked into Agnus Dei, who knocked
into Kyrie. Gloriae charged at the mimic, but it swung its
remaining arm and drove her back. Its blade whirled.

The severed arm squirmed, and its hand caught Lacrimosa's
hair. It pulled her to her feet. Lacrimosa wriggled and tried to pry
herself loose, but could not. Unnaturally strong, the arm tugged
her toward the body it had been attached to. The creature snarled
at her, spraying her with drool.

"Lacrimosa," it hissed. "I was made with the blood of your
husband." It spat a glob of blood onto her chest. "Do you
recognize it? My master took it from his blade."

Agnus Dei, screaming and weeping, ran forward. She
barrelled into the mimic, and it fell. It howled and its teeth sank
into Agnus Dei's shoulder, but she seemed not to notice. She

grabbed its head and slammed it against the floor again and again. The skull cracked, and centipedes spilled from it.

Gloriae slammed her blade down, severing the mimic's second link of arms. Kyrie set fire to it. The arms squirmed and screamed like a blazing snake.

Lacrimosa still struggled with the first severed arm; it was clutching her throat now. Kyrie rushed forward, set it ablaze, and its fingers opened. Lacrimosa breathed raggedly.

"Agnus Dei!" she whispered, hoarse.

The mimic's head had shattered. Blood and bone fragments spread across the cobblestones. And yet its jaw would not release Agnus Dei's shoulder. Kyrie grabbed the jaw, twisted, and managed to pry it off. He tossed it down and stomped on it until the teeth broke off.

Agnus Dei was screaming and sobbing. She drew her sword and began stabbing the mimic's torso, again and again. Its legs kicked and cockroaches fled from it.

"You have to burn it!" Gloriae said, but Agnus Dei seemed not to hear. She kept stabbing and weeping and screaming.

Kyrie touched her shoulder, but she seemed not to notice him.

"Agnus Dei," he said. "Kitten."

She spun toward him, eyes red and puffy. "It said... about Father, did you hear? It said...."

"It was lying, Agnus Dei," Kyrie said. "Don't listen to it." He handed her a torch. "Burn its body, Agnus Dei. Finish it."

Agnus Dei took the torch and stared down at the mimic. There was nothing left but twitching legs and a shredded torso.

A voice rose from it.

Kyrie gasped. How could it still speak? And yet its blood bubbled, and strange, gurgling words rose from it.

"We will... return... more of us... thousands... we will make you mimics too...."

Agnus Dei tossed the torch onto it.

The remains caught fire, and a scream rose from them, high-pitched. Kyrie covered his ears and grimaced. The scream went on and on, and the ruins shook.

Finally silence fell.

Kyrie breathed out shakily.

His wounds ached, his lungs burned, and he nearly collapsed.

"It's over," he said hoarsely. Agnus Dei crashed into his arms, and he held her. Gloriae and Lacrimosa joined the embrace. Blood and ash covered them.

"We beat them," Kyrie whispered into the embrace. Agnus Dei's hair surrounded his face like a pillow, scented of smoke. "We defended our home."

He looked to the eastern horizon. Red wisps spread across it. Dawn had arrived. It looked to Kyrie like rivers of blood.

One battle had ended. The war against the mimics, he knew, was only beginning.

LACRIMOSA

The young ones huddled under the archway, embracing one another. She had washed their wounds with spirits, bandaged them, and prayed for them. Now, as the youths whispered in the dawn, Lacrimosa could be alone with her thoughts, her grief, and her memories.

She walked to the edge of the courtyard. A bit of old wall, three feet tall, jutted there like a last tooth in the gums of an old dragon. Lacrimosa climbed atop it and stared into the dawn. Wind played with her hair. Snow fell lightly, kissing her cheeks. She looked toward the valley where her husband lay buried.

"I miss you, Ben," she whispered.

She missed his strong arms around her; his laughter, deep and rolling like distant thunder; the stubble on his face; the softness in his eyes when she kissed him.

"Watch over me, Ben. You walk now in our halls beyond the stars, with our parents, with our siblings. You're at rest now. I continue the fight for you."

The wind gusted, opening her cloak, chilling her. Lacrimosa hugged herself. It would be so easy, she thought, to lie down in the snow, close her eyes, and wait for warmth to take her. It would be like falling asleep, and she would be with Benedictus again. But Lacrimosa turned her head, looked back at Kyrie and her daughters, and knew that she must be strong for them.

"I must survive," she whispered into the wind. "I must guide them, and heal them, and fight for them. Who else would?"

They had so much to live for, she thought. Kyrie and Agnus Dei wanted to get married, to raise a family. Gloriae still dreamed of becoming a great leader, a queen of Requiem and defeater of Osanna. The youths spoke of rebuilding Requiem, of killing Dies Irae, of changing the world. In all this darkness, they saw light.

And what of myself? Lacrimosa thought. *Do I still see light in the world? My light died and lies buried in that valley. My children are my light now--my daughters, and Kyrie, my adopted son.*

"I don't know what strength I still have, Ben," Lacrimosa spoke to the distant valley. "But so long as I can, I will carry your torch. I will keep our children alive and their hope burning. I will do this for them and for you." Suddenly she was trembling, and tears flowed down her cheeks. "I miss you, Ben. I wish you were here with me. I love you."

When the wind gusted again, ash from a mimic's body swirled around her boots. Lacrimosa looked at the burned body, which lay in the courtyard, and saw a red glint. She frowned.

Wrapping her cloak around her, she stepped off the wall and approached the body. It was but a pile of ash and old bones. She stirred the ash with her boot, and saw the glint again-- something red and glistening like a ruby. Thankful for her leather gloves, Lacrimosa reached into the ash and retrieved a gemstone the size of a chicken's egg.

She brushed it off and held it up. It sparkled strangely in the light. Shadows and stars seemed to swirl inside it, blood-red. It was heavy. Though small enough to fit in her palm, it felt much larger, like lifting a gourd.

"What's that, Lacrimosa?"

Gloriae walked toward her, eyes narrowed. Inwardly, Lacrimosa winced. *She still won't call me Mother. I saved her from Dies Irae moons ago, but I'm still only Lacrimosa to her.*

She hid her disappointment. "A gemstone," she said, holding it out. "I found it inside a mimic's body."

Gloriae frowned at the stone. "This looks familiar. I've seen this before somewhere." She scrunched her lips. "Yes. *Artifacts of Wizardry and Power* spoke of glowing red stones."

Lacrimosa nodded. "Gloriae, would you stay here and watch? You have the sharpest eyes. Call us if more mimics arrive. Kyrie, Agnus Dei! Come downstairs, into the cellars. We have some reading to do."

Soon the three stood underground by the hearth. The cellars looked strangely empty without the wood they'd been collecting for weeks. Her footfalls echoed. Sap, twigs, and pine needles covered the floor. They had few furnishings: A table and chairs Kyrie had built, a bearskin rug, and beds of straw. They had no shelves; their belongings, including their books *Mythic Creatures of the Grey Age* and *Artifacts of Wizardry and Power*, lay in the corner.

Lacrimosa set the gemstone on the table, then fetched *Artifacts of Wizardry and Power.* She placed the ancient, leather-bound tome beside the gemstone, blew off the dust, and opened it.

"Let's see," she said and sat by the table. Kyrie and Agnus Dei stood behind her, looking over her shoulders at the book.

"Does it say anything about gemstones from mimic guts?" Agnus Dei said. She reached toward the pages. "Give it here."

Lacrimosa slapped her hand away. "Be patient. I'm looking." She flipped to the first chapter. "This chapter is about the Griffin Heart."

Agnus Dei groaned. "We know all about the Griffin Heart. We destroyed it already. Come on, Mother, get to the gemstones."

Lacrimosa turned her head and glowered at her daughter. "Agnus Dei, calm down. I'm looking."

She flipped the parchment pages and reached the second chapter. "And this chapter is about the Summoning Stick...."

Agnus Dei groaned louder. "Mother, we already used the Summoning Stick when fighting the nightshades. Give me the book. I'm a fast reader."

Lacrimosa glared at her daughter. "Agnus Dei, you're making me angry. Will you please let me--"

Lacrimosa froze.

The table was shaking.

"Earthquake?" she whispered. The gemstone and book rattled on the tabletop.

Kyrie shook his head. "Only the table is moving. Look! Its legs."

Lacrimosa gasped. The table legs were curling inward, forming a shape like animal legs. Before her eyes, the table began to creep across the floor, insect-like.

"What the--?" Kyrie said. "Agnus Dei, look what you did. Even the table is mad at you."

"I did nothing!" Agnus Dei objected.

Lacrimosa rose from her chair and stared. Her heart raced and her fingertips stung. She didn't like this. The table crawled, reminding her of a spider. It seemed to... turn to face her. The book and gemstone slid and fell onto the rug.

The table froze.

"Look, the rug!" Lacrimosa said.

They crowded around it and watched. The bearskin rug twisted. Its head rose to glare at them with its beady eyes. Its mouth opened, fangs glinting, and roared. The body of the rug squirmed, as if the bear were struggling to rise and surprised to find that it had no bones left.

Kyrie whistled. "First the griffins and nightshades. Then the mimics. And now the furniture is turning against us. Can't we ever win?"

Agnus Dei punched his shoulder. "Pup, this is no time for being smart."

Lacrimosa lifted the gemstone off the rug. The bear gave a last growl, then fell flat onto the floor. Once more, it was still, its eyes dead and its mouth shut. The gemstone was now ice cold, nearly freezing Lacrimosa's hand. Red liquid swirled within it; it looked like blood.

"The gemstone brings things to life," Kyrie whispered, voice awed.

Agnus Dei snorted. "Sir Obvious saves the day again."

He glared at her. "You sound just like your sister, do you know?"

They raised their fists, and their eyes flashed. Lacrimosa stepped between them.

"Children! Stop fighting."

Agnus Dei flushed. "I'm not a child, Mother, I'm *nineteen*. The pup is only seventeen. He's a child."

Kyrie opened his mouth to object, but Lacrimosa put a finger against his lips.

"Kyrie, not now. No arguing. You two *are* children, and intolerable children at that." She placed the gemstone in Kyrie's hand. "Hold this. Now let's try this book again--quietly this time."

Lacrimosa turned several more pages, then nodded. "Here we are."

This chapter was entitled "Animating Stones". It featured an illustration of a battle. On one side fought knights, swordsmen, and archers. On the other side, a wizard commanded an army of statues. The statues seemed to move; they were tossing javelins and waving swords.

Lacrimosa read out loud.

"As there is no greater crime than taking a life, so is there no greater Magik than giving it. In all the lore of Ancient Artifacts, the Animating Stones are the most powerful, and the most dangerous. An Animating Stone can cause a river to rise like a serpent; a statue to march and fight; a corpse to escape the grave; or any other dead matter to take life, to move, to serve its master. Such is their might, that around Animating Stones, all other Magiks and Artifacts lose their power, and--"

"Look at this part," Agnus Dei interrupted. She pointed at the next paragraph. "About the Ancient Days."

Lacrimosa sighed and skipped forward. She kept reading. "In the Ancient Days, when the world was in chaos, the Ocean Deities created the Animating Stones, so they may mold the species from fire and water, and create a male and female from each. First they created the fish, then birds, and finally creatures to crawl upon the earth. They created Man and Woman last, him of fire and her of water, and placed the last two Animating Stones within their hearts."

Agnus Dei scrunched her lips. "It doesn't say when they created Vir Requis."

Kyrie shoved her. "The Draco stars created us, not any Ocean Deities. You should know that."

"Pardon me, oh wise scholar pup."

Lacrimosa continued reading. "When all creatures swam, flew, crawled, and walked, the Ocean Deities collected all the Animating Stones. They took them to a dark forest, and dug deep tunnels, and scattered them underground. None have seen them since."

The chapter was finished. Lacrimosa closed the book.

"So where is this dark forest?" Agnus Dei demanded. "How did Dies Irae find the buried Animating Stones?"

Kyrie mussed her hair. "If the book told us that, it would be too easy. And things are never easy. Haven't you learned that yet?"

"Stop messing up my hair, pup."

Lacrimosa stood up. She looked at the youths--Agnus Dei with her flushed cheeks and flashing eyes, and Kyrie who was like a son to her now. She thought of Gloriae, her golden daughter, who guarded above, strong and brave. For the first time since the mimics had attacked, Lacrimosa saw hope for her children.

"Let's return to the courtyard," she said. "We have Animating Stones to collect... and life to create."

TERRA

"Kyrie!" he called, flying over the hills of dead. "Brother! Kyrie!"

Lanburg Fields lay below him, a field of blood, shattered weapons, and shattered bodies. Five thousand dead Vir Requis lay here, the last of their kind, cut with arrows, talons, and griffin beaks.

Dead. All dead.

"Kyrie!"

Terra's eyes stung, and his wings shook so badly, he could barely fly. His sister flew beside him, weeping.

"Kyrie!" she cried too, flying over the desolation, trembling. "Kyrie, where are you?"

They landed among the bodies and shifted into humans. The stench of blood and death rose around them, spinning Terra's head. His fingers shook. Desperate, he began to rummage through the bodies, turning them over, shoving them aside.

"Kyrie!"

No. He couldn't be dead. Couldn't be.

"We should have been here," he said hoarsely. "We should have died with them."

But the tunnels had collapsed around him and Memoria. The darkness had trapped them. The Poisoned had fought them. They had spent a day digging for light and life... only to find darkness and death.

"I should have been here with you, Kyrie," he whispered, limbs shaking. He remembered bandaging Kyrie's knee only a week ago, after he had fallen. *When you needed me most, I wasn't here.*

He pushed over the body of a child, but it was a girl, her body burned, her face torn. As he held the girl, the wind died.

For a moment, the killing field was silent.

Memoria spoke behind him, her voice strangely soft, strangely beautiful.

"Terra... I found him."

He turned and saw her looking toward him, but not at him. She seemed to be staring a thousand yards away, her eyes huge and glistening. She cradled a small body in her arms. It was burned so badly, Terra could not recognize it.

But it had yellow hair. It was the right size. It wore the same orange scarf.

Terra... I found him.

Terra clenched his fists.

No.

He took a deep, shaky breath. *Do not remember, Terra. Memories are wrong. Memories are pain. That life is behind you. Kyrie has been dead for eleven years; let him rest in peace.*

Terra looked around him. No blood. No fire. Just ice, snow, and frost. Whale Hall rose around him, its pillars like ribs. The sun shone softly, a mere smudge behind the ceiling of ice. *An end to pain,* he thought. No more memories. No more blood. His life was ice now. He would fill his memories and soul with nothing but this endless ice.

Pain stung him. He winced and cursed.

Amberus, the Elder of Elders, smiled and clucked his tongue. He was sprinkling green powder into Terra's wound; the stuff burned like ilbane. As he worked, the old man chanted prayers to the Wind Goddess, or maybe it was the Sky Eagle or Old Walrus. Terra no longer cared about deities, not those of the north, nor the stars that had abandoned him.

"You will heal now," Memoria said, voice soft. She sat beside him, wrapped in furs, a hood pulled over her head. "Amberus is a wise healer."

Her eyes, large and brown, brimmed with concern. Terra felt his pain melt, both the pain of his wounds, and the pain within him. No, not everyone lay as burned skeletons. Memoria still lived. *And it's for you that I still live,* he thought. *It's for you that I don't walk into the ice and never return. I'll stay alive for you, sister, and watch over you.*

Amberus bandaged the wound and furrowed his brow. "Your wounds will heal, Son Terra, but an evil caused them. The Ice Mother weeps for them. There is dark magic in them, and poison, and secrets from far away. What caused these wounds, Son Terra? They trouble me greatly."

"Demons from under the ice," Terra said. His throat tightened at the memory, and he swallowed. "They were like dolls, sewn together from the body parts of dead men. They seemed to have dark magic to them, yes. Memoria and I could not become dragons around them, as if their magic undid ours."

Amberus closed his eyes and mumbled prayers. His feet tapped, silent against the ice. He chanted to Father Whale, a god of ancient times, and to Mother Turtle, whose northern lights glittered upon the Ice City.

Terra looked at his sister. Memoria stared back, her doe eyes so large, so sad. He could see his fear reflected in them. Was Dies Irae back? Was he hunting them again?

Finally Amberus opened his eyes. They were startling blue and glowed like the moon. Staring at nothing, he drew black powder from a hidden pocket, tossed it onto the floor, and slammed down his staff.

Terra watched, eyes narrowing. He caught his breath. The black powder stirred and raised smoke. The smoke swirled, flowed toward the distant ceiling of the palace, and raced around the columns of ice. Moaning like wind, the smoke dived to the floor, gathered, and formed into ten figures like men. *No, not men,* Terra decided. The smoke looked like mismatched bodies sewn together, their hair swarming like worms.

"The creatures we saw," Memoria whispered. She clutched her fur cloak.

The smoke dispersed, swirled in a maelstrom, then formed new figures. This time it formed thousands of small, smoky creatures that marched across the ice. *More rotting demons,* Terra thought. *An army of them.* The creatures howled, then dispersed into snakes of smoke. The smoke rose, swirled and raged, and finally collapsed into powder again.

Silence filled the hall.

"What does it mean?" Terra asked, looking up at Amberus.

"They are mimics," Amberus said. Wrinkles deepened around his eyes. "Mimics of life... and mimics of death. They flow with the stench of it. They hunt your kind, the sky warriors that you call dragons. They do not sleep. They do not tire. You cannot kill them. They will never stop hunting you and your kind."

"Do you see more of our kind, Amberus?" Memoria asked. She clutched Terra's hand. She looked at him, and Terra knew she was remembering the names the creatures had spoken.

Agnus Dei.
Kyrie Eleison.

Amberus shook his head, his necklace of icicles clinking. "That is hard to see now, as it always has been. If there are more dragons, they hide well; the Mother Turtle cannot see them. But these mimics... they hunt for dragons everywhere. Most flow to the old ruins, the place you call Requiem. If there are more dragons, they hide there."

Terra closed his eyes. His chest tightened, and cold sweat trickled down his back. He could barely breathe, and his pulse pounded in his ears. War. Destruction in Requiem again.

Terra... I found him.

For years he had struggled to forget, to banish those words from his memory. Now, once more, Terra felt the fire around him, smelled the stench of death, saw the small burned body.

"We have to go back," Memoria whispered.

Terra opened his eyes. "What?" he demanded. "Memoria, we do not return. Not now. Not ever. When we left, we left for good."

Memoria breathed heavily and her cheeks flushed. She glared at him. "Terra, when we left, we thought that we were the last. That they all had died at Lanburg Fields. But they didn't. Two at least still live. Agnus Dei... and our brother."

Terra clenched his fists and shook his head. His chest felt tight. "Kyrie is dead, sister. We buried him."

Memoria's eyes flashed. Her chest rose and fell as she panted. "We buried a body. The body of a burned child his size, with the same hair and scarf. But we don't know it was him." She clutched his shoulders, tears in her eyes. "Kyrie is alive, Terra. Kyrie and the princess Agnus Dei. I know it."

He looked away, throat burning.

Terra... I found him.

He looked back at Memoria, her face so pale, so sad. He couldn't let that happen to her. The loss of his brother still haunted him. How could he lose his sister too, see her body also burned, cry over her grave?

"Memoria," he said, and for a moment he could say no more. He tightened his jaw. For the first time since he'd buried Kyrie, he felt ready to cry. He refused to. He would shed no more tears. He had vowed to remain strong. It was a long moment before he could speak again, voice strained. "Memoria, I led us here to protect you. To hide you. To--"

"You fled here to escape death!" she said. "You came here
to escape memory. To escape pain. To escape... to escape what we
found at Lanburg Fields."

He shouted, voice echoing in the ice hall. "We ran to save
our lives!"

She shook her head wildly, hair swaying. "That doesn't
matter anymore. Our lives are threatened here too. Those
creatures found us even here, a thousand leagues north of
Requiem."

"Three mimics found us. Thousands march to Requiem."

"So we will return to defend it!"

Terra laughed mirthlessly. "With what? Our swords? We
couldn't shift around those things, Memoria. Their claws tore
through my armor as if it were wool." He looked at Amberus,
who was watching them silently. "Elder of Elders, please. Tell her
it's dangerous. Tell her she cannot go chasing that evil."

The old man nodded slowly, lips pursed. He looked at the
powder on the ice, and his brow furrowed. His eyes darkened, and
his wrinkles deepened. His knuckles whitened around his
whalebone staff. Terra had never seen the old man look so
troubled.

Finally Amberus looked up, nodded, and spoke in a low
voice.

"It is time to reclaim Adoria's Hands."

Terra stared at him. "Adoria? Is this another deity of the
north?"

Ambrus shook his head. His voice was soft, as if lost in
memory. "She was an iceling sorceress who lived many seasons
ago. She created magic to stop other sorcerers from casting spells
upon her. She could hold out her hands... and stop magic. Fearing
sorcerers, the giants killed Adoria and cut off her hands. The
Giant King wears those hands as amulets; they hang on a chain
around his neck. They still repel magic."

Terra felt the blood leave his face. "The Giant King...."

Amberus stared at him, his eyes suddenly blazing. "You
cannot shift around mimics. Their magic stops your own. But if
you owned Adoria's Hands, mimic magic would not touch you.
You could become dragons around them. You could burn them
all with dragonfire. If you want to save your friends, you must
face the Giant King... and reclaim Adoria's Hands."

Terra turned away from Amberus. He looked at his sister--his small, frail sister, the person he loved most, the person he was sworn to protect. He lowered his head and embraced her.

"How can I face this again?" he whispered. "Memoria, how can I face the dead, their souls that still hover there? I was a bellator, a knight of Requiem. I vowed to defend them. How can I face their ghosts?"

Memoria held him, her grip tight, fingers digging. She whispered into his ear. "We don't return for the dead, Terra. We return for the living."

Kyrie! he had cried. *Kyrie, do you hear me?*

Could it be?

Could he still live?

Terra took a deep, shaky breath. His stomach knotted, and he could barely breathe. Kyrie, a child with yellow hair, only six years old, a somber child who saw too much war, too much pain. Kyrie, who'd be seventeen now, a grown man. Kyrie, who lived forever in his mind, even here, even as he struggled to forget.

Are you still out there, Kyrie? Do you still need me?

He tightened his jaw.

He nodded.

Agnus Dei. Kyrie Eleison.

"We'll need Adoria's Hands." He held his sister's shoulders. "We'll need to kill the Giant King."

GLORIAE

As Gloriae worked, collecting Animating Stones, she did not speak. The others conversed excitedly, imagining where Dies Irae was mining the stones, and how they could animate their own warriors, and about finding more firewood, and... Gloriae ignored it. She kept separate from the others. As they scoured the courtyard for Animating Stones, she walked along the mountainsides, rummaging through the ashes of the mimics her arrows had killed.

Mimics. Monsters. Creatures of death. Dies Irae's latest creations.

Before them, he had sent nightshades upon Requiem, creatures of darkness and evil.

And before the nightshades... he had sent her. Gloriae the Gilded.

For the first time she understood. She looked at the ruin around her, the ashes of demons, monsters, rotting things. She had just been one of his monsters.

"I am Gloriae the Gilded!" she would cry from her griffin. "I fight for light and life."

And thus she had killed. Thus she had tortured, and burned, and dealt death to Requiem. To her own people. Thus she had let Dies Irae mold her into just another monster, a creature of darkness and death. No different than the nightshades. No different than the mimics.

Gloriae came upon the burned, smoking body of a mimic. It rustled at her feet in the breeze. She kicked it, and the body scattered. She reached into the ash--it was still warm--and found another Animating Stone. The stone's innards pulsed red in her hand like a heart.

My heart too was made of stone, she thought. *I was a creature like this.*

Gloriae looked into the stone. Liquid seemed to swirl inside it like blood. In its patterns, she imagined the eyes of a child, a young Vir Requis wounded by griffin claws.

"Kill it," Dies Irae had said to her. "Draw your sword and kill the weredragon."

Gloriae had not wanted to. She wanted to go home. She wanted to look away from the child's weeping eyes, from the blood on his stomach.

"Run the creature through, daughter," Dies Irae had said.

"Yes, Father," she told him. He was a father to her then. She drew her thin sword, and stabbed the child, and stared at the blood with dry eyes. She was six years old.

Gloriae looked back at the ruins of Draco Murus. Her sister was chasing Kyrie, yelling at him for getting ash in her hair. Lacrimosa was trying to stop the girl, but it was like trying to stop a charging mare. Gloriae wanted to smile. She wanted to run too, to laugh, to play. But... those were fragile emotions, weren't they? Emotions regular people felt. Not warriors of ice. Not maidens of steel.

If I smile, if I laugh, if I love... I am human. I am guilty. My hands are bloody.

She stared. She kept her face still. She had to remain this warrior of steel; warriors did not feel pain, guilt, or shame.

"I must remain Gloriae the Gilded," she whispered to herself. "Hard as steel, ruthless as my blade. I will allow no weakness. I will not allow those child's eyes to haunt me. Dies Irae raised me a killer; to change would hurt too much, confess too much blood. I will remain what he made me. But I will not kill more Vir Requis." She turned to look east, toward the distant lands where Dies Irae ruled. "I will kill you, Irae. You made me a killer, and this killer will be your death."

"Gloriae! Gloriae, have you found the last ones?"

Lacrimosa was waving from the ruins, calling her. Gloriae stared back, hand on the hilt of her sword, and nodded.

Stay strong, she told herself. *Even if she is your mother. Even if you love her. Love leads to joy, to memory, to guilt... and then pain.*

"I found them," she called back. She walked uphill, the Animating Stones in her pack, and joined the others in the ruins.

They brushed off a few ashy cobblestones and placed their Animating Stones there. Gloriae counted them. A hundred shone and trembled at her feet. What ash blew toward them formed strands like snakes, which writhed until the wind blew them away. The cobblestones beneath them trembled.

Kyrie stared down at the Animating Stones and shuddered. "Nasty things, they are. Black magic."

Gloriae looked at him and raised an eyebrow. "Black magic, Kyrie? According to our book, they created early life in this world. Death and life are closely linked; they are sides of the same coin. Or stone, in our case. Don't judge so quickly what is evil and what is good."

She stared back to the stones, and wondered: *Am I talking of this magic, or of myself?*

Lacrimosa lifted one stone and held it to the light. It glimmered. "If we create life with them, will our creations serve us? Or will their loyalties still lie with Dies Irae?"

Gloriae remembered her days at Flammis Palace, serving the man she thought of as Father. Hunting for him. Killing for him.

She put her hand on Lacrimosa's shoulder and stared into her eyes. "Whatever beings we animate--they will not serve him. He animated creatures from dead soldiers who feared him; their loyalties continued in their mimicry of life. But we will animate the stones of Requiem. Our creations will fight for us." She nodded. "Broken statues cover this land. Let us find what statues are still whole, even if ash and dirt cover them. They will be Requiem's new soldiers."

Lacrimosa nodded. "King's Forest lies several leagues north, nestling the ruins of our palace. We will find statues there. Most will be smashed, but we might be lucky and find some whole. Kyrie. Agnus Dei. You two travel there, and take fifty Animating Stones with you. Raise us soldiers of stone. Gloriae, you will travel with me south, where our old temples once stood. We might find more statues among their ruins."

Gloriae nodded. "When Dies Irae returns with more mimics, and he will, he will find us ready this time. I hope he himself leads the next charge." She drew her sword and raised it. The light of Animating Stones painted it red. "If he does, he will meet this blade."

They collected the Animating Stones into packs, and with quick embraces, they parted. Gloriae and her mother began walking down the southern mountainside. Her sister and Kyrie disappeared down the other way.

For a long time, daughter and mother walked in silence.

They walked across valleys strewn with shattered blades, arrowheads, and cloven helmets. They moved through forests of charred trees, skeletons, and fallen columns. Silently, they passed by mass graves, where the wind whispered and yellow weeds rustled. Gloriae tried to imagine Requiem in her glory days: Proud columns of marble rising among birches, stone pools and statues among flowers, and white temples where priests played harps. Mostly, she imagined herds of dragons in the sky, roaring their song, a stream of color and fire and music.

I destroyed this land, she thought, remembering the dragons she had slain in her youth.

But no. She had been only a child when Dies Irae started his war. Three years old, that was all. By the time she was eight, most dragons were dead; only a handful of survivors remained for her to hunt.

"He did this," she whispered and clenched her fist around Per Ignem's hilt. "Not me. Him alone."

The memories swirling through her, Gloriae had forgotten about her mother beside her. Lacrimosa now touched her hair and smiled sadly. There was no accusation in her lavender eyes, only pain and love.

"I know, sweetness," she whispered.

For the first time, Gloriae realized that she looked like her mother. Lacrimosa had the same pale skin, the same golden hair, the same face Gloriae knew people said was beautiful.

"What do you know?" she whispered, and a tightness gripped her chest. She had spoken little; she had thought a lot. Could Lacrimosa see into her heart?

Lacrimosa took her hand. "You are my daughter, Gloriae. You don't have to speak for me to know your pain. You shield this pain in ice, but it pulses red as fire, and I can see its light."

Gloriae stopped walking. A tremble took her knees. "I hide nothing," she whispered.

But suddenly Lacrimosa was embracing her, and Gloriae allowed it. Suddenly tears stung at her eyes.

"I love you, Gloriae," her mother whispered into her ear. "You don't have to speak of your pain. Not until you're ready. I know what he did to you. I know what he made you do. And I still love you. I always have and I always will." She pulled back and looked into Gloriae's eyes. "You are forgiven, Gloriae."

Something salty touched her lips. She was crying. She, Gloriae the Gilded--crying. Her fingers trembled. *No,* she told herself. *Stay strong. You are Gloriae the Gilded. You are a killer. You are a warrior of steel. You... you....*

She fell to her knees, and another tear flowed, and Gloriae reached out to clutch at something, anything, and Mother was there kneeling beside her. She clung to her.

"I'm sorry," she whispered, her tears on Mother's shoulder. "I'm sorry, please. Please. I didn't know, I...."

She bit back her words. She knuckled away her tears.

"No," she said. "No pain. Not now. I'm not ready. We still have to be strong. To kill him. We must kill him, Mother."

Lacrimosa nodded and brushed back locks of Gloriae's hair. "We will kill him. Now let's keep moving. We have statues to find."

They continued walking through the ruins. Crows cawed above, the first sign of life Gloriae had seen all day. She look at Lacrimosa, this woman of pale frailty like starlight, and realized: *For the first time, I called her Mother.*

AGNUS DEI

"Pup, you're walking too slowly," she said. "Can't you hurry up?"

Kyrie glared at her. He looked to Agnus Dei like a porcupine, all bristly with weapons. A sword hung from his right hip, a dagger from his left. A bow, a quiver of arrows, and two torches hung over his back. Dented armor covered his forearms and legs, and he wore a helmet that was too large. With all this covering him, he sloshed through the snow like a drunkard.

"Agnus Dei," he said, "I swear. If you complain about one more thing, I'm going to--"

"What, give me a black eye?" She smiled crookedly. "Maybe a fat lip? I'd like to see you try, pup. I'm stronger than you, deadlier than you, faster than you--well, obviously faster than you, seeing how slow you're walking. Look at me. I'm bearing just as much armor and weapons, but I'm walking straight and fast."

"I might be slower, but you're whinier," he said, adjusting the strap of his quiver. "That's for sure."

"Who's whiny?" she asked and mimicked him. "Ow, Agnus Dei! My feet hurt. I'm hungry. I'm thirsty. I love you so much, that my heart aches, and my loins are about to burst into flame."

He groaned. "And what about you?" He spoke in falsetto. "Oh pup, I want to fight! No wait, I want to fly now. Actually let's kiss and roll in the hay!"

She snorted. "You wish." But in truth, she did want to fight, and fly, and... as Kyrie put it, roll in the hay. Any one of those things beat crying. Sometimes Agnus Dei felt that no more tears could flow from her, that no more pain could fill her. And yet the pain was always there, a rock in her stomach, ropes around her heart, smoke in her eyes. Fighting, flying, loving--that was better than pain. Wasn't it?

She sighed and took his hand. It was gloved in leather, and she squeezed it.

"All right, pup," she said. "I'll walk a little slower to match your small puppy steps."

They walked through the ruins, snow swirling around their boots. Soon they passed the mossy boulders that reminded Agnus Dei of dragons, and she looked to her right and saw the cemetery there. The ropes around her heart tightened, and she gave Kyrie's hand another squeeze.

I'm still fighting, Father, she thought. *I'll be strong like you. Like you taught me.*

Tears filled her eyes, and she wiped them with her fist. Kyrie saw, and his eyes softened, and for a long time they walked in silence. She looked at him once, and wanted to pester him, tease him, kiss him even... but none of it felt right. Not before, not now. How could she still find joy in this world, when her father lay buried, and monsters crawled the ruins?

But there was something she could do. *I can fight.*

"Do you think we'll find any statues?" she asked. She hefted her heavy leather pack, where she carried Animating Stones. "I've seen only pieces of statues in Requiem, feet or hands or heads."

Like the body pieces Dies Irae sews together, she thought with a shudder.

Kyrie scanned the northern horizon, as if he could see statues from here. "I don't know. But the ruins of Requiem's palace are a good place to look. If we find them anywhere, we'll--"

A howl pierced the air.

Agnus Dei and Kyrie drew their swords with a hiss.

A second howl sounded--closer this time.

Scanning the ruins, Agnus Dei lowered her blade.

"Wolves," she said. "They would roam my old mountain hideout; I'd recognize their howls anywhere."

She wished she could shift--she'd rather face a hungry wolf pack as a dragon--but the Animating Stones in her pack meant facing them as humans.

"Those aren't wolves," Kyrie said. He stared from side to side, as if seeking them. "There are no more wolves in Requiem."

A third howl rose, this one even closer. More howls answered. They still sounded like wolf howls, but... deeper, crueler. Agnus Dei shivered.

"Look!" Kyrie said and pointed with his sword.

Agnus Dei saw six figures in the distance. They seemed like men--they ran through the snow on two legs--but they howled like demon wolves.

"They saw us," she said. "Kyrie, let's light some arrows."

He already had his tinderbox in hand. "I like the way you think."

They switched from swords to bows, lit their arrows, and nocked them. The figures raced toward them. Their stench carried on the wind--the stench of bodies.

"More mimics," Agnus Dei said, jaw tight.

When the creatures were close enough to see clearly, she nearly gagged. Their bodies were from dead humans, stitched and stuffed. Their heads were the heads of dead wolves, sewn onto human necks, fur matted and eyes dripping pus.

"Let's burn those bastards," Agnus Dei said. "Fire!"

She loosed her arrow. Kyrie did the same. The flaming missiles flew in an arc. Agnus Dei cursed; her arrow missed. Kyrie's hit a mimic's leg. It screeched, fell, then rose and kept running.

"Fire again!" Agnus Dei shouted.

They lit more arrows. They shot again. This time, Agnus Dei hit a mimic in the chest, and she shouted in rage and triumph. The creature fell, and the fire spread across it. Kyrie's arrow grazed another's shoulder, searing but not killing it.

"Agnus Dei, light your torch!" Kyrie shouted. He was busy lighting his, and soon swung it as a flaming club. Agnus Dei managed to light hers as the five surviving mimics reached them.

She swung her torch and hit a wolf head. Sparks blazed. A second mimic bit at her left. Its stench stung her eyes and twisted her stomach. She leaped back and raised her arm. Its teeth banged against her vambrace, and it howled. She shoved the torch against its face. Its fur kindled and it screamed.

From the corner of her eye, she saw Kyrie battling his own mimics. Then one leaped onto her, knocking her down. She hit the snow and crossed her arms over her face. Wolf teeth bit at her armor. Drool dripped onto her face, thick with dead ants. Agnus Dei grimaced and kicked the creature's stomach.

The mimic fell off, and Agnus Dei jumped up. She slammed the torch into the fallen mimic, but another one leaped onto her back. Teeth ripped at her shoulder, and she screamed. Her thick, woollen cloak absorbed most of the bite, but those teeth still tore flesh.

She spun, swinging her torch, but was too slow. The mimic barrelled into her, and she fell again. Teeth closed around her forearm, pressing into the armor. The creature snarled, steam rising from its nostrils. Worms filled its fur.

The words of the mimic last night returned to her. *We were made with drops of Benedictus's blood....*

Rage filled Agnus Dei. She dropped her torch, drew her dagger, and shoved it into the wolf's eye.

It screamed and released her. She scrambled to her feet and shoved her torch into its rotting face. The head caught flame, and soon the whole body burned and writhed. She stared down at it, the fire stinging her eyes, and spat onto its body.

"Agnus Dei," Kyrie said, panting. "Agnus Dei, you're hurt."

She turned to see three mimic bodies at his feet, burned dead. Teeth marks peppered his arm; he clutched the wound.

"I hate these bastard mimics," she said and tightened her jaw. The smoke and heat stung her eyes. "I hate the damn things. I *hate* them."

He nodded. "I know. I do too. More than anything--other than Irae, maybe."

Agnus Dei tossed her torch aside, took three large strides, and embraced him. He held her in the snow and smoke, and she rested her head against his shoulder. His hand, bloody, smoothed her hair.

"I hate them, by the stars," she whispered, throat tight. "I hate their lies. I want to burn them all."

"We will," Kyrie promised.

She stared into his eyes. She touched his cheek, smearing ash and blood across it. "I love you, Kyrie. I'm sorry if I tease you sometimes, or call you a pup. You're a good fighter. And you're strong. Don't forget that, Kyrie."

"Okay, kitten," he said, and gave her a smile and wink.

She couldn't help but laugh. It felt good. She kissed his cheek, and pushed him back, and said, "Let's bandage these wounds, then keep walking. And try to keep up this time."

LACRIMOSA

The mimic scurried toward them like a starfish. It had no torso, no legs, no head. It was nothing but five human arms growing around a mouth.

Nausea filled her, and Lacrimosa screamed.

The creature raced toward her on five hands. The mouth in its center snapped open and closed, making sucking noises.

Gloriae shot her bow. A flaming arrow flew and hit an arm. That arm collapsed and burned, but the creature kept racing on its four good arms.

Lacrimosa wanted to gag. She wanted to run. Instead she raced toward the creature, shouted, and swung her torch.

The flames hit the creature between two arms, and it squealed, a sound like a child crying. She had expected a howl of rage; this high, pained mewl shocked her, and Lacrimosa lowered her torch.

The mimic leaped and wrapped its arms around her. It hugged her, crushing her, and its mouth came in to bite.

"Get off her!" Gloriae cried and stabbed it. The mimic squealed--a child's squeal. Blood gushed from it.

Lacrimosa struggled. The arms felt like they could snap her ribs. The mouth opened before her face, screaming, full of teeth. She tried to push it back, but it pinned her arms to her sides. Her torch fell to the ground.

"Burn, you freak," Gloriae said, lifted the fallen torch, and held it to the creature.

It screamed. The flames rose, intolerably hot. Lacrimosa grimaced and closed her eyes. She struggled and writhed, freed an arm, and shoved the burning mimic off.

It curled up at her feet, scurried, and fell. Flames and smoke rose from it. Still it cried, the sound of a human girl.

Gloriae nocked another arrow. Lacrimosa wanted to stop her. *No*, she wanted to cry. *No, it's only a child! Don't kill it.* But she knew that death was mercy for this thing, this starfish of arms growing from a crying mouth.

Gloriae shot her arrow into that mouth.

Blood flowed, and the creature convulsed, then lay still.

"Hideous thing," Gloriae said and spat onto it. "Disgusting."

Lacrimosa said nothing. She stared down at the burning mimic, wondering who it had been in life. Who had given it these five arms, this mouth? Soldiers? Farmers? Was one a child?

She forced a deep, shaky breath. "Let's get its Animating Stone."

Once they had its stone, they continued to walk between the ruins. Snow began to fall, coating their cloaks. Soon they entered the Valley of Stars, where the temples of Requiem had once stood.

Lacrimosa walked silently, head lowered. This was a holy place. Bricks lay strewn around her, white mounds under the snow. The capitals of columns lay fallen, glimmering with icicles. Part of a wall still stood, as tall as Lacrimosa, still showing the grooves of griffin claws. Lacrimosa clutched the hilt of her father's sword. Diamonds shone in that hilt, arranged like the Draco constellation. In the Valley of Stars, the diamonds seemed warm against her hand. *This place still has some power, even as it lies in ruin.*

Gloriae looked around with narrowed eyes, her mouth open, her cheeks kissed pink with cold. She turned to Lacrimosa.

"I remember this place!" she said. "I... I remember temples. They stood tall, as tall as Flammis Palace, all of white stone. Birches grew here." She knelt, reached into the snow, and lifted a glass crystal. "This crystal! It was part of a chandelier. Many of them hung in the temples. I remember."

Lacrimosa looked at her daughter, and memories flooded her too, but not memories of temples and crystals. She saw again a laughing toddler, her hair all golden curls, her eyes green and full of wonder at the world.

"I love you so much, Gloriae," she said, tears in her eyes. "Then and now. My heart broke when Dies Irae stole you. Let our hearts heal now. Together."

Gloriae opened her mouth to speak, but seemed to see something. Her eyes widened, and she pointed behind Lacrimosa. "Look!"

Lacrimosa turned, and a smile spread across her face. She had missed the statue at first; snow and icicles covered it. She walked toward it, cleared off the snow and ice, and her smile widened. It was a statue of a dragon, six feet tall. One of its wings had fallen, it was missing a fang, and a crack ran along its chest, but it was otherwise unharmed. It was the most complete statue she had seen in these ruins.

"Do you think it would work?" Gloriae whispered, coming to stand beside her. Snow sparkled in her hair.

Lacrimosa nodded. A tingle ran through her. "This one will be a warrior of Requiem."

She ran her fingers over the crack along the dragon's chest. It was the work of a griffin talon, or perhaps a knight's war hammer. *In this wound, I will place its heart.*

She took an Animating Stone from her pack. It thrummed in her palm, glowed, and its red innards swirled. It felt hot, so hot it almost burned her. Lacrimosa wedged the stone into the crack, until it stuck. It pulsed and glowed in the statue's chest, a heart of stone.

Lacrimosa took her daughter's hand, and they stepped back, watching.

The dragon statue was still.

Lacrimosa exhaled, feeling deflated.

"It's not working," Gloriae whispered.

"Just watch," Lacrimosa said, still daring to hope.

She stared and frowned. Was Gloriae right? The Animating Stone still glowed and swirled, but....

The stone dragon's wing creaked.

Gloriae gasped and squeezed Lacrimosa's hand.

The statue moved its head, just an inch. The stone creaked, and for an instant Lacrimosa thought the head would snap off. But the stone moved like a living thing—creaky and stiff, but alive.

Then the dragon lifted its arms and arched its back, and snow fell from it. The icicles on its arms snapped. It tossed back its head and roared, and Lacrimosa wanted to draw her sword or flee. Would it attack them?

"Stone of Requiem!" she called to it. "I am Lacrimosa, Queen of Requiem. Do you hear me? I raise the stones of our land. Requiem calls for your aid."

The stone dragon looked at her, and its eyes narrowed. The Animating Stone in its chest blazed. The statue's mouth closed, opened, and then it roared again.

It was a roar of pain, of grief, and of joy.

"It's thanking us," Lacrimosa whispered, her eyes moist. "It saw the death of this land. It sings for memory, and for new life."

The clouds parted, and beams of sunlight fell upon the ruins of Requiem. The stone dragon, chipped and broken, roared its song.

Lacrimosa turned to face her daughter and saw that Gloriae's green eyes shone. The girl panted, her hair golden in the sun.

And there is new life here too, grief and pain and finally some joy. As I bring life to the stones of Requiem, let me bring new life to my daughter, to my beloved, to my Gloriae.

She smiled at her daughter, and Gloriae smiled back, the rarest of smiles. *She has a beautiful smile, a smile like sunlight on snow.*

"And now, daughter," Lacrimosa said, "we will build an army."

AGNUS DEI

They entered King's Forest at dawn, five days after leaving their mountain ruins, and Agnus Dei's throat tightened.

"The hall of Requiem's kings," she whispered.

Kyrie took her hand. They stood on a hill and gazed silently upon the ruins. Dead, burned trees lay covered with snow. Requiem's palace lay fallen between them, the palace where Father had once ruled. It had once boasted a hundred columns. They lay smashed now, buried in snow. Only one still stood, two hundred feet tall, its capital shaped as bucking dragons. It rose from the ruins into sunbeams, kissed with light, its marble brighter than the snow.

"King's Column," Agnus Dei said, voice soft. "That is what it's called. They say even Dies Irae himself, atop his griffin Volucris, could not topple it. They say it is star blessed. I thought it a legend."

Kyrie nodded. "It won't fall so long as there are living Vir Requis. While it stands, there is hope for Requiem."

Agnus Dei lit her torch. "Let's move carefully. We might find statues in the ruins. We might also find mimics."

Kyrie lit his torch too, and they walked downhill toward the palace ruins. The snow glittered under the dawn like a field of stars. It was quiet. Agnus Dei heard only a soft wind, the crackle of their torches, and the crunch of snow under their boots. Lumps rose under the snow. Agnus Dei and Kyrie began brushing snow aside, searching. They found many bricks, fallen blades, a broken lance, a shield, the skeletons of men, and even a griffin's skeleton. They found statues too, but they were smashed: a marble head here, an arm there, pedestals with feet still attached, but no more.

"Do you think we can repair them?" Agnus Dei asked. She lifted a statue's hand, twice the size of her own, and held it.

"With what?" Kyrie said, his clothes white with snow. "We have no tools."

Agnus Dei sighed. It seemed hopeless. Some of the war's largest battles had been fought here. Everything here was smashed, aside from King's Column.

She turned to look at the pillar. It towered above her, so wide three men could not hug it. Scenes of flying dragons were engraved into the marble. Agnus Dei walked toward the column and touched the stone. It was cold, colder than ice; she could feel that even through her gloves. She ran her fingers over old words carved into the marble. *Requiem! May our wings forever find your sky.*

"King Aeternum built this column," she told Kyrie. "He was the first of our line, and among the greatest kings, Father would say. Father was descended from him, did you know? Aeternum ruled seventy-four generations before Father, and his line ruled continuously until the war." She swallowed.

Kyrie put an arm around her. "The line still stands. You are descended from Aeternum too. When you or Gloriae are crowned, you will be the seventy-seventh monarch of Aeternum's house."

She raised an eyebrow. "Me or Gloriae--queens? Pup, we are fighters. Survivors. We are no queens. What is there to rule here?" She swept her arms around her. "Nothing remains."

Kyrie jutted his chin toward King's Column. "That remains. Aeternum's pillar. And we remain, don't we? You and I. Your mother and sister. Lacrimosa is our queen; this is her pillar now, her place to rule. And after her, you and Gloriae will rule."

Agnus Dei laughed and pinched his cheek. "Pup, you'd hate me as your queen. If you think I'm bossy now, you'd be running to the hills then. And if Gloriae is queen, I think you'd hate that enough to jump off a cliff."

He grinned. "Maybe you're right. I think a rebellion is in order. I think it might be time for Kyrie Eleison to take power." He laughed, then sighed and took a deep breath. "You're right, kitten. There's not much left here, and not much point for queens, and kings, and palaces. But I like talking about it. It makes me feel like... like it's honoring old Aeternum, if he's watching from the Draco stars. And I feel like we're honoring Benedictus too. When we remember their prayers, their customs, and their lines of power, we're keeping their memory alive. We're carrying their torch. Even if Requiem lies in ruin, and we can never rebuild her,

I'll keep carrying this torch. For him. For Benedictus. I loved him."

Agnus Dei looked at him with damp eyes. She sniffed and nodded. "I loved him too. More than I ever told him in life. I wish he were here, that I could tell him that. I wish.... Oh, pup. There are so many things I wish for. The world seems so dark sometimes, doesn't it? But I'm not giving up." She took his hand and held it tight. "And I'm glad you're with me. I love you too, Kyrie. Don't forget it. If anything happens... if mimics arrive, or Dies Irae himself, and if we lie wounded and dying... know that I love you."

Her lips trembled and she took deep breaths. Kyrie shoved their torches into the snow, embraced her, and kissed her. She wrapped her arms around him, and her body pressed against him. They kissed deeply, desperately, and it was long moments before they drew apart and stood, silently holding hands, staring at the ruins under the snow.

Suddenly Agnus Dei gasped. "Look, Kyrie!"

The clouds parted, and the sun emerged. It shone behind King's Pillar, casting a long shadow. The shadow stretched five hundred feet across the snow, like a path. It ended at a hillock of snow beneath burned trees.

"King Aeternum is showing us something," Agnus Dei said. "Let's look."

They followed the path of shadow. It led them out of the palace ruins, and into deep snow where birch trees once grew. The way was tricky, with many bricks, old helmets, and shattered weapons hiding under the snow to trip them. When they reached the path's end, they found piles of snow that rose five feet tall. Just then the clouds gathered, and the shadowy path vanished.

Agnus Dei cleared some snow away. She found herself staring at a woman's marble face.

"A statue!" she breathed.

They kept clearing away the snow, and soon revealed the rest of a statue--a nude woman holding a jug.

"She's perfect," Kyrie said.

Agnus Dei frowned at him. "Perfect, huh? Keep your eyes off her naughty bits, pup."

"I mean she's not damaged. There are a few chips, but... the statue is whole. Let's keep digging."

They kept clearing away snow, and found many pieces of statues--hands, heads, legs, torsos, and pedestals. They placed these parts aside and kept digging. Soon they unearthed a second, complete statue--a warrior holding a marble sword and shield.

They kept digging and finally found a third complete statue. This one was a king; he sported a crown, robe, and beard.

"This one is a statue of King Aeternum," Agnus Dei said. "See the two-headed dragon on his shield? It was his sigil."

Kyrie lifted a hammer and three chisels from the snow. "This place must have been a workshop. A sculptor lived here. King's Column knew we should look here." He closed his eyes. "Thank you, King Aeternum. If you truly watch over us, thank you."

They found no more whole statues. Grunting and straining, they dragged the complete statues into clear snow and stood them side by side. A nude maiden. A warrior in armor. A proud old king.

"The girl looks just like you," Kyrie said and reached toward the statue's breasts. Agnus Dei slapped his hand away and glared.

"This isn't time for jokes, pup," she said. "Give me that chisel and hammer."

"Hey, what did I do? Don't hammer me over the head."

"It's not for you, pup. Not yet, at least. We need to give these statues their hearts."

She began to chisel. It was slow, careful work. She hated damaging these statues, but knew she must. *You will be warriors of Requiem.*

Finally she had carved chambers in their chests, where hearts would pulse in living beings.

"Ready, pup?" she whispered. "I'll animate the warrior and the king. You can animate the girl statue you're so smitten with."

He nodded. Fingers tingly, Agnus Dei pulled two Animating Stones from her pack. They trembled and thrummed. The light inside them, like red liquid, swirled and reached toward the statues, as if craving new homes. Suddenly Agnus Dei was fearful; sweat beaded on her forehead, and her pulse quickened. If the magic worked, would these statues attack them?

The Ocean Deities created these stones in the Age of Chaos, she thought. *They are as old as the world, and all that's in it. And I hold them in my palm.* She took a deep breath. *I am a princess of Requiem. Gloriae and I are the last of King Aeternum's line. I will never fear the stones of Requiem.*

She placed one Animating Stone into the marble warrior. Before her courage could desert her, she placed the second Animating Stone into the king. Kyrie planted his stone into the woman, and they stepped back.

The statues were still.

"It didn't work," Agnus Dei whispered.

"Just a moment," Kyrie whispered back. "It--"

A shrill scream, like crackling ice, rose behind them.

Agnus Dei spun around, waving her torch.

Mimics.

"Oh, stars," she said.

Kyrie was already nocking an arrow. "More like star*fish*. Ugly bastards."

The mimics were emerging from the ruins like spiders from under an upturned rock. They had no heads or torsos; they had only human arms, sewn together into rotting creatures like nightmarish starfish. They squealed and raced across the ruins toward her and Kyrie. There were a dozen at least.

Agnus Dei lit and fired an arrow. Kyrie fired too. The two arrows shot like comets, but the creatures moved too fast. Both arrows missed. Agnus Dei loaded another arrow, shot again. Her arrow grazed one mimic starfish, but it kept running. Kyrie's second arrow missed.

They had no time for thirds. The mimics leaped and flew toward them.

Agnus Dei swung her torch. She hit one starfish as it flew. It squealed, pulled its arms together, and fell into the snow. A second starfish jumped and wrapped around her.

Agnus Dei screamed and struggled, but the starfish pinned her arms to her sides. One arm was hairy and broad. Another was the thin arm of a young woman. She could not see the others. They squeezed her, crushing her. She dropped her torch and couldn't breathe.

"Kyrie!" she whispered. She could speak no louder. "Kyrie, help!"

She managed to turn her head. Stars floated before her eyes. She saw Kyrie lying in the snow. Four mimic starfish wrapped around him. She could see only his left foot and some of his hair. They were biting, squealing, *eating* him.

"Kyrie, no!" she cried, eyes burning. "Please...."

She fell to her knees. Three more mimics jumped and wrapped around her. One's mouth--they had mouths in their centers--opened before her. Its tongue licked her cheek, and its teeth came in to bite.

It screamed and pulled back.

Agnus Dei took a ragged breath, kicked, and shouted. The mimic was ripped from her body. Its fingernails scratched her, clinging to her, then were torn free.

The stone warrior stood before her, its Animating Stone pulsing in its chest. It held the mimic in marble hands, regarded it blankly, then tossed it aside.

"Get the others!" Agnus Dei shouted. Two other mimics were wrapped around her, one around her stomach, the other around her legs.

The stone warrior regarded her. Its Animating Stone glowed so brightly, it nearly blinded her. With stone fingers, it cut into the mimic around Agnus Dei's stomach. Pus, worms, and black blood spilled from it. The statue pulled it back. The mimic's fingers clung to Agnus Dei, ripping her cloak and tunic, but the statue managed to pull it free. It ripped two arms off, and blood showered. It tossed the rest aside.

Agnus Dei kicked and clawed at the starfish around her legs, and managed to free herself. Her legs were scratched and her pants shredded. She found her torch extinguished in the snow. Mimics scuttled toward her. She drew her sword and swung it. Rotting arms flew.

"Kyrie!" she cried.

The stone girl was pulling the mimics off him. He was alive, coughing in the snow, bloodied. The third statue, the stone king, was fighting mimics beside him. They wrapped around it, but it kept tearing their limbs off.

Agnus Dei kept swinging her blade. The severed arms did not die, but kept crawling through the snow toward her. Finally she managed to beat them back long enough to reignite her torch. Snarling, she began to burn them. The arms twitched, hissed, and curled up.

Finally all the mimics were torn apart, burned, and dead.

Kyrie rushed to her, blood trickling from a gash on his forearm. "You're hurt."

She nodded. Her clothes were tattered, her skin bleeding. "What are a few more scratches?"

They shared a quick embrace, splashed their wounds with spirits, and bound them. Pain filled Agnus Dei, but she ignored it. She was a warrior. She could take pain and keep fighting. Kyrie was pale, and sweat soaked his brow, but he too stood straight, ignoring his wounds. *We've become like statues too,* she thought. *We barely feel pain anymore.*

She turned to look at the statues. The three stood together, splashed with black mimic blood. They stared back, faces blank.

"We'll need more," Kyrie said, voice hoarse. Mimic blood soaked his clothes.

Agnus Dei looked at the smashed columns. They lay everywhere, their segments as large as boulders. She gave Kyrie a crooked smile.

"We have marble. We have tools. We have three statues who will work hard." She patted Kyrie's helmet. "They will build more."

Would it work? she wondered. It seemed crazy, but... this whole war was crazy. She lifted a hammer and chisel and shook the snow off them. She approached the statue of the king, her ancestor, and placed the tools in his hands. The statue's fingers closed around them, and he stared at her with stone eyes.

"For years, you lay hidden in ruin," she said to him. "For years, Requiem lay fallen. Today her stones will live. Today you will build brothers and sisters. The fabled columns of Requiem lie smashed now. We cannot rebuild them, but we can raise them to life. Carve them into men and women. Carve them into warriors who can reclaim our glory."

The statue stood still. Agnus Dei exhaled slowly, feeling like a deflated bellows. *He doesn't hear,* she thought. *Or he doesn't understand. He can move, but not help us.*

She turned to Kyrie. "I don't know how Dies Irae commands them. I don't know how--"

Kyrie's eyes widened and his mouth fell open. "Look."

Agnus Dei spun around. The stone king was walking through the snow, steps slow and creaking. He approached a piece of fallen column. It was larger than him. The statue stood over it, tools in hands.

"Go on," Agnus Dei whispered. "You know what to do."

The statue turned to look at her. Agnus Dei stared back. Light filled the king's eyes--starlight. The statue turned back to the marble and began to carve.

Agnus Dei felt a lump in her throat. She put an arm around Kyrie and kissed his cheek.

"For the first time in years," she whispered, "Requiem will have an army."

DIES IRAE

He stepped onto the parapet, stared down to the courtyard, and beheld an army of rot and worm.

"Mimics!" he shouted and raised his arms. "Soon you will feast on weredragon flesh!"

They howled, shrieked, and slammed swords against shields. Pus dripped from their maws. Maggots swarmed across them. Congealed blood covered their bodies like boils.

My children, Dies Irae thought. *My lovelies.*

"Hail Dies Irae!" one mimic cried, a creature with six arms and blades for hands.

"We will feast!" cried another, a creature with a bloated head like a rotting watermelon.

A thousand screamed below. Their stench rose to fill Dies Irae's nostrils. He breathed it in lovingly. It was the smell of dead weredragons, of victory.

"The weredragons murdered your brothers," he called down to them. "With cowardly fire, they burned all mimics who drew near."

They hissed and screamed. They banged their blades, and their teeth gnashed.

"But you are not mere scouts!" Dies Irae cried over the din. "You are an army. You are an army bred to kill weredragons."

Their howls rose. They waved their weapons and screamed for blood.

"You will eat their bodies! You will suck up their entrails. But bring me their heads. I will sew their heads onto the bodies of women, so that you may take them, and hurt them, and plant your seed inside them. They will be your slaves."

The mimics screamed and drooled. Some dropped their shields and began rubbing themselves, moaning and screaming. Dies Irae watched and smiled.

"Who do you serve?" he cried.

"Dies Irae! Hail Dies Irae!" Their voices shook the ruins.

Smiling thinly, Dies Irae turned and stared at the mimic who stood beside him on the parapets. His most beautiful mimic. The crown jewel of his army. His proudest creation.

"And you, Teeth, will lead them," he said.

The mimic stared back, bared its sharp teeth, and hissed. Its burly, hairy arms reached out and flexed. Centipedes crawled over its stilt-like legs. Dies Irae touched its cheek.

"You are my sweet killer," he said. "Built fresh. Of young bodies. Young freakish bodies. You are strong. You will lead. You will kill."

It snarled. A worm crawled between its teeth. "Yes, master."

Dies Irae smiled when he remembered building this mimic. The two boys had come to him with a fresh body, a friend of theirs, one of their gang. The dead one had long, hairy arms like an ape's. The leader had sharp teeth and a powerful jaw. The third one was stupid, but had long legs made for running, for towering over enemies.

The Rot Gang, that was their name, he remembered. An appropriate name.

He plucked a worm from Teeth's head and crushed it between his fingers. It squirmed, its juices spilling. Dies Irae tossed it aside and licked his fingertips. Teeth snarled.

"Take your army," Dies Irae told him. "Take these thousand warriors. Lead them to Requiem... and to triumph."

Teeth tossed back its head and howled, saliva spraying from its mouth. It raised twin blades in its hands. They caught the light and seemed to shine with the Sun God's fury.

Dies Irae stood on this crumbling wall of Flammis Palace, crossed his arms, and watched his army leave the bloody courtyard. The mimics snaked through the ruins of his city. *Yes, Confutatis lies in ruins now,* he thought. *The weredragons destroyed it. I will make them suffer for it.*

When the army disappeared into the distance, Dies Irae descended the wall and entered the ruins of his palace. He walked down halls smeared with blood, rotting guts, and the old ash of dragonfire.

He stepped down a stairwell, plunging into darkness. The air grew colder. Frost covered the walls and stairs. The smells of fear and blood filled his nostrils. The stairwell kept twisting, burrowing into the darkness that lurked under his palace. Finally he stepped into the dungeons. The old kings of Osanna had kept barrels of wine here. Dies Irae kept sweeter treats.

Torches crackled, lighting a craggy hallway lined with cells. Dies Irae stepped toward a cell with iron bars. He heard the prisoners whimper, and he smiled.

"Yes, darlings, you should whimper," he said. "I like it when you whimper."

The keys hung from a peg on the wall. Dies Irae opened the cell's door and stepped inside.

Five women stood chained to the walls. The torchlight danced on their nude bodies. Dies Irae felt his blood grow hot and his loins stir. The women were ripe, with rounded hips, teary eyes, and trembling lips.

"My mimics are creatures of rot and worm," he said to them. A smile spread across his lips. "When I sent them on the hunt for ripe women, I didn't know what they'd bring. Crones? Corpses? But it seems mimics have the lusts of men. You are like summer fruit, full of sweetness and juices."

He stepped toward one woman, a peasant girl by the look of her. Her hair was red, and tears filled her grey eyes. Dies Irae caressed her cheek.

"Please, my lord," she begged.

Dies Irae touched her hair. "Please?" he asked. "What do you wish to beg of me?"

She trembled. "Please, my lord. Is my father.... The creatures dragged him away, and.... Please release me, my lord, I beg you."

He kissed her forehead. His hands travelled down her body, caressing her. Her flesh was icy but soft. Goose bumps rose under his fingertips.

"You should be proud, sweetness. You will do what so many have dreamed of. You will hurt weredragons. When my mimics bring me their heads, I will sew one onto your body."

"My lord, please...." Tears streamed down her cheeks.

"I think for you, the boy Kyrie will do. His head will look nice on your soft, ripe body. When my mimics take you, and hurt you, and plant their rotting seeds inside you, Kyrie will know more pain and terror than any being before him. Does it not please you, precious, that your body will hurt a weredragon so?"

Sobs racked that body and she could not speak. Finally she blurted out, "Silva will kill you! The Earthen will save us!"

Dies Irae nodded with a smile. "Ah yes, the Earthen, the group of ragtag Earth God followers who've been killing all those mimics." He grabbed the girl's cheeks and squeezed them. "They are pesky flies, and my creations whisper that this Silva, this leader of theirs, has some skill with the blade. He will make a good mimic some day."

The girl opened her mouth to speak more. Dies Irae backhanded her, so hard that blood splattered, and he felt her jaw crack. Her eyes rolled back and she hung limp on her chains.

He left the girl and turned to another prisoner, an angel of soft blond hair and red lips.

"I think... the weredragon Lacrimosa should work for you. She has always been so thin, and you are luscious. Yes. Her head will be for you."

This girl too wept, and begged, and Dies Irae smiled. What a glorious end it would be for the weredragons! He licked his lips.

A voice spoke behind him, soft and cold.

"And I want the head of the golden weredragon."

Dies Irae turned, eyebrows rising. One of the women had spoken. She stood chained like the others, but did not weep. She did not tremble. Her dark eyes stared at him, simmering with anger.

"The golden weredragon?" he asked her. "Gloriae the Gilded?"

The woman nodded. "When the dragons flew upon this city, it was the golden one who torched my home. The weredragon Gloriae killed my brothers. She killed my husband. Cut my head from my body, my lord. Place her head upon me and make me a mimic. Let the others hurt me. I will do this to make Gloriae suffer."

Dies Irae approached her and examined her in the torchlight. Among the chained women, this one was the fairest. Her hair was black satin, hanging down to her chin. Her eyes were pools of midnight. She looked older than the others--a woman, while the others were mere girls. Her body was lithe and strong, decorated with several knife scars. This was no peasant.

"Who were your brothers?" he asked her, narrowing his eyes. "Who was your husband?"

She raised her chin. "Blood Wolves," she said, eyes spiteful. "Will you kill me for that? I think not. Not if you want my body fresh for your dear Gloriae."

Dies Irae nodded, eyebrows raised, and scratched his chin. "Common thieves, you mean."

She spat onto the floor. "Blood Wolves are no common thugs. We are the shadows in the night. We are the daggers in the alley. We are the terror that strikes in darkness."

Dies Irae ran his fingers along her chest, tracing a scar. It ran from her left collarbone, between her breasts, and to her bottom right rib. He touched her hip, and traced the length of a second scar, which ran down her thigh. She stared back at him, chin raised, lips tight.

"Terror in darkness, you say." He pursed his lips. "Shadows in the night. Perhaps I could find another use for you."

She gritted her teeth. "From the way your fingers touch me, I know how you would use me. I have no interest in serving you so, great emperor. I am a Blood Wolf too. I can fight like my brothers and husband, the men the weredragons slew. I will hurt them."

Dies Irae nodded and rubbed his chin. Five women were chained here. But only four weredragons remained. Benedictus was dead, his body stolen. *Yes. Yes, I can spare this one. The four others will be toys to my mimics. This one will be mine.*

He unchained her wrists from the wall, and then her ankles. She moved her limbs, hissed, and gritted her teeth. She rubbed the raw flesh, and sweat beaded on her brow. A snarl found her lips. Dies Irae couldn't help but smile. This one was feral. A wolf indeed.

"What is your name?"

"Umbra," she said and glared.

He grabbed her wrist. "Come with me."

She pulled her wrist free and bared her teeth at him. "I will walk. You will not drag me."

Yes. Yes, I like this one.

They left the dungeons, climbed the stairwell, and walked across the crumbling halls of Flammis Palace. Everywhere were strewn bricks, stains of ash, smeared blood, and guards with sallow eyes. Those eyes lit up when Umbra walked by, still nude.

Umbra stared back at them, chin raised, as if challenging them to speak. Her eyes said, *Make a move, and I'll tear out your throats.*

He led her upstairs and into his bed chamber. The nightshades, griffins, and dragons had destroyed half the palace, but this room remained untouched. It was a large chamber, large enough to house a dragon. Golden tapestries covered his walls. His bed was ten feet wide, made of pure gold inlaid with diamonds. His tables, chairs, and vases were gilded and shone with emeralds, rubies, and sapphires. Priceless swords of steel and jewels hung everywhere.

"Like gold, do we?" Umbra asked. Her eyes darted from gemstone to gemstone. They lit up like the eyes of a starving man who stumbled upon a feast. She reached toward a jewelled dagger which lay on a giltwood table.

Dies Irae caught her wrist. "Do not touch anything. You will have gold too, if you earn it."

She looked up at him. A crooked smile touched her lips. "And how do I earn it, my lord?"

He twisted her wrist and pulled her close. "I will show you."

She spat in his face. "Let me go. My husband hasn't been dead a moon."

He slapped her face. He'd wanted to knock her down, but she stayed standing... and punched him.

Her fist hit his cheek, and he fell. White light blinded him. He blinked and struggled to rise, but Umbra pressed her foot against his chest, pinning him down. She grabbed the dagger, drew the blade, and pointed it at him.

"This dagger is mine," she said. "I take payment in advance. I will kill for you with this dagger. Give me a name, and he is dead. But I will not be your slave. Those women underground? Rape them if you will, not me."

Dies Irae lay looking up at her. His blood pulsed. "I do not want those women underground. I want you. I want your daggers in the night. I want your hands covered in the blood of my enemies. And I want your body under mine."

He reached up, grabbed her waist, and pulled her down toward him. Her dagger scratched his side, but he barely noticed. She snarled, and he rolled her onto her back and lay atop her.

"Get off me," she said.

"No."

Dies Irae was not a young man. He was twice this woman's age, but she made him feel young. He reached down and found her ready for him. She moaned beneath him, and snarled, and wrapped her arms around his back.

"You will kill weredragons," he hissed as he thrust into her.

"I will cut off their heads!" she cried and panted.

"We will kill the beasts and make them suffer like none have suffered."

She screamed.

Their voices echoed.

He rolled off her and stared at the ceiling. Gold and jewels covered that ceiling too. These chambers were the only place where glory and light still shone. The weredragons had destroyed the rest of the empire. *But they will pay. They will pay.*

Umbra nestled against him and ran her fingers across his chest. "For an old man, you have a lot of fire in you."

Dies Irae looked at her, silent. Suddenly he did feel old. Here beside him lay a woman half his age, a woman of midnight beauty. Her hair was silk, her eyes pools of shadow, her body lithe and tanned and intoxicating as summer wine. And him? An old cripple. Benedictus had taken his left arm; he wore a steel mace there instead. His brother had taken his eye too. Yes, he felt old. He felt ugly.

I should have beaten her, he thought. *I should have made her bleed, made her fear me, and raped her as she screamed.* Then it would not matter that he was old or deformed. Then he would be powerful, a tyrant to fear. But this.... She had given herself willingly. She had *enjoyed* it. That meant that she could judge him, see not only his power, but his weakness too.

Dies Irae looked away and gritted his teeth.

"How many men have you killed?" he asked.

"In bed?" She considered. "Three."

"I mean in a fight."

She snorted. "Your common soldiers fight. They hack and slash with clumsy blades, and wear armor that slows them. I don't fight, my lord. I sneak in the darkness and stab in the back. I poison and strangle. I have killed thirty men. Now I will kill weredragons."

Dies Irae rose to his feet. He stepped toward his window and looked outside at the ruins of his city. "A thousand mimics march toward Requiem. I know the weredragons. They will not stay to defend their home. They will leave. And I know where they will go."

He turned to look at Umbra. She lay on his rug, staring up at him hungrily.

"Where, my lord?"

"To darkness," he said. "To death. And to your daggers."

MEMORIA

They flew over plains of ice, snow, and rock. The clouds stretched like fingers above them.

"Remember your training," Terra said. Frost and icicles covered his bronze scales. "We've killed griffins. We can kill giants."

Memoria nodded. She let fire fill her mouth and dance between her teeth. Yes, she had fought, and she had killed. She had blown her fire, and lashed her claws, and bitten with her fangs. She had let blood wash her.

"We can kill giants," she agreed.

Her wings were steady and her jaw tight, but her insides trembled. Would giants beg for mercy too? Would they look at her with wide, terrified eyes like the boy she had killed? And, when their eyes met hers, would she find only hatred in her heart and fire on her breath?

Memoria stared ahead at the plains of ice and rock. *No. Do not remember that boy. You had to kill him. If he was old enough to ride a griffin, and old enough to kill dragons, he was old enough to die. Giants will not have such large, frightened eyes.*

They flew for hours. They crossed leagues. They soared over plains of ice, snow, and black boulders; over seas where whales swam; over icebergs where seals would once gather and now only snow whispered. They flew through wind and cloud. Frost covered their scales and icicles hung from their mouths. Finally, after what seemed a lifetime of flying, they saw the Jet Mountains ahead.

They rose like fortresses, black as memory. No snow covered them. Their surfaces were polished, like shards of black glass glued together. When the light caught them, it nearly blinded Memoria. She remembered Amberus's parting words. *The Giant King lives upon the mountaintop. It's him you must face. He has Adoria's Hands.*

"Remember your training," Terra repeated. "We've killed griffins. We can kill gia--."

A howl tore the air.

Memoria narrowed her eyes, and her heart pounded. She looked around but saw nothing.

"Giants," she whispered.

Terra nodded. "Keep flying."

The Jet Mountains were getting closer. The sunlight blazed against them, shooting toward the two dragons. Memoria grimaced and squinted. She could barely see.

The howl rose again. A second, then a third howl answered it. The mountain seemed to shake. Memoria covered her ears. The howls were deep, guttural, and ached in her chest. Memoria had heard armies of griffins shriek, but she had never heard anything so loud, so cruel, a sound like tumbling boulders.

"Do you see them?" she called over the roars.

Terra flew beside her, eyes narrowed. The light from the mountains turned his bronze scales white. He growled and blew fire.

"No!" he called back. "They've seen us. They--"

"Terra!"

Something came flying through the light toward them. She could barely see it. She grabbed Terra and pulled him down. Air whooshed above them.

"What was that?" Terra cried.

"Fly up! Higher."

They soared and emerged from the blinding light. Snow and ice rolled beneath them. When she looked ahead, she saw the Jet Mountains closer than she'd ever seen them. Shadows raced across them. Panes of stone moved, and light drenched her again.

"They're using some kind of stone mirrors," Terra said and cursed.

The giants' howls rose. A boulder flew from the mountains, tumbling through the beams of light toward them.

"Watch out!" she cried. She swerved right. Terra swerved left. The boulder passed between them, flames coiling around it.

"Not the most pleasant welcoming," Terra said.

Memoria flew higher, shooting up in a straight line. The air grew thin and cold. She could barely breathe. She looked down and saw giants scurrying across the mountainsides, adjusting their stone mirrors. Memoria had always imagined giants to be slow, lumbering beasts, but these creatures were so fast, her eyes barely caught them.

"Higher, Terra!" she shouted. "Fly out of their boulders' range."

He flew beside her, and they kept soaring, until Memoria gasped for breath, and darkness clawed at the corners of her eyes. She had never flown so high.

Are we safe? she wondered... then saw more boulders flying toward her.

She cursed and swerved, but a boulder hit her leg. She screamed. Pain blazed, and tears sprang into her eyes. More boulders flew. She dived, whipped around them, and swooped.

"New plan," she growled, the wind roaring around her. "Let's burn the bastards."

Terra swooped beside her, flames dancing between his teeth. The giants howled below them. Beams of light blazed, nearly blinding Memoria. The clouds swirled. From the mountains, twenty flaming boulders came flying.

Memoria spun. Three boulders missed her. One grazed her back. A second boulder slammed against her wing. She screamed and tumbled, plummeting toward the mountains.

"Terra!"

More boulders flew. Though her wing blazed, she forced herself to fly. She dipped sideways just in time. Boulders shot around her, their flames licking her. She swerved, dived, spun, and swooped.

"Memoria! Fly with me."

Terra swooped beside her, claws outstretched. His scales were chipped along his left side. They veered left and right, up and down, dodging the boulders. The beams of light kept hitting them, blinding them. A boulder hit her tail, and she screamed, but kept swooping. She saw two giants scurrying across the mountain beneath her.

She was close enough.

She blew flame.

The giants leaped behind boulders. Her flames rained against the mountain. The giants screamed.

Terra blew his own fire. The flames hit the mountainside and cascaded like a river of lava. A giant burst out from behind the boulders, hair blazing, a club in his hands.

For an instant, Memoria faltered. It was the first giant she had seen up close. *He's hideous.* The giant stood thirty feet tall, each foot covered in boils and coarse white hair. He wore only a ragged loincloth, and a stench of stale sweat rose from him. His nose was bulbous and red, sprouting white hair from the nostrils. Crooked teeth, each the size of a sword, grew from his mouth. His eyes were small and mean, the color of dried blood.

Howling, the giant swung his club at her.

Memoria flew backwards and blew flame.

The inferno hit the giant. He screamed and fell back, skin crackling.

"Watch out!" Terra said, grabbed her, and pulled her down. They landed on the mountainside. A boulder flew overhead, missing them by an inch.

Terra shot a jet of flame. A giant screamed behind Memoria. Three more giants ran ahead, boulders raised in their hands.

Memoria bathed them with fire. Two dropped their boulders. A third tossed his. Memoria leaped aside, and the missile grazed her shoulder. She grunted with pain. Her leg still throbbed.

"I don't like this," Terra said. Memoria whipped her head from side to side. A hundred giants were emerging from holes, tunnels, and the cover of stone outcrops. They bore clubs studded with bones, boulders that crackled with fire, and gleaming stone daggers. They climbed from below, from above, from each side.

"Fly!" Memoria said and leaped into the air. She flapped her wings as fast as she could. "Over the mountaintop."

Terra flew beside her. Boulders shot after them. One hit Terra's wing. He howled.

"Terra!" Memoria cried. She spat fire down at the giants and flew to her brother. He was wincing, but still flying. She held him and helped him fly higher. All around them, the barrage of stone continued. Memoria swerved, dodging most of the boulders. One slammed into her side, knocking the breath out of her. Pain bloomed. She could not breathe. She could not see.

No, don't kill me! the boy had cried. *I beg you, please. I have parents and a sister. Please. Please....*

Only a boy. No older than fifteen. A boy with scared eyes, with soft cheeks that had never grown stubble. A boy in armor. A boy riding a griffin. A boy who flew for Dies Irae, who killed and destroyed.

He is old enough to die.

She burned him.

He screamed. He screamed for what seemed like eternity.

Die already, stop screaming and die! Memoria wanted to cry, but she only watched him burn, until finally he screamed no more. A boy. With parents, with a sister. Silenced.

"Memoria!"

She wept. "I had to do it. I had to."

"Memoria! Fly! *Fly!*"

Her eyes snapped open. Terra was shaking her, struggling to fly with one hurt wing. Boulders still flew around them, and giants howled. Memoria gritted her teeth and flew.

They soared up the mountainside. Their reflections raced along the smooth, black stones--one green dragon, one bronze. More giants emerged from holes and behind rocks. There were thousands.

Blue sky burst before her. They reached the mountaintop, flew over it, and saw the city of giants.

Memoria's breath died.

LACRIMOSA

"No more tears," she whispered to herself. "Now is my turn to be strong. To lead. For our children, Ben. For you."

She stood under the orphaned archway, above the ruins of the fort where they made their home. The wind streamed her hair, kissed her cheeks with snow, and whispered of the growing threat in the east. *There will be war,* she knew. Dies Irae knew they were here; she did not doubt that now. Hundreds of mimics would march here. Blood would spill.

"Mother," Agnus Dei said. She came to stand beside her. Her mop of curls was white with snow. Her clothes were tattered, and bandages covered her wounds. Shadows filled her eyes, and she looked too thin to Lacrimosa, too weary, too haunted.

"Are you eating, Agnus Dei? You look thin."

She narrowed her eyes. "We're mustering forces for war, and that's what you worry about? That I'm not eating?" She sighed. "Mothers will be mothers."

The snow flurried. Lacrimosa shielded her eyes with her palm and stared down the mountainsides. Their forces seemed too few. *They cannot stop the tide,* she thought. *Am I mad to stay here? Am I mad to make a stand? Will this be another Lanburg Fields?*

"We used every Animating Stone we have," Lacrimosa said. "One hundred and twenty. Will it be enough?"

The stone dragon she had animated stood on the eastern hillside, unmoving, a sentinel of stone. Kyrie and Agnus Dei had animated three more statues. The stone maiden stood to the north, the warrior to the south, the king to the west.

Between them stood over a hundred warriors carved from the smashed columns of Requiem. They were crude figures; they had only the rough shapes of men, their surfaces craggy. The four true statues had carved them, and they were ugly things, but Animating Stones pulsed within them. They lived. They would fight.

"Time for dinner," Kyrie announced, climbing out from the cellars. He held two steaming bowls. "I cooked. Gloriae helped a bit. Tonight we have a delicious, lovingly simmered stew of turnips, oats, and sausages."

Gloriae emerged from the cellars behind him, holding two more bowls. "Kyrie, have we eaten anything but turnips, oats, and sausage stew for the past month?"

He nodded, handing out bowls. "Yesterday was more of a soup, what with all the water you added."

"Soup with some Gloriae hairs added for flavor," Agnus Dei muttered. "I nearly choked on one. Sister, you might be the deadliest warrior among us, and you are also the deadliest cook."

Soon the four sat in the courtyard, wrapped in their cloaks, eating as the sunset painted the world red. Lacrimosa was glad to see them eating hungrily, even Agnus Dei. *They'll need what strength they can get*, she thought. *More than ever.*

As they ate, the statues moved across the mountainsides, arranging firewood in a ring around the ruins. *Fire and stone,* Lacrimosa thought, watching the statues work. *This is how we fight in the ruin of the world. This is all we have left. Fire and stone.*

She looked at her children, one by one. Agnus Dei, of fiery eyes, of skinned knees, of grumbles and tears and kisses and flames. *She looks so much like Ben.* And Gloriae... her lost daughter, finally returned. Gloriae, of icy green eyes, of pain, of fear, of hidden love and light. Finally, Lacrimosa looked at Kyrie, who was like a son to her now. Kyrie, the boy who'd survived Lanburg Fields; no, not a boy but a man now, full grown, a man who would father her grandchildren.

I will protect them, Ben, she thought and looked up to the sky. *I won't let them die.*

They were still eating when howls sounded in the distance.

They froze. Lacrimosa lowered her spoon, rose to her feet, and stared east.

"We can't even enjoy one good meal," Agnus Dei said. She grabbed a torch from the ground. "My stars."

The howls rose, some deep and guttural like dying boars, others high like the screeches of ghosts.

"Weredragons!" they cried. "We will eat you alive. We will have your heads."

Lacrimosa drew an arrow from her quiver, tightened the kindling around its tip, and lit it. She walked toward the eastern ruins of the fort, to war, to blood.

"Fire and stone," she whispered. "They fight for us today."

She stepped onto the remaining few bricks of the fort's wall and saw the mimic army.

She felt the blood drain from her face.

"Bloody stars," Kyrie said, coming to stand beside her, bow in hand.

Even Gloriae, always stony like a statue, seemed shaken. She gritted her teeth.

"So many," she whispered.

Agnus Dei snorted, blowing back a curl of her hair. "Come on, we can take em," she said, but Lacrimosa noticed that the girl's fingers trembled around her bow.

She returned her eyes to the mimics. A hundred had attacked Draco Murus last time, and nearly killed them. A thousand now howled ahead, charging through the snow. Their stench carried on the wind, the stench of rot and worms and old blood. They bore swords and shields. A towering mimic ran at their lead, his legs like stilts, his arms ape-like and swinging.

"Weredragons!" this leader of mimics howled. "Your heads are mine."

Lacrimosa smiled a crooked, mirthless smile.

"Let them taste fire first," she said. "Then stone."

She loosed her arrow.

The three young Vir Requis gave wordless cries and shot three more arrows.

The flaming missiles flew through the sky, and each hit a rotting torso. Those mimics screamed, pulled the arrows out, and kept running.

"Damn," Agnus Dei said. "These ones are tougher than the last."

Lacrimosa nodded. "We'll see how much fire they can take."

She ran toward the ring of firewood, which surrounded the fort, and lit it. It crackled into life at once, flowing around the fort like a flaming serpent. The mimics screamed and kept charging.

Lacrimosa climbed onto a pile of fallen bricks. She saw the horde closer now, three hundred yards away. She shot an arrow and hit a mimic's shield. It kept running.

"Statues of Requiem!" Lacrimosa shouted. The statues stood outside the ring, unmoving. Kyrie and the twins were still firing arrows, but their missiles did not faze the mimics.

"Statues, hear me!" Lacrimosa shouted. "I am Lacrimosa, wife of King Benedictus, Queen of Requiem. Fight for Requiem. Fight the enemy, tear them apart, destroy them! Fight them now."

The statues began to move. They walked slowly, limbs creaking. The crude statues, those carved from the columns, barely moved at all.

"Charge at them!" Lacrimosa shouted. "Give them no mercy. Fight for the Draco stars, for the rebirth of your home."

They began to move faster. Soon they were running. Their feet thundered, kicked up snow and dirt, and they shouted. Their cries were like cracking stone, like weeping forests, like the pain of Requiem. It sounded almost like the deep, mournful cries of dragons.

"Fire, then stone," Lacrimosa whispered, and watched the statues crash into the army of mimics.

Blood, chips of stone, and gobbets of flesh flew. There were ten mimics for each statue. The rotting creatures hacked at the marble warriors, breaking off arms, heads, and legs. The mimics were made of flesh, but their blows bore the strength of ancient magic. The marble statues swung at them, their arms tearing through rotted flesh, scattering limbs and heads. Black blood and rot sprayed the snow.

Hope filled Lacrimosa. *We can do this. We can defend our home.*

Then she heard cries that chilled her blood.

"For Requiem!" Gloriae cried. She brandished her sword in one hand, a torch in the other.

"For Queen Lacrimosa!" cried Agnus Dei and Kyrie, raising their own swords and torches.

The three youths leaped over the fiery ring, howled, and charged into battle.

"No!" Lacrimosa shouted, horror clutching at her. "Stay with me. Here!"

They did not hear. Swinging their weapons, the youths crashed into the battle and began hacking at mimics.

Lacrimosa cursed and began running across the courtyard. *Stupid children!* They had raised warriors of stone so they would not have to fight themselves. *If the mimics don't kill them, I will.*

She reached the ring of fire. The flames rose around her, blocking her view. They were lower in one spot; that was where the youths had jumped out to battle. Cursing, Lacrimosa jumped over the fire and ran toward battle. *The children might be dumber than doorknobs, but I must protect them.*

She drew Stella Lumen, her father's sword. Its blade hissed and reflected the firelight. Two mimics rushed at her, pus oozing from the stitches that held them together. They swung jagged blades.

Lacrimosa was no soldier. She had not trained in swordplay like Gloriae. But she had fought enough battles to muster courage if not skill. She parried left and right, screaming. She swung a torch in her left hand, her blade in the right. She let them taste steel and fire. They fell back.

"Daughters!" she called. "Kyrie! Back to the fort. Do not meet them in open battle."

She could not see them. Everywhere around her, the statues and mimics fought. Severed mimic limbs crawled across the battlefield, clutching her boots. She stomped them and burned them with her torch.

"Requiem!" Kyrie called somewhere in the distance, his voice nearly drowned under the roar of battle. Lacrimosa did not know what she craved more; to kill mimics, or to clobber the boy over the head.

A mimic skirted around two statues and raced toward her. Lacrimosa cursed and raised her blade. The mimic was shaped as a monstrous centaur. Its lower half was a headless, rotting man running on all fours. Sewn onto the man's shoulders, rose the nude torso, arms, and head of a woman. Her hair was made of snakes, and her teeth were jagged metal. In each hand, the rotting woman wielded an axe.

Horror, white and burning, spread through Lacrimosa. She tightened her grip on her sword.

"Stella Lumen, burn with the light of stars," Lacrimosa whispered, holding the blade before her. "Father, be with me today."

The strange centaur charged toward her, squealed, and swung an axe.

Lacrimosa dropped to her knees and slid forward through the snow. The axe whistled over her head. As she slid, Lacrimosa swung her blade and cut the mimic's leg.

It screeched, a sound that seemed to shake the mountain. Snow cascaded. Lacrimosa leaped to her feet, and the mimic charged toward her. It swung both axes at her head. She leaped back. The centaur raced toward her.

Lacrimosa lobbed her torch. It hit the centaur's upper half, then fell into the snow. The mimic screamed. Its chest reddened and crackled. Before it could recover, Lacrimosa shouted, ran toward it, and swung her blade.

Stella Lumen opened the creature's stomach. Snakes spilled from it like entrails. They squirmed around Lacrimosa's feet, hissing.

An axe swung. Lacrimosa parried and sparks flew. She thrust her sword and hit the mimic's neck.

Blood showered. The mimic screamed. Lacrimosa slashed again, and the mimic fell. She stabbed it again and again, but still it kicked and squealed.

Fire. Lacrimosa thought. *I need fire.*

Her torch had extinguished in the snow. She grabbed it, looked up, and saw Agnus Dei fighting beside her. A mimic with four arms was attacking her. Lacrimosa ran and touched her torch to her daughter's. It crackled back into flame.

"Agnus Dei, you are the most numbskulled girl I've ever seen!" Lacrimosa shouted.

Agnus Dei grunted. "Not now, Mother. I'm busy."

The centaur mimic, lacerated and burned, was struggling to rise. Worms squirmed across it. Lacrimosa ran and shoved the torch against its head. The snakes of its hair caught fire, and soon the entire creature burned. It twisted and screeched in the snow.

Lacrimosa did not stay to watch it die. She ran back toward Agnus Dei, and found that the girl had slain the four-armed mimic. Statues and mimics still battled around them.

"Where's your sister?" she cried. "Where's Kyrie?"

Agnus Dei pointed. "There."

The two were fighting back to back, five mimics surrounding them. Beyond them, dozens of mimics and statues lay smashed and burned. Dozens more still fought in every direction.

"Gloriae! Kyrie!" Lacrimosa called. "Back to the fort."

She ran toward them. Agnus Dei ran too. With swords and torches, they slew mimics that clawed and bit from each side.

"Back to safety," Lacrimosa commanded, her head pounding, her limbs shaking. "The statues will finish our work here."

Cuts and scrapes covered the youths. They nodded, panting, and began heading back uphill.

A thundering howl rose before them.

Snow cascaded.

A great mimic came running downhill toward them, shoving aside statues and other mimics. It towered over the others on freakishly long legs, and had hairy arms that rippled with muscles. When it opened its mouth to scream, it revealed sharp teeth like a wolf's. It seemed sewn from three bodies--the legs of one, the arms of another, and the torso and head of a third. In each hand, it held a flanged mace.

The mimic's leader, Lacrimosa remembered.

"Kyrie! Agnus Dei!" she yelled. "Attack it from its right. Gloriae! We'll take its left side."

The mimic grinned. Drool dripped down its chin and steamed when it hit the snow. With a mocking howl, it swung its maces.

Lacrimosa leaped back, but Gloriae charged and swung her sword. A mace hit her breastplate and dented it. Gloriae cried and fell.

"Gloriae!" Lacrimosa cried. She ran and swung Stella Lumen at the mimic.

It swung its mace, and Lacrimosa ducked and raised her arm to protect her face. The mace hit her vambrace, and she screamed. One flange dented the steel and bit her arm.

"Mother!" Agnus Dei cried and attacked at the mimic's other side. She swung her torch at it, but it lashed its mace, holding her back.

"Lacrimosa, down!" Kyrie said, nocking a flaming arrow.

She fell to her knees, and the arrow flew over her head. It slammed into the mimic, plunged through its chest, and extinguished. The mimic grinned and ran toward Kyrie, swinging its maces.

Kyrie shot another arrow. He hit the mimic, but the creature only grunted and kept charging. Lacrimosa and Agnus Dei slammed their swords against its back, but the cuts did not slow it.

Was Gloriae alive? Lacrimosa had no time to check. The mimic reached Kyrie and swung a mace. Kyrie ducked, and the mace glanced off his helmet. He fell into the snow and his eyes closed.

"Pup!" Agnus Dei screamed, eyes widening. She jumped onto the mimic's back and pushed it into the snow. She began slamming her sword's pommel into its head. The mimic thrashed and howled.

Lacrimosa ran. The mimic rose to its feet and shook Agnus Dei off. It dropped one mace, clutched Agnus Dei's throat, and began to squeeze.

"Let her go," Lacrimosa said, snarled, and swung her blade. Stella Lumen severed the mimic's arm with a shower of blood and starlight.

Agnus Dei fell to her knees, scratching at the hand that still clutched her throat. Lacrimosa helped pry the fingers loose. Agnus Dei sucked in breath and coughed. Her face was deep red.

"Behind you!" she managed to say.

Lacrimosa spun around and hurled her torch. She hit the advancing mimic in the face. It howled, dropped its second mace, and brushed the sparks off its face.

"Pup, pup, get up!" Agnus Dei was crying, shaking Kyrie. The boy was coughing and struggling to rise. *Hurt but alive,* Lacrimosa thought in relief. *What of Gloriae?*

The mimic lashed its remaining arm at her. Lacrimosa ducked and swung her sword. She sliced the creature's elbow. It snarled and reached its claws toward her.

A flaming arrow slammed into its head.

Gloriae came walking downhill, already nocking a second arrow. Her eyes were ice, her face emotionless. The wind streamed her hair. She drew the bowstring.

My daughter. She's alive. Such relief swept over Lacrimosa, that her eyes blurred.

The mimic screeched.

Gloriae shot her second arrow. It pierced the mimic's neck, and it fell to its knees.

Lacrimosa stepped toward it. It snarled, oozing pus and rot.

"Fire," she told it. "Stone. And steel."

Lacrimosa swung her blade and severed its head.

The other Vir Requis burned its body with their torches, until it did not move. But Lacrimosa held onto the head, keeping it at arm's length. It shouted and snapped its teeth. An arrow still thrust out of it.

"We will keep this piece alive," she said. "Now back to the fort."

Holding the head, she raced up the mountainside. The other Vir Requis followed. Around them, as if disheartened by the loss of their leader, the mimics were falling fast. The statues were tearing into them, killing them left and right. Only twenty statues remained standing; the rest were smashed and lay still on the ground. Many lay in pieces no longer than a foot.

The Vir Requis stepped back into the ruins, looked down the mountainside, and watched the statues kill the last mimics. Lacrimosa tossed the severed mimic head onto the cobblestones, then turned to face the youths.

"You three are the stupidest Vir Requis who ever lived. If Ben were here, he'd clobber you harder than the mimics."

Lacrimosa had promised herself she would stop weeping; she could no longer cry, not now, Benedictus having left her to lead. Tonight she could not help it. The tears filled her eyes, and she embraced Kyrie and her daughters.

"Never do anything so foolishly brave again," she said as she embraced them. "I love you too much to see it."

Agnus Dei squirmed in the embrace. "Mother, really."

They broke apart and breathed deeply. Lacrimosa's body ached. The fire crackled in the night, raising sparks like fireflies.

Laughter sounded in the shadows.

Lacrimosa turned and saw the severed mimic head. It lay on the cobblestones, glaring at her. Its sharp teeth reflected the firelight as it cackled.

"You have won this battle," the mimic said and spat out blood. "You killed a thousand of us. Fifty thousand are gathering as we speak. With each he builds, our master makes us larger, stronger, smarter. You cannot win, weredragons."

Lacrimosa walked toward the head. She pointed her sword at it.

"Where do the others gather?" she asked. "Where does Dies Irae find the Animating Stones?"

It cackled and spat at her. Its gob of spit landed on her boot.

Lacrimosa placed the tip of her sword against its face, but did not break the skin.

"Talk to me," she said, "or you will die."

It cackled. "Kill me, weredragon. It will not save you."

Lacrimosa felt a hand on her shoulder. She turned to see Gloriae. The young woman was covered in blood, ash, and mimic gore. She stared down at the head, her eyes emotionless, her face as cold as one of the statues.

"I will make it talk," she said, her voice strangely soft. "Mother, take Agnus Dei and Kyrie into the cellars. Leave me with it. I promise you; it will tell me all it knows."

Lacrimosa shivered. What would Gloriae do? Had she tortured prisoners before? Lacrimosa did not want to think about it, did not want to imagine what skills Dies Irae had taught her daughter.

"Gloriae, are you sure?" she whispered.

The young woman nodded, eyes icy.

Lacrimosa looked away. Her eyes stung. *I must be strong. For you, Ben. For our home.* She took a deep breath.

"Agnus Dei," she said. "Kyrie. Come with me underground. We'll bandage your wounds. Gloriae will join us soon."

As they walked downstairs into shadows, Lacrimosa looked back one more time at Gloriae. The wind billowed her daughter's hair, swirling snow around her. Then Lacrimosa stepped into the cellars and saw nothing but darkness.

GLORIAE

She stood among the ruins, staring down the mountainside at the battlefield. A thousand mimics lay burned and torn apart. Nearly a hundred statues lay smashed. The last few statues, including the stone dragon, were searching for mimic body parts and crushing them.

It smells wrong, Gloriae thought. *I was raised to savor the smell of fresh blood. To dream of it, crave it. Yet here I fight, in a field of rot and stone.*

She raised her eyes from the carnage and stared into the eastern horizon. Dawn was rising, sending pink tendrils across a cloudy sky. Beyond that horizon lay home. *What used to be my home, at least.* The empire of Osanna lay many leagues from here, across crumbled cities, burned fields, and wilted forests. The nightshades had ravaged it, but Dies Irae still ruled over the ruins.

"He's still out there somewhere," Gloriae whispered into the wind. "The man I called Father. The man who banished me. The man I will kill."

Hoarse laughter sounded behind her. Gloriae turned. The severed mimic head lay on the cobblestones, oozing its juices. It cackled, eyes mocking her.

"You will not kill Dies Irae," it said, coughed, and spat. "He has a new body waiting for you, Gloriae the Gilded. Yes, I know your name. And I know your fate. He will cut off your head, and sew it onto a new body, and turn you into a mimic. Then he will let a thousand other mimics thrust inside you, until you bleed and beg for a death that will never come."

Gloriae stared at it silently, waiting for it to finish speaking.

"You like talking," she said. "That is good. You will talk more. You will tell me everything you know."

It spat a glob of maggoty saliva. "I know that you will be a slave to mimics."

"How lovely," Gloriae said. "But enough about me. Let's talk about you, my toothy friend. Tell me about that Animating Stone that gave you life. Where did Irae find it?"

She knelt before the head, torch crackling.

"Will you torture me now?" it asked. "Burn me? Cut me? Pull out my teeth? Do it. I fear no pain."

A centipede emerged from its mouth and scurried along the cobblestones. Gloriae watched it flee into shadows, then stared into the mimic's eyes.

"Pain won't make you talk. Memories might." She narrowed her eyes, examining it. "Who were you?"

It cackled. "I am mimic. I am death and despair. I am rot and worm. I am your future."

Gloriae shook her head. "That is what you are now. Who were you once?"

It glared at her. "Weak."

"Life," she said. "You were life once. Real life."

It coughed blood onto her boots. "What would you know of life? I know you. All beings do. You killed children when you yourself were a child. You killed countless in your chase of weredragons. You unleashed the nightshades. You destroyed the world."

Gloriae stared at it with dry eyes. *Stay strong. No feelings. No pain.*

"Yes," she said. "I am a giver of death. I deal in blood and steel. I have killed many, and I will kill many more before they burn my body in a great pyre." She touched the mimic's head, leaned down, and whispered to it. "But I was not always a killer. Once I too was life. I too was a child."

The head hissed and tried to bite her fingers. "You will beg for death, mortal. You will be one of us. You--"

"You were a child too once," she said. "You were a boy."

"I am mimic! I am stronger than life. You will join us. You--"

She clutched its cheeks, lifted the head, and stared at it levelly. "Who were you? You have rotted less than the others. You were killed fresh. Who were you in life?"

"Teeth!" it screeched. "I-- No. I am only death, I..."

She brought its face close to hers. "Teeth? What does that mean?"

"They... Teeth! Legs. Rot Gang, and Arms. He betrayed us. He had to die. I had to kill him. Teeth! It hurts, Teeth. It hurts. He hit our head with his mace. He lied to us. Silver! I brought you death, I brought you rot, we are Rot Gang. We are three. Pay me my silver."

She shook the head. "Who was to pay you? Who hurt you? Was it Dies Irae?"

Blood filled the mimic's eyes and flowed down its cheeks like tears. "Do not speak of him! He will hurt us again. He wields a fist of steel. He hit our head. He killed our Legs. He.... He...." The head trembled in her hands.

"What did he do?" Gloriae demanded. "Did he kill you?"

The creature wept its tears of blood. More blood poured between its sharp teeth. "I have teeth. Sharp teeth. Teeth, they call me. I had to kill Arms. Long arms, he had, arms for silver, silver coins, that's what I asked of him. But... his fist of steel. He took my head. He hurt Legs. It burns! He burns us."

Gloriae held the head steady, though its blood covered her hands. "He killed you," she whispered. "And he made you into a mimic."

The head shook. "No, master! Not the needles. Not the strings. It burns in our chest, the stone. Not his legs! Give him back his legs. I don't want them. Not his arms, please. I don't want his arms. I killed him for silver, not arms. Where are my legs? Where are my arms? The needle burns!"

Gloriae stared at the weeping, trembling, bloody creature. Was this what Dies Irae planned for her too? To kill her and sew others' parts onto her?

"How many were you?" she said.

"Three. Rot Gang. Rot. We deal in death and silver. Not needles. No, please not needles, and not stones that burn."

She shook the head. "Animating Stones. Where are they from? Where is he finding them?"

"I must serve him. I must kill for him. I must never betray him. He will hurt us, Arms. He will cut us. He will burn us, Legs. We must not tell her. We must never speak of the stones."

"You will speak," Gloriae said. "You will tell me everything."

It cackled, spraying saliva. "You cannot hurt us like he did."

Gloriae shook her head. "No. I cannot. But I can end your pain, Teeth. I can free you. I can separate you from Legs and Arms."

It froze.

Its breath died.

For a long moment, it stared at her with narrowed eyes.

"We... we were Teeth once. We do not want his legs. We do not want his arms. They scream inside me. They still burn! I hear their voices in my skull. Free them from me. Cut them off me! Cut them off. I will speak to you then."

Gloriae glared. "First you will speak to me. Then I will end your pain. Then you will be a boy again, only Teeth. No more mimic."

It wept like a child. "Only Teeth. No Legs. No Arms. No silver. No rot. Just Teeth. Only Teeth, Rot Gang, yes."

"Will you speak?"

It nodded, seeming to wilt in her hands. "We will speak of stones, yes. Animating Stones. Things that burn. Stones of fire; they bind us, they move us. They serve him. Oh, they serve him, Arms. They do not stop. We cannot stop it inside us, clawing us, moving us."

Gloriae narrowed her eyes. "Where did Dies Irae find them?"

The bloody tears kept flowing; Gloriae could not believe it had so much blood. "I have seen them, Arms. Yes, I have. A wagon driving through the city. A wagon that glowed red. Animating Stones were there! They took them into his dungeon, Legs. He took one. He put it inside us. He took my legs. He took my arms. He used yours, he sewed us together, Rot Gang, no silver, only mimic. Only mimic."

"Where did the wagon come from?"

"A mine! A mine in a burned forest. A mine where Animating Stones glow. A mine of mimics, yes. A mine of stones. A mine of pain, and death, and rot. Rot Gang. Free them! Cut them off me. Cut off his legs. Cut off his arms."

Gloriae dug her fingers into the head. "Not yet. Where is the mine?"

It bared its bloody teeth. "Master would laugh of it. The same forest, he said, where the weredragon king once hid. He mined for Animating Stones in a crater, a crater where no trees could grow, and where the earth sank. And he laughed, Arms. Yes, how he laughed."

"The weredragon king? Do you mean Benedictus? Is the mine in Hostias Forest, where Benedictus once hid?"

The head coughed and trembled. "We don't know, Legs, do we? We don't know, Arms. Hostias Forest, he called it, yes, right under the crater where King Weredragon hid. And he laughed. But we only screamed. Our stone burns. It burns us. He hurt us. He laughed and sewed us. Free us!"

Gloriae tossed the head aside. She turned to leave.

Hostias Forest. The crater. Gloriae clenched her jaw. The place she had burned when hunting Benedictus and Kyrie. She would have to return there.

"You promised!" the head screamed behind her. "She promised to free us, Legs. She promised to make us Teeth again, to make us Rot Gang."

Gloriae drew an arrow and lit it with her tinderbox. She nocked the arrow in her bow.

"You lied!" the head shrieked, eyes blazing. "You swore to free them, to cut them off!"

Gloriae shut one eye, drew, and aimed.

"Yes," she whispered. "I lied."

She loosed her arrow. It shot like a comet and hit the severed head. It burst into flame.

"You will burn with us!" it screamed from the fire. "You will burn too, Gloriae. You will burn forever. You will burn in the Sun God's fire."

The flames overcame its words. Gloriae watched it burn, until it was nothing but a skull. Still its jaw moved, and its teeth clacked. Gloriae walked toward it and kicked with her steel-tipped boot. She kept kicking until the skull shattered.

"I did not make you a boy again," she said. "But I freed you. I ended your pain. That is more than what Dies Irae will do to me, if he catches me." She clenched her fists. "But he will not catch me. He will burn too."

She turned around and stepped underground into the cellars.

TERRA

His wing and leg blazed in pain, but Terra kept flying. The city of giants spread beneath him.

"Stars," Memoria whispered.

She flew beside him, blood staining her green scales. Terra clenched his jaw. The sight of her blood hurt him more than his wounds. *I will not let her die too. I will fight and burn and die if I must, but I will protect her.*

He returned his eyes to the city. It spread like a labyrinth. Leagues of grey brick walls wound across the mountaintop. Giants ran between them, shouting and howling and pounding their chests. There were thousands, maybe tens of thousands.

"Look," Terra said. He pointed a claw and grunted with the pain; his knee felt swollen and burned. "The fort."

"I see it," Memoria said, eyes narrowed. "The king must live there."

The fortress loomed taller than an Ice Palace, taller than the old courts of Requiem; Terra guessed that it stood a thousand feet tall. Built of grey, frosty bricks, it was a simple structure; it had no bridges, towers, or courtyards like the forts of men. It was but a great cube of stone. It rose from the city, a sentinel over the mountain.

Hundreds of spikes lined the fort's parapets, holding the decapitated heads of icelings. The heads gazed with eyeless sockets, their mouths open, their skin frozen blue. Giants stood there too, boulders in hands. They howled, and soon those boulders flew toward the two dragons.

Terra cursed, flew sideways, and dodged a boulder that grazed his leg. More boulders flew.

"Fly above the fort!" he shouted. "We'll be harder to hit."

Memoria nodded. They flapped their wings hard, shooting between the boulders. They flew higher and higher. The cold, thin air spun Terra's head. He righted himself, flew north, and circled above the stone fortress.

One giant tossed a boulder. Terra and Memoria scattered. The boulder flew between them, reached its zenith, and tumbled down. The giants below howled, and the boulder crashed between them, punching a hole into the fort.

The boulders ceased flying.

"Good," Terra said, flapping his wings. "We're safe if we hover right above them. I..." A closer look at the fortress made his breath die.

"Stars above," Memoria said, flying beside him. "Look at the *size* of him."

Terra clenched his jaw. Ice seemed to form along his spine. Fire filled his mouth, flicking between his teeth.

"I see him," he said, voice low. "He's a big boy, that one is."

A massive, deformed creature stood atop the fort, howling and pounding his chest. He towered over the giants who manned the parapets around him, twice their size. Tufts of hair grew from his squat, misshapen head. His body was all muscles overgrown with boils and scars. Claws grew from his fingers, each the size of a man. He wore a loin cloth, a belt decorated with iceling heads, and a crown of icicles.

"He must be a hundred feet tall," Memoria whispered.

Terra nodded. "Twice our size. He's their king."

The Giant King howled and reached his claws toward them. His cry shook the air; Terra could feel it pound against his chest. In his mind, he heard the howls of dragons, and the shrieks of griffins, and Memoria's voice. *Terra... I found him.*

"Look at his neck," Memoria said.

Terra frowned and stared. A golden chain hung around the giant's neck. Two small, white objects hung from it. When Terra squinted, they came into focus. Hands. A woman's hands, pale and dainty, folded into fists.

"Adoria's Hands," he said. "Those are the toys we want. Let's burn him, then grab them."

The smaller giants leered and waved their arms. The king pounded his feet, snapped his teeth, and cried out to them in a guttural language.

Memoria shook her head. "No fire, Terra! What if flames burn Adoria's Hands?"

The Giant King spat and shouted. His eyes blazed. Terra imagined that he was insulting them, calling them weak, inviting them to fight. Terra's head spun. He grinded his teeth.

What am I doing here? he thought. *I vowed to nevermore fly to war. To nevermore see fire, blood, a loved one die.* He wanted to turn and leave, to fly back to the ice palace. To hide from war. From pain. From those soft, echoing words.

Terra... I found him.

But had she found him? Had that small body, burned beyond recognition, truly been Kyrie?

Are you still there, Kyrie? Still in the ruins of Requiem, waiting for me to find you?

"If you're alive, Kyrie, I'll help you," Terra whispered, quiet enough that Memoria could not hear. "I'll burn the mimics who hunt you. I'll take Adoria's Hands."

His sister flew around him, green scales splashed with blood. "Ready, Terra?"

He nodded, staring down at the giant. "We dive. I'll fly to his front, you to his back. Let's claw out his neck."

Terra bared his fangs, outstretched his claws, and swooped.

Dragons! To me!

Requiem, rally here!

Griffins! They killed the children, they--

The words of old battles screamed in the wind. Terra snarled and swooped. He swooped like in the old days, like he would swoop against Osanna, diving to kill, to burn, to fight for his life. To death. To glory. To pain.

Kyrie! Kyrie, do you hear me?

His howl rang. He reached the Giant King.

Claws flashed. The giant swung his fist. Terra dipped, flew under the blow, and lashed. His claws hit the giant's thigh.

Nothing. No blood. No mark. The giant's skin was tough as the thickest leather armor. Memoria flew behind the giant. She bit his shoulder, then cried. Her fangs would not pierce his skin.

The Giant King roared. Terra and Memoria flew up. The giant's fists swung, and one hit Terra's tail. It knocked him into a spin.

"Terra!" Memoria cried. The lesser giants cheered around them.

The king reached out, fingers thick and bloated like dead seals. Terra flapped his wings, narrowly dodging the blow, and soared.

"The damn thing seems made of boiled leather," Terra muttered. He circled a hundred feet above. The giant howled and stamped his feet below, grinning and drooling. Boulders flew. Terra flew left and right. One boulder grazed his side, chipping a scale.

"Leather? It felt like biting into iron," Memoria shouted. She flew beside him, wincing.

Terra growled. "Let's burn the beast."

"No fire, Terra! We can't harm Adoria's Hands."

"Then we'll burn the smaller ones."

Terra soared, spun, and dived. Boulders flew around him. One hit his left horn, knocking it off. He howled in pain and blew fire at a row of lesser giants. They blazed. More boulders flew. Terra soared, spun, flew at them again. He roared more fire. More giants burned and fell.

"Memoria, you all right?" he shouted.

She flew alongside the fort's parapets, blowing more flame. Giants caught fire. Their boulders fell, cracking the parapets.

"I'm fin--" she began, and a boulder slammed into her side. She fell.

"Memoria!"

Terra flew across the fortress, moving toward her. He flew too low. The Giant King reached out. Those bloated fingers grazed him. Terra flew higher. For an instant, he thought he was free. Then the king's hand closed around his leg.

The giant pulled him down like a man tugging a struggling bird. Terra howled and lashed his tail. He hit the king's face, but the giant only laughed. His fingers tightened around Terra's leg, nearly breaking the bone.

"Memoria!" he cried. Where was she?

The king pulled him near. His mouth opened, showing rotten, yellow teeth. His breath assailed Terra, as foul as mimics. His tongue reached out. *He's going to eat me alive.*

Terra blew fire, not caring if he harmed Adoria's Hands. His flames hit the king's face, crackling and showering sparks. The king howled, released Terra's leg, and brought his hands to his face.

113

Terra flapped his wings. The giant was rubbing his eyes, slapping the fire off his face. Terra swooped, shouted, and drove his remaining horn into the Giant King's left eye.

The giant roared so loudly, Terra thought his eardrums would tear. He pushed, driving the horn deep into the giant's head. The giant howled. His hands clutched him.

Terra couldn't breathe. The giant wrapped his arms around him and squeezed. Terra had never felt such pain. His ribs creaked. He felt one crack. He thought his organs would burst. The world turned black. Stars floated.

I'm dead, he thought. *It ends here. I'm dead and so is Memoria. I'm sorry, sister. I'm sorry. I love you.*

He flapped his wings. Somehow he kept kicking. He clawed, but the arms kept squeezing.

His eyes rolled back.

"Terra!"

He heard thudding wings. He heard cries, howls, tearing flesh. The arms released him.

Terra fell to the floor. He looked up and saw Memoria slashing the giant's face. She was like a raven attacking a bear. Her fangs and claws dug into the giant's eyes, nose, mouth. The king howled and swiped at her. Blood covered her scales; she was more red than green.

Up. Up! Fly, dragons of Requiem!

Howling, Terra pushed himself to his feet. His chest blazed. It felt like knives were digging inside him. He flapped his wings and soared.

He slammed into the giant, clawing. One claw caught the giant's slobbery lip, and tugged, and tore. Blood showered.

"It won't die!" Memoria shouted.

"It will! Bring it down!"

The king's hands thrashed. One fist hit Memoria. She cried and fell back. Another fist thudded into Terra's side, but he ignored the pain. For an instant, he saw the king's face. There was barely anything left; his head was a mess of blood and burned flesh. Disgust filled Terra. He flew, spun, and lashed his tail.

His tail's spikes drove into what had been the giant's head. One pushed through the ear, deep into the brain.

The king howled.

Terra pulled back. Memoria flew beside him. They hovered, panting, staring.

The Giant King swung his arms uselessly. He mewled. Mucus and blood flowed down him. He took one step toward them, knees shaky. He took a second step... and faltered. His knees hit the fortress roof, shaking the structure. He reached out feebly, swinging his hands as if swatting flies.

"Let's put him out of his misery," Terra said.

He flew to the giant's right. Memoria flew to his left. They clawed, lacerating the giant's neck.

The Giant King gave one last, gurgling yowl. He clutched his face and mewled like a demonic baby.

Then he fell.

He hit the fortress, cracking the stone. He kicked his legs, then lay still.

Terra collapsed beside the body. Breathing hurt. Memoria landed beside him and nudged him.

"More giants are climbing the walls," she said. "Let's grab Adoria's Hands and get out of here."

Terra nodded and grunted. He limped toward the dead Giant King. The body lay facedown, hiding Adoria's Hands beneath it. Terra shoved the body, but it felt like shoving a mountain.

"Come on!" Memoria shouted, shoving with him.

Giants howled behind them.

Boulders came flying.

Terra and Memoria leaped aside. The boulders hit the Giant King, shoving the body several feet back.

Terra roared fire. The flames shot across the fortress and hit a dozen giants. Memoria blew fire behind him, burning more giants. More boulders flew. The two dragons scattered, and the boulders hit the dead king again.

"Terra, the hands!" Memoria shouted.

The boulders had shoved the king, revealing Adoria's fingertips. The king's body still buried the palms.

"Hold them back!" he shouted to his sister.

Memoria nodded and flew in circles, blowing fire at the climbing giants. Flaming rocks flew around her. Terra shoved the giant's body, pushing with his feet. He howled with the pain. The body barely moved.

"Hurry, Terra, more are climbing!"

Terra grunted, shoving, driving forward. White pain blinded him. He shouted... and the body moved a foot. Terra reached down, snapped the chain, and tugged it. The hands came free.

"I've got them!" he called hoarsely. "Fly!"

Clutching the hands, he flapped his wings, shooting straight up. Memoria flew beside him, eyes narrowed, blood trickling. Boulders blazed around them like flaming comets.

In his mind, Terra saw the flaming arrows, the hordes of griffins, the fire upon Requiem. He saw their old home: the mosaic floor, the balcony in sunrise, the vineyard at sunset, the garden where he'd play with Memoria and Kyrie.

"I never left you," Terra whispered as he flew. His eyes stung. "You're still with me, Requiem. Now. Always."

If Memoria heard him, she said nothing, but she gave him a sad smile.

They flew from the Jet Mountains. They flew over plains of ice and snow. They flew over this land of exile, this frozen world where they hid from fire and pain. Blood had spilled here today, and fire burned, and for the first time in years, Terra felt the ice inside him melt.

I remember. I was a soldier. I was a brother. I am that man still.

He looked at Memoria, his little sister, the person he'd stayed alive for. He nodded at her.

"It's time to go home."

GLORIAE

She knew this place. She had hunted here. She had burned here. She had shed her mother's blood here and nearly killed her father.

Hostias. Once a shadowy, ancient forest. Today it was a land of burned trees and memories of war.

I rode my griffin Aquila over these woods, she remembered, *cutting the sky, the wind in my hair. I was a warrior of glory, of gold, of grandeur... and of lies.*

"Are you sure you know the way?" Gloriae asked her mother. "The land looks different now."

Lacrimosa nodded, walking beside her. "I know. I visited your father here every new moon. I will find the crater."

Her mother's tunic and leggings were tattered, her cheeks were ashy, and her lavender eyes looked too large, her face too thin. When Gloriae looked at her own body, she saw more dirt, more tatters, more scratches and bruises and thinned limbs.

I was a huntress of jewels and might, a light upon Osanna, a champion of justice. And now... now we are humble, and dirty, and gaunt. Gloriae missed those old days, missed the glory. But what glory had that life truly held? *Only glory to the blind,* she thought. *And I was blind. Dirt and hunger, when suffered for truth, are nobler than gold and lies.*

Gloriae looked over her shoulder and drew comfort from the sight of their host--marching statues with pulsing Animating Stones in their breasts. Roughly hewn from boulders and columns, they were craggy, bulky things, slow to move and rough to touch. Frost and snow covered them. Their features were mere chips, eyes narrow slits, mouths harsh lines. Though their first statues--the dragon and the maiden--had carved them only recently, they seemed to Gloriae like ancient things, gods of earth and stone and wisdom. The age of the stone appeared in every nook and bump upon them.

"They make a bloody racket," Agnus Dei muttered, walking beside Gloriae. The statues crackled with every step, a sound like grinding rubble. "The mimics will hear."

117

Kyrie was walking with an arrow in his bow. He snorted. "Let them hear. Our statues beat them to pulp last time. They can do it again."

But last time we fought on our turf, and now we march upon theirs, Gloriae thought, but said nothing. She knew that attacking a place was harder than defending it. Kyrie would learn that today, she suspected. She pulled down her helmet's visor, a gilded mask of her own face. Behind it, she felt like a statue herself, blank and expressionless, made for killing.

"I recognize this place," she said. She pointed at a frozen stream that snaked between craggy boulders shaped like trolls. Rushes had once grown along it; they had burned away in the war, but the boulders were unmistakable. She had camped here with her griffins once. "We're almost there."

Lacrimosa nodded. "Ben's hut was near. We would walk here many times."

And this is the place where I nearly killed Kyrie, Gloriae thought, but said nothing. It seemed so long ago. *Dirt for gold. Truth for glory.*

They kept walking. The charred trees rose around them, creaking in the wind, heavy with snow and icicles. Soon Gloriae heard a sound from ahead: creaking, hammering, grunting. She sniffed and smelled rot on the wind. *We're near.*

"Gloriae," said her twin, and placed a hand on her shoulder. "You are a brave warrior. You will fight well today."

When Gloriae turned her head, she saw Agnus Dei staring at her with somber eyes. *She's afraid,* Gloriae realized. *And so am I.*

She nodded. "You will as well. You are a warrior, Agnus Dei. I've seen you fight. I have fought you myself. Yours is a steel heart."

The sounds grew louder as they walked. *Thump thump* and *twang.* Hammering. The creaking of ropes. And above it all the grunting, squealing, and screaming of mimics.

"Stop," Gloriae said, raising her hand to halt the others. The statues too ceased walking; when still, they looked like nothing but boulders with the hint of men's shapes.

"What is it?" Kyrie asked.

"We make too much noise. I'll scout ahead. Wait here."

She left them between the burned trees. As she walked, she drew Per Ignem, and the blade caught the light. *My blade is thirsty for your blood, Irae,* she thought as she walked. *You gave me this blade.*

You gave me these steel-tipped boots. You gave me this steel armor and this steel soul. A snarl found her lips. *If you are here today, these weapons you gave me will be your death.*

The sounds from ahead grew louder. *Thump. Twang.* Squeals and shouts. *Move faster, maggots. Get this dirt out of here.* Screams and clashing metal. And above it all, a stench of rot that filled Gloriae's helmet and made her growl.

She stepped over a fallen bole, climbed a hill of burned birches, and beheld the Animating Stone mine. She knelt behind fallen trees and watched.

A ditch and wooden palisade surrounded the mine. Behind these crude fortifications, Gloriae saw a crater the size of the amphitheatre in Confutatis. It was clear of brush and dust rose from it. Tents, scaffolding, and wagons of dirt covered the crater. In the center, a shaft led underground.

Gloriae narrowed her eyes, examining Dies Irae's forces. Mimics patrolled the crater, their arms burly, their chests broad. Some seemed to be workers; they carried shovels and buckets. Others were warriors; their arms ended with blades instead of hands. Gloriae counted thirty workers and fifty warriors.

"Is that all?" she whispered, raising an eyebrow. *This mine is the key to Irae's power. Are these all his guards?*

Frowning, she walked back to the others. She found them ahead of the statues, lighting their torches and arrows. Their faces were somber, their eyes dark, their fingers tight around their weapons.

"What did you see?" Kyrie asked her. Ash and mud covered his face.

"Fewer than a hundred mimics," she said. "This worries me."

Kyrie snickered. "You're worried about a hundred mimics? We smashed a thousand back in Requiem."

Lacrimosa seemed to understand faster. "Exactly, Kyrie," the queen said. "That's what worries Gloriae. This mine is valuable to Irae. Why guard it with a mere hundred mimics? Where is his army?"

Kyrie rolled his eyes. "Didn't you hear me? We smashed his army in Requiem."

Agnus Dei groaned and punched his arm. "Pup, you are denser than a statue's backside. Don't you remember what the mimic head said when Gloriae questioned it? Irae has thousands of mimics left. Why aren't they guarding the mine?"

Kyrie rubbed his arm and glared at her. "Because they're preparing to invade Requiem, that's why. Maybe they're invading it already, while we're here in Osanna. Dies Irae underestimates us. He always has. So he guards this place with a hundred mimics and thinks it's safe."

Gloriae nodded slowly. "Maybe, Kyrie. Maybe. But I'm worried. Let's proceed cautiously."

"You mean, let's be extra careful not to die?" Kyrie snickered again. "I think we've all become rather good at that already, Gloriae. If you think it's some elaborate trap and want to turn back, say so. Otherwise, let's storm the damn place and smash it."

Gloriae looked at Lacrimosa. "What do you say, Mother?"

Lacrimosa stared toward the mine. Her lips tightened and she drew Stella Lumen. She nodded.

"We need that mine. Whatever horrors await us in its darkness, we will face them." She raised the blade, and stars seemed to shine within its steel. "Fire and stone."

Gloriae bared her teeth. "Fire and stone."

She spun around and drew Per Ignem. She raised the blade in one hand, her torch in the other. With a shout, she began running. The others answered her cry, and she heard their footfalls behind her. The statues ran too, their feet shaking the earth, their cries like mournful thunder and cracking mountains.

Waving her torch, Gloriae leaped over a fallen bole and charged toward the mine.

The mimics below howled. Their stench hit Gloriae like a fog. Balls of flame flew over the sharpened stakes that surrounded the mine. Gloriae batted one aside with her torch. Another hit her breastplate and fell to her feet. Gloriae spat. It was a flaming human head.

"Bring down the walls!" she shouted. A thousand statues of Requiem ran around her. "Knock them down!"

The statues jumped into the ditch that surrounded the mine. As they crashed down, the mine shook. They began smashing the palisade, cracking and toppling the sharpened logs. More flaming heads flew from within the mine. Gloriae snarled as she dodged them.

Soon the palisade fell, and statues filled the ditch like stones filling a mote. Behind the smashed fortifications, Gloriae saw the mimics waiting. They waved blades, howled, and leered.

"Kill them all!" Gloriae shouted and ran toward them. She ran over the mimics in the ditch, as if they were stepping stones, and leaped through the smashed palisade.

Two mimics ran toward her. They had no hands; their arms ended with blades. Those blades swung at her. Gloriae ducked, dodging one blade, and parried the second with her sword. She tossed her torch and burned one's face. She leaped up, spun, and swung her sword. The second mimic's head flew. Before the first mimic could recover, she thrust her blade and pierced its chest. As it howled, she lifted her torch and swung it left and right. Soon the mimics burned.

The battle raged around her. The other Vir Requis were swinging their torches and swords, holding back dozens of the undead. The statues were pouring into the mine behind her, and their stone hands tore mimics apart.

Three mimics raced toward her, only three feet tall. Gloriae grimaced. Were they children or dwarves? She could not tell; their heads were too rotten. They lashed at her with daggers. Gloriae parried and swung her weapons. Soon they lay dead around her, oozing pus. She stared down at them. *If they were children, well... I've killed children before.*

It only took moments. Gloriae slew two more mimics, these ones with the heads of horses, and it was over. The mimics all lay torn across the mine. Their limbs, torsos, and heads still twitched and crawled. The statues moved across the crater, stomping the mimic parts and grinding them.

"Is that all?" Agnus Dei said and laughed. She kicked aside a crawling arm. "Is that all Irae's got?"

Gloriae stared around, eyes narrowed. *This was too easy.*

"All right!" Kyrie said. He began walking toward the shaft. "Into the mine. Let's kill whatever creatures crawl down there and be done with."

No, Gloriae thought. *No, this is wrong.* She knew Dies Irae. He would not leave this place so vulnerable. This had to be a trap, or--

A grumble sounded below.

The crater trembled.

Kyrie paused outside the shaft. He took a step back and raised his weapons. Gloriae clutched her sword and snarled.

"Here we go," she whispered. "Whatever terror Irae prepared for us... it's waking up."

A stench rose from the mine, worse even than the dead mimics across the crater.

"Come near me," Lacrimosa said, voice strangely calm. She raised Stella Lumen, her sword of Requiem steel and diamonds. "Let us stand together."

The crater trembled. The strewn mimic arms began to crawl toward the trees, as if fleeing what evil lurked below.

Gloriae moved to stand at her mother's left. Agnus Dei and Kyrie moved to her right. The queen of Requiem held her sword before her, and its blade glimmered.

Gloriae raised her own sword, Per Ignem, a blade of northern steel and gold. "I fight beside you, Lacrimosa, Queen of Requiem."

Agnus Dei and Kyrie had no ancient, legendary blades. Theirs were common swords found in abandoned castles, their steel unadorned, their grips simple leather. Kyrie had named his "Irae's Fate", and Agnus Dei had dubbed hers "Pup Killer" after an argument with Kyrie. Common swords, but as the two raised them, they shone with just as much light.

"For Requiem," Kyrie said.

"For Father," whispered Agnus Dei.

A howl rose from the mine.

Cracks ran along the crater. Burned trees snapped and fell. Red light beamed out of the shaft. Thousands of cockroaches fled from it and scurried across the crater. Thunder boomed and lightning rent the night.

A shadow rose from the shaft.

Gloriae gasped. Her legs shook. She panted and growled and hissed. Beside her, she heard the others curse.

"What the stars is it?" Agnus Dei asked, disgust twisting her words.

"Irae's insanity," Gloriae answered softly. "And all his malice."

The creature unfurled before them, and Gloriae screamed.

KYRIE ELEISON

"Stay near me, kitten," he whispered. "I'll look after you."

Beside him, Agnus Dei clutched her sword and torch. "Pup, focus less on protecting me, and more on killing that thing. All right?"

Grimacing, he watched the creature unfold itself, rise to its feet, and roar to the heavens.

"Deal," he said.

The creature from the mine stood twenty feet tall, maybe thirty. It was a mimic, but unlike the others. It seemed stitched together from gobbets of flesh. Its limbs were huge, ten feet long, wide as barrels. They were made of many smaller limbs braided together. Its muscles were woven of human legs and arms bundled into strands of oozing flesh. Its torso was stitched together from a dozen rolled up bodies; Kyrie saw three faces peering from its stomach like fetuses trying to emerge from a womb. A helmet the size of a barrel covered the mimic's head. Kyrie was grateful; he did not want to see its face.

For a moment, the world was silent. The mimic giant stood before them, watching them.

Then Lacrimosa's voice pierced the night.

"Burn it."

Kyrie nocked a flaming arrow and fired.

It slammed into the mimic's chest, and it roared. Bricks rolled and the earth shook. The other Vir Requis shot arrows too. They slammed into the mimic, and it screamed and pulled the arrows out.

"Statues of Requiem!" Lacrimosa called. "Bring it down."

The statues raced toward the undead giant. Howling, it swiped its arms, and statues flew. Kyrie cursed and leaped aside. A statue flew over his head, a missile of chipped stone. He glanced behind him and saw the statue crash into its brothers, scattering them.

"Damn thing's going to ruin my day," Kyrie muttered and nocked another arrow. He aimed at the giant mimic's head. The helmet had only a thin slot for the eyes. *If I can only shoot my arrow in there....*

The giant kept moving, lashing its arms at statues. Kyrie stayed still. He closed an eye. He aimed. He caught his breath... and fired.

The flaming arrow pierced the night. It slammed into the helmet, an inch above the eye slot, and fell.

"Stars damn it!" Kyrie said. He gritted his teeth and reached for another arrow, but had no time. The giant howled and leaped toward him.

Kyrie cursed and jumped back. The mimic giant swiped a hand at him. Each finger, Kyrie realized, was made of a man's arm. He ducked, and the hand flew over his head. He raised his sword and sliced into the hand. Blood showered.

"Pup!" Agnus Dei shouted somewhere in the battlefield.

The giant tossed back its head and howled. Kyrie leaped, ran, and sliced his sword across the giant's calf. It roared, and Kyrie ran behind it. Before it could turn toward him, he nocked an arrow. When it started racing toward him again, he had aimed and fired.

The arrow glanced off the giant's helmet.

"Damn it all!" Kyrie shouted.

He raced across the crater. The statues were hacking at the mimic's legs, but it kept kicking them away, like a man kicking away nipping dogs. Lacrimosa and the twins were firing arrows, but they barely fazed the giant. A dozen arrows soon covered its torso, but it seemed not to feel them.

"Aim for its eyes!" he shouted at the girls.

Agnus Dei groaned. "Pup, I don't tell you how to kill mimics."

The giant heard her and ran toward her, feet cracking the earth. It swung its hands at her. One finger slammed into her shoulder, knocking her down.

"Agnus Dei!"

Dread filled Kyrie like a bucket of ice inside him. He shouted, ran, and leaped onto a pile of fallen statues. He vaulted forward and landed on the giant mimic's back.

The stench assailed him. Kyrie thought he might pass out. The mimic bucked and reached over its back, and its hands slammed against Kyrie. He grunted. Each blow felt like a hammer.

He dug his fingers into the mimic's flesh. Its back was woven of a dozen human bodies slung together, a jumble of arms and legs and gasping faces. The giant kept leaping, and the blows fell onto Kyrie, but he clung on. He drew his dagger. He drove it into the mimic's back.

Rot sprayed. The giant screamed. Kyrie grimaced and twisted the blade.

"Pup!"

"Kyrie!"

The giant thrashed and its hands slammed against Kyrie's back. The pain bloomed. Kyrie thought he might pass out. Statues kept attacking the giant's legs, but it kept kicking them aside. Arrows kept piercing its chest, but it barely noticed. It kept reaching over its back and lashing at Kyrie, knocking the breath out of him.

"No way," Kyrie managed to say, the blows raining against him. "No way, my friend. You are going down."

He pulled his dagger free. Blood and halved worms covered the blade. Kyrie shoved his fingers into the creature's back and pulled himself up, until he reached its neck. With a cry, he shoved the dagger down.

Blood flowed from the giant's neck.

It wobbled.

It pitched forward.

"Pup!" Agnus Dei cried.

The giant hit the ground. The world shook. Kyrie tumbled off it, rolled across the ground, and stopped at Agnus Dei's feet. She knelt over him, ran her fingers over his cheek, and her eyes were red. He could barely see her. His eyes fluttered and stars floated before him. Gloriae and Lacrimosa rushed to him too.

"Pup, are you alive?" Agnus Dei shook his shoulders. "Get up! Get up, pup, or I'll kill you!"

Kyrie pushed himself to his feet. He turned to face the fallen giant. It was struggling to rise. Its arms, each one woven of a dozen severed limbs, flexed as it pushed itself to its knees.

"This one's mine," Kyrie said hoarsely.

He reached over his back and took his last arrow. Legs trembling, he walked toward the giant mimic.

It stared at him. Kyrie could see red, blazing eyes inside its visor, each the size of a human head.

He lit and nocked his arrow.

The giant roared.

The arrow flew.

This time Kyrie shot true. The flaming arrow flew through the slot in the visor--it was only three inches wide--and drove into the giant's eye.

Its scream was so loud that the crater cracked, and Kyrie fell. He grunted, struggled to his feet, and walked forward. The mimic giant floundered at his feet, its head burning. Kyrie drove his sword into its visor, and clenched his jaw as the blood poured.

The giant gave a last cry, and its limbs hit the dust.

It lay still.

Covered in its blood, Kyrie stared down at it, sword in hand.

"Bastard," he said.

And then Agnus Dei was hugging and kissing him, and Lacrimosa was tending to his wounds, and even Gloriae gave him a curt nod that said, *Well done.*

When they burned the giant's body, it raised black smoke that seemed to never end. Kyrie watched it burn, and thought about the men, women, and children who had died to form it.

"We have to kill Irae," he said, jaw clenched. "We have to kill him once and for all."

Agnus Dei stood by him, her arms around him. "We will."

AGNUS DEI

She raised her sword. Pup Killer, she had named the blade after a fight with Kyrie. A silly name, she knew. A silly fight. Tonight she wished she had a legendary sword like Gloriae's Per Ignem or like Mother's Stella Lumen, swords with history, glory, and might. Tonight she would need all the might she could get.

"We enter the mine," she said. "If we find Animating Stones, we'll take them. If we find Dies Irae, we'll kill him. I'll climb down first. If Irae is down there, I want him to meet my sword first."

Gloriae stepped up beside her. "I'll enter behind you. We are twins. We will wield twin blades."

With a small smile, Gloriae raised Per Ignem and touched its steel to Pup Killer.

Agnus Dei nodded. "Time of the twins."

Lacrimosa joined her blade to the salute. "The statues will enter behind you. I'll bring up the rear. Kyrie, you go with me. If anything enters the mine behind us, we'll kill it."

Kyrie touched his blade to the other three. Thunder rolled. It began to rain.

Agnus Dei approached the shaft leading into the mine. When she listened, she heard nothing from below. No hammering. No cries. Silence.

"There are more mimics down there," she said. "They're waiting. I'm ready for them. Come, Gloriae. Behind me."

With a deep breath, Agnus Dei climbed into the shaft.

A ladder led into darkness. Agnus Dei held the rungs with one hand, her sword with the other. She began to climb down. Cold air blew from below. When she looked down, she saw nothing but darkness.

Gloriae climbed above her. "Do you see anything?" she said.

"Yeah, I see your smelly feet above me. Nothing but darkness below."

It seemed that she descended forever. The air became so cold, Agnus Dei's teeth chattered. Wind moaned around her, ruffling her hair. The stench of rot grew as she descended. Above her, she heard creaking and thumping, and dirt rained onto her.

"Gloriae, what's going on up there?" she asked.

Gloriae's voice answered in the darkness. "The statues are digging their hands into the sides of the shaft. That's the only way they can climb down."

"Just make sure the bloody things don't make the mine collapse, all right? At least, not before we grab some Animating Stones."

They kept descending into the darkness. Agnus Dei remembered the last time she had plunged underground. She had crawled through caves in Fidelium Mountain. Father had been with her. Dies Irae and his nightshades had waited for them.

I wish you were with me here too, Father, she thought. *The darkness seems colder without you. Your spirit now dines in our halls beyond the stars. If you can see me down here, please watch over me.*

Finally the shaft ended. Agnus Dei let go of the ladder and stood on shaky feet. The darkness was complete. When she held her hands before her face, she couldn't see them.

"The shaft ends here," she said. "Be careful, Gloriae. Come stand beside me."

She felt in the darkness. Her hands touched craggy walls and slats of wood. She inched forward and found herself walking into a tunnel.

"Let's light some fire," Gloriae said.

Agnus Dei nodded and rummaged in her pack for her tinderbox. Soon she and Gloriae held crackling torches. The light revealed a tunnel that sloped into darkness. Wind blew from it, cold and rank with the smell of mimics.

"I used to come to this crater every moon," Agnus Dei said. "Mother and I would travel here to meet Father. I never understood why no trees or grass grew from it. Now I know. It's because Animating Stones pulsed beneath it. This place is evil."

Gloriae shook her head. "No. Animating Stones are only tools. Tools are rarely evil; the men who wield them often are."

"So let's find our man. Let's shove our swords into him."

She began walking down the tunnel, her torchlight dancing against craggy walls held with wooden slats. As she walked, she couldn't help the thoughts that whispered. *Our man. Dies Irae.* Was he... could he be... her father?

Agnus Dei growled. No. Impossible. True, Dies Irae had raped her mother nine moons before she and Gloriae were born. True, Dies Irae believed that he was the true father, not Benedictus. But Agnus Dei refused to believe.

"I am nothing like him," she whispered, jaw clenched. She had brown, fiery eyes like Benedictus. She had black hair like him, a temper like him, skin that tanned gold like his. And Gloriae... true, Gloriae had blue eyes and golden hair like Dies Irae, but so what? Lacrimosa was fair; Gloriae must have inherited her eyes and hair from her, not Dies Irae.

I will never believe that he's my father, she thought. *And even if he is... I don't care. I still hate him, and I'll still kill him.* She couldn't wait to thrust her sword into his flesh and watch him die.

Her footfalls echoed down the tunnel. When she looked over her shoulder, she saw statues walking behind Gloriae. She could only see several feet into the darkness; if Mother and Kyrie walked behind, the shadows hid them.

A growl sounded ahead.

Agnus Dei whipped her head forward and snarled. She raised her torch but saw nothing. She stopped walking and stared.

The growl sounded again.

The tunnel shook.

Dust fell from the ceiling and wooden beams creaked. More growls filled the tunnel, and something cackled.

"Time to kill," Agnus Dei said. With a wordless battle cry, she ran into the darkness, swinging her torch and sword.

A beam snapped to her right. A boulder crashed above. Dust rained.

"Come face me!" she cried. Shadows scurried ahead, laughing. She ran toward them, but they fled. All around her, wooden beams snapped, dust showered, and rocks fell.

"Agnus Dei, back!" Gloriae cried behind her. "Turn back."

"I can see them ahead!" Agnus Dei answered. "They're running away. After me, Gloriae!"

She raced into the darkness, leaping over falling stones. The tunnel shook violently. Agnus Dei fell, scraping her knees. She pushed herself up and kept running. She saw a mimic ahead. Its eyes blazed, it leered, and then it turned and fled.

"Come face me!"

Gloriae shouted behind her. "Agnus Dei, the mine is collapsing! Boulders are falling."

Agnus Dei looked over her shoulder and gasped. The ceiling was crumbling, burying the animated statues. Boulders crushed them.

"Mother!" Agnus Dei screamed. "Kyrie!"

Boulders crashed and began rolling toward her.

"Run, Agnus Dei!" Gloriae cried.

Agnus Dei ran deeper into the darkness. Rocks buffeted her back and helmet. A boulder crashed ahead of her. She leaped over it and kept running. More boulders rolled behind. The mimics were gone. She couldn't even hear them laughing anymore.

"Gloriae!"

She grabbed her sister's hand. The two ran together, heading deeper into the tunnel. A beam crashed before them, and dust blinded Agnus Dei. She leaped over the wood and rocks and plunged into darkness. She fell. Rocks rained. Dust filled her nostrils. Statues cried behind her.

"Mother," she whispered.

A rock hit her shoulder, and she fell onto her chest. Gloriae fell beside her.

Her hand opened.

Gloriae's hand slipped from her grip.

Rocks covered her, and Agnus Dei reached out, trying to grasp something, anything.

"Pup. Pup...."

Mimics laughed in the darkness.

Stars shone.

A blow struck her helmet, and her face hit the ground. All sound and light faded from her world.

LACRIMOSA

She had reached the bottom of the shaft, and begun to walk down the tunnel, when the mine collapsed.

My daughters.

Stones fell, beams snapped, and dust rained.

My daughters!

No other thought filled her mind. She raced forward. Debris crashed around her. A rock hit her shoulder, and she shouted. She had to get through. She had to save them.

"Agnus Dei!" Kyrie shouted beside her. He began tossing rocks aside.

"There, move that boulder!" Lacrimosa said. A boulder the size of a man blocked their way. "Help me."

My daughters. No. Please, stars, please, don't take them from me.

She grabbed the boulder and pulled. Kyrie strained beside her. It wouldn't budge.

"Statues of Requiem!" Lacrimosa called. "Do you hear me?"

Had any statues survived? They had all entered the mine before her. Were they all crushed, as dead as the burned mimics?

"Statues, come help us," Kyrie shouted, but they did not emerge from the wreckage. A few more rocks tumbled, and then the dust settled.

Lacrimosa released the boulder she'd been pulling.

"It was a trap," she said.

Kyrie was still tossing rocks aside. In the light of her torch, Lacrimosa saw that his eyes burned and his cheeks were red.

"Agnus Dei!" he shouted. "Do you hear me? Gloriae!"

Lacrimosa wanted to scream too, to attack the wreckage, to cry and shout. *No.* She steeled herself. She refused to panic. *Stay calm. Think. If the twins are alive, I have to stay calm to save them.*

"It was a trap," she said again. Her fingers trembled, but her voice was steady. "This was not the main entrance to the mine. It was built for us."

"What are you talking about?" Kyrie demanded. "Lacrimosa, come on, help me move these boulders. Hurry!"

She clutched his shoulders and forced him to stare at her. "Kyrie Eleison! Listen to me. Think. Dies Irae knew we'd come here. He knew we'd crawl down the shaft. He rigged the tunnel to collapse onto us. But he wouldn't destroy his only entrance to the mines, not if he wants more Animating Stones. There must be a back entrance somewhere. If the girls survived... if they're trapped somewhere down there... we have to find it. Now come, hurry! Back to the surface."

Kyrie's eyes blazed. He looked ready to argue. Then he squared his shoulders and nodded.

"Let's go."

They began climbing the ladder out of the collapsed mine. Scratches and bruises covered them, but Lacrimosa barely felt the pain. *My daughters.* A vision of them crushed and broken flashed through her mind. Lacrimosa tightened her jaw and banished it. *Don't panic. Stay calm. Save them. There must be another entrance to the mine. There must be. If the girls are alive, I'll find them.*

Soon she and Kyrie climbed back onto the crater.

Mimic dogs awaited them there.

The creatures howled and lunged at them.

They were stitched together from various dead animals. Their heads were canine, but some had the bodies of goats, and one had human arms instead of legs. One had the body of a flayed pony, and another had an arm for a tail. They all barked, drooled, and bared their teeth.

Lacrimosa swung Stella Lumen, slicing into them. Kyrie fought beside her. They swung their torches too, burning the creatures. The dogs swarmed and leaped, their eyes blazing in the night. Their fur burned, but they kept attacking. One bit Lacrimosa's arm, and she screamed and beat it off.

"Lacrimosa, look!" Kyrie said. "Between those burned trees. It looks like a path."

Lacrimosa torched another dog and stared. *Yes.* She had missed it earlier, but now, with the blazing dogs casting their light, she saw it. A rough path led from the crater between the burned trees.

"You think Irae made the path?" she shouted over the howling dogs.

"It might lead to another shaft. Let's go! This dog and pony show is getting boring anyway."

They began to run, slicing and burning their way between the throngs of mimic dogs. Her arm bled, and her head spun, but Lacrimosa forced herself to keep running. They raced out of the crater and onto the path, the dogs in hot pursuit. Burned branches snapped under her boots.

My daughters. Please, stars, please. Don't let me lose them like I lost my husband.

The dogs yapped behind her. As she ran, Lacrimosa nocked an arrow. She spun, knelt, and fired. A dog yelped and fell. She kept running.

"Damn it!" Kyrie shouted and skidded to a stop.

Lacrimosa fired her last arrow. Another dog fell. "What is it?"

"A hole in the ground. I nearly fell in."

Lacrimosa ran forward and held her torch over the ground. Hidden under charred logs, a shaft led underground.

"Climb down," she said. "I'll hold back the d--"

Before she could finish, three dogs leaped onto her. She beat one back with her torch. The other two knocked her down. They snapped their teeth, and Lacrimosa banged one's face with her sword's hilt. The other bit her arm before Kyrie stabbed it. A hundred more mimic dogs came running from the forest.

"Into the mine!" she shouted. "Hurry."

Kyrie nodded and climbed down. "Come on, after me."

Lacrimosa clubbed two dogs with her torch, then leaped into the shaft. A ladder led into the darkness, and she began scurrying down. The dogs surrounded the opening, barking, but dared not jump down.

"Think we'll find the girls down here?" Kyrie shouted below her. She could barely hear him over the howling dogs.

Lacrimosa closed her eyes as she climbed into darkness. *Please, stars. Please. Don't take my daughters from me.* Her fingers trembled around the rungs of the shaft's ladder.

"I don't know, Kyrie. Hurry."

The ladder seemed endless. She descended into darkness-- the darkness of the earth, and of her fears. She had only just buried her husband. If she now had to bury her daughters, how would she continue? How could she revive Requiem, if only she and Kyrie now lived? How could she find strength to live on?

"No," she told herself again. "No, don't despair. Not when your daughters might still breathe, might still need you."

She forced herself to think only of every new rung, every new step into the belly of the earth. They descended until finally, shivering with cold and fear and injury, they reached solid ground.

"Agn--!" Kyrie began, but Lacrimosa elbowed him.

"Quiet, Kyrie," she whispered. "Let's move quietly."

They ran down a tunnel, struggling to keep their footfalls as soft as possible. Soon they heard hammering, grunting, and digging ahead. Red light glowed in the darkness. They rounded a corner, and Lacrimosa cursed and leaped back.

"Wait," she whispered and held up her arm, stopping Kyrie. "Peek."

They stuck their heads around the corner, and Lacrimosa exhaled slowly. *Stars.*

"There must be hundreds," Kyrie whispered, knuckles white around his sword hilt.

Lacrimosa nodded. "And hundreds more get their hearts here every day."

The cavern ahead was as large as Requiem's old halls. Torches and scaffolding covered its walls. Wooden bridges criss-crossed its depths like spider webs. Iron wagons screeched in and out of a dozen tunnels, moving on tracks, their wheels sparking. Everywhere she looked, Lacrimosa saw mimics. They covered the walls like bats. They dug in the cavern floor. They rode the wagons and manned the bridges and hollered as they worked.

"Look, Lacrimosa," Kyrie said and pointed. "That tunnel, over there."

Lacrimosa squinted. A fist seemed to grip her heart and squeeze. Far below and across the cavern, twenty or thirty mimics crowded around the entrance of a tunnel. It was hard to see in the darkness, but it seemed like the tunnel was blocked. Rocks and boulders filled it, and dust still poured from it.

"That must be the tunnel that... that...."

That my daughters escaped from? That my daughters died under? She did not know how to finish that sentence. Before she could say more, the mimics around that collapsed tunnel shifted, and Lacrimosa glimpsed two figures on the ground.

"No," she whispered, tears budding in her eyes. "Please, stars, no."

Lying on the ground by the tunnel, covered in dust and blood, were her daughters.

Kyrie made to race down into the cavern. Lacrimosa grabbed him and pulled him back.

"No, Kyrie!" she hissed.

He looked at her with wild eyes. "Lacrimosa, they... stars, they might be hurt, they need us, they...."

"We can't help them by dying," she said. "Wait, Kyrie. We watch. We hide. If we rush into this cavern alone, we're dead. If they're still alive, we'll save them, I promise you, Kyrie, I promise you. Now is not the time to rush to battle."

Panting, Kyrie knelt beside her. His fists clenched around his weapons. Lacrimosa placed her hand on his shoulder, and they stared silently from the darkness.

As they watched, a figure emerged from shadows and walked toward the collapsed tunnel. Cloaked in darkness, the man stood over the bloodied girls. A mimic held a torch near him. Its light glinted on jewelled armor and an arm of steel.

Lacrimosa's heart seemed to shatter inside her.

"Dies Irae," she whispered.

DIES IRAE

He stood in the cavern, arms crossed, and stared down at the girls.

The twins.

His daughters.

Finally, after all this time, he had them.

Gloriae was unconscious. Blood speckled her armor, and when Dies Irae removed her helmet, he saw her eye and forehead swelling.

My beautiful sweet Gloriae, Dies Irae thought. *Why did you have to disobey me? You were once so beautiful, so pure. You could have ruled this glorious empire at my side. Now you will serve me as a mimic.*

He turned to look down at Agnus Dei. Blood trickled down her forehead. Her eyelids fluttered weakly, and her mouth kept opening and closing. Bandages covered wounds on her arms and legs. Fresher scrapes peeked from the tatters of her clothes.

And Agnus Dei, my freakish daughter. You have never served me. You have always hated me. You will too will become a mimic of rot and worm.

Dies Irae turned to stare at Lashdig, chief of his miners. The hunchbacked, warty mimic stared back, his one eye large and blue, the other squinty and black. Matted red hair grew between scars on his head.

"Tie them up," Dies Irae told him. "And gag them."

Lashdig bowed his head. "Yes, master."

The stooped mimic barked a few commands, mimics shuffled, and soon ropes bound the twin girls. Lashdig stuffed bloody cloths into their mouths, which he secured with more rope. The girls began coming to, and started to struggle, but their screams were muffled, their limbs too weak to break free.

Dies Irae caressed Gloriae's cheek. "Why do you struggle, sweetness? You will become a beautiful mimic, a slave girl to my warriors' desires."

Her eyes blazed with hatred, and Dies Irae laughed. He turned to Agnus Dei, the dark twin.

"And you, Agnus Dei, why do you struggle so?" He chuckled at the sight of her squirming and screaming into her gag. He leaned down and kissed her forehead. "You too will become a beautiful mimic, Agnus Dei. Lashdig himself here will enjoy thrusting into you, he and all his miners."

He straightened and faced Lashdig again. "What of the other weredragons?"

Lashdig stared from his mismatched, rheumy eyes. "The tunnel swallowed them, my lord, as you planned. Their beastly stone mimics are crushed too."

"Find me bodies. If you have to scrape them off stones with a shovel, do it. I want their blood. I want what's left of their bones. Find me the weredragon whore and the boy."

Lashdig bowed. "Yes, my lord." He turned toward his workers. "Mimics! Dig. Dig well. Find us the weredragons. Their blood will feed our new children."

A voice spoke behind him.

"The blond one. Is that Gloriae?"

Dies Irae turned to see Umbra, the Blood Wolf assassin, walk toward him. She held a drawn dagger, and her eyes blazed. In his chambers, at his insistence, she was always nude. Today she wore black leggings, a black bodice, and five more daggers around her waist.

"This is her."

Fast as a panther, Umbra pounced atop Gloriae. She snarled and backhanded the young woman's cheek. Gloriae grunted into her gag. Her lip split, and blood trickled from it.

"You murdered my husband," Umbra hissed. "You burned my brothers." She backhanded Gloriae again. "I will make you suffer." She brought her dagger close to Gloriae's face. "I will make you suffer like they did."

"Umbra!"

Dies Irae's voice rang across the cavern. He grabbed her shoulders and pulled her off Gloriae. She struggled in his grasp, but he held her tight.

"Umbra, control yourself. That is an order."

She hissed and spat. "She will pay for her crimes."

Dies Irae nodded. "But not at your hands, Umbra. If you kill her, her pain ends. Once we make her a mimic, her pain will last forever."

Gloriae moaned, blood trickling down her chin. Agnus Dei screamed into her gag and thrashed. Umbra laughed.

"Very well, Irae," the Blood Wolf said. She tossed back her hair and sheathed her dagger. "I will keep her alive. But once she is a mimic, Irae... I will hurt her, again and again, a thousand times for every Blood Wolf she slew."

Dies Irae nodded. *And I will hurt you, Gloriae, for every nightshade you released from the abyss. And I will hurt you, Agnus Dei, for every man a weredragon has slain.*

He turned toward Warts and Bladehand, two of his finest warrior mimics. They rustled with bugs and stared at him with bloodshot eyes.

"Lift the girls," he told them. "While Lashdig and his miners dig for the others, we'll take these two to the camp. We'll dissect and stitch them there. Soon you will have fine, rotting bodies to enjoy."

Warts and Bladehand hissed and drooled. "Yes, master. As you command."

Bladehand grabbed Gloriae and slung her over his shoulder. Warts lifted the writhing Agnus Dei. Both girls screamed into their gags, a beautiful sound. Dies Irae began walking across the cavern, and the mimics followed behind. All around him, the miners dug, tunnelled, and sifted for Animating Stones. The red crystals glowed in wagons, thousands of them, thousands to keep building his armies.

One will be for you, Gloriae. And one for you, Agnus Dei.

As Dies Irae walked across the mine, the twins screaming behind him, he smiled thinly.

GLORIAE

Everything hurt. Bruises and cuts covered Gloriae. Her head pounded. Stars shone above between naked branches. As the mimics carried her through the burned forest, every jostle shot pain through her.

"Move faster, my lovelies," Dies Irae called out, marching ahead of the column. "I want to hit the camp by sunrise."

The mimics growled around him. Fifty of them, maybe a hundred, snaked through the forest. They carried crackling torches. Tied up and gagged across one's shoulder, Gloriae couldn't see much, only burned trees, thumping mimic feet, and glimpses of Agnus Dei tossed across a second mimic's shoulder. She kept trying to meet her sister's eyes, but only caught glimpses of the girl's flopping, dusty hair.

Are Mother and Kyrie dead? Or are they captured too? Worry for them gnawed on her, worse than her pain. The entire tunnel seemed to have collapsed behind her. It seemed unlikely that Mother and Kyrie could have survived.

"You will be my slave," hissed the mimic who carried her. His hand grabbed her thigh and squeezed. "I will take you deep, and break you."

Gloriae glared down at its chest, the only part she could see. Oozing wounds stretched across that chest, slapping against her cheek as it ran. Gloriae closed her eyes and tried to ignore the stench and pain.

If Mother and Kyrie are dead, so is Requiem, she thought. *Kyrie is our last male. Unless... unless his child truly quickened within me, and is a boy, and can still survive.* That too seemed unlikely to Gloriae. She had not bled since lying with Kyrie two moons ago, or was it three now? But she had also barely eaten, barely slept, barely rested from battle. Those more likely dried her blood than any life within her. Tied and gagged across a mimic's back, Gloriae lowered her head, and her soul seemed to sink into her belly.

So it's over. We lost the war. And soon... soon I and my twin will be mimics too, maggot-ridden and cursed for eternity.

Gloriae wanted to find hope. She struggled to grasp any ray of it she could find. But how could she? How could she escape death yet again?

A bird cawed.

A second bird, across the road, answered it.

Whistles cut the air.

With thuds, flaming arrows slammed into a dozen mimics.

"The *Earthen.*" Dies Irae spat the word in disgust. "Mimics! Find them."

More flaming arrows flew. Gloriae grimaced. One arrow flew so close, it singed her hair. She stared through narrowed eyelids, but saw only shadows in green cloaks darting between the trees. *Green cloaks. Earth God priests.*

Twenty mimics raced into the woods, firing their own arrows and swinging their swords.

"Bring me their heads!" Dies Irae shouted. "A hundred slaves to any mimic who brings me Silva."

Gloriae sucked in her breath. Silva the Elder? She had heard his name whispered in the halls of Flammis Palace. Dies Irae had called him an outlaw, a crazy old man, a disgraced follower of a false god. He had killed Silva's siblings, toppled his temples, hunted him across the land. Did the priest still live?

More arrows flew. Three mimics fell dead. The battle raged through the forest, mimics and Earthen clashing swords and firing arrows.

Green shadows leaped from the burned trees, racing toward Gloriae with raised swords. *Will they free me from the mimics? Or will they kill Gloriae the Gilded, she who had hunted and killed so many of their number?* She remembered the tavern last summer, where she had hunted Kyrie; she had killed an Earth God priest there, one Tilas, or Talis, or Taras. She had forgotten his name, but would these Earthen remember her crime?

Bladehand grunted and tossed her down. She landed with a grimace, banging her elbow against a rock. Warts tossed Agnus Dei down; her sister slammed against her, yelping. The two mimics snarled and clashed blades with the Earthen.

She lay, Agnus Dei atop her, watching the fight. It only lasted minutes. Growling, Bladehand tore into an Earthen's face, then stabbed his chest. Warts sliced off a woman's arm, grabbed her throat, and clawed out her eyes. Soon they were feasting on

Earthen entrails. The other mimics came walking back from the forest, carrying severed heads, chewing on human organs.

Dies Irae nodded. Blood covered his mace and splashed his armor.

"Good, lovelies, good," he said. "Now grab the weredragons. Our camp lies just ahead. Soon the weredragons will taste needle and stitch."

They began to march again. Dawn rose around them, spilling red stains across the sky. The burned trees creaked in the wind, their icicles glimmering red. *A dawn of blood,* Gloriae thought and closed her eyes. *Perhaps the last dawn of my life.*

The mimics crested a hill and began to descend. They grunted and howled around her, and Agnus Dei screamed into her gag. Gloriae opened her eyes to see a camp sprawled across a valley below. Stench rose from it like steam. A palisade of sharpened logs surrounded the camp, protecting dozens of huts. Chained humans shuffled between those huts, mimics howling and whipping them.

Dies Irae led them into the valley, and soon they marched through the camp. Gloriae looked around, nausea twisting her gut. Blood soaked the snow and the huts' walls. When a mimic cracked a whip and entered one hut, Gloriae glimpsed prisoners inside, thin and shivering, their backs lashed. Many prisoners were missing limbs, their stumps wrapped with bloody bandages.

Between the huts rose piles of body parts, sorted into arms, legs, torsos, and heads. The piles rose thirty feet tall. Mimics walked atop them, rummaging through them, like ants scurrying over hives. Gloriae saw one mimic lift a woman's arm, lick it, and toss it aside. She gagged and coughed, her head spinning.

What has he turned into? she thought. How could Dies Irae, an emperor once devoted to gold and light and beauty, sink to such evil? This was not the man she had known. True, the Dies Irae who'd raised her had hunted, killed, and brutalized his enemies. But he had done it for order, light, and justice. This... there was no light here. There was no glory or justice. *You became worse than any enemy you've imagined.*

Past the piles of bodies, Gloriae saw ditches where fires burned. The mimics were tossing body parts into the flames: limbs that were frail, torsos that were thin, heads with no teeth.

They crackled in the fires. Gloriae understood. *He collects what he needs. He burns the rest.*

Finally Dies Irae stopped by a group of chained, whipped prisoners who stood barefoot in the snow. He raised his hand, and the mimics carrying Gloriae and Agnus Dei stopped too.

"Put them down," Dies Irae said.

The mimics tossed Gloriae and her sister onto the bloodied snow. They rolled, grunted, and shivered in the cold.

"What have we here?" Dies Irae asked, examining the prisoners. He caressed the hair of a chained toddler. "Why, this one is too small. He is useless to me. Burn him." He moved on to a woman with a bruised face. He squeezed her arms. "This one is strong. Take her limbs. Her teeth are crooked; burn her head." Next he frowned at an old man. "Burn this one, all of him."

He went from prisoner to prisoner, choosing parts to keep and parts to burn. Gloriae watched, her head spinning, the taste of vomit in her mouth. She struggled against the ropes binding her, but only chaffed her skin bloody. Beside her, Agnus Dei also struggled. She screamed into her gag, and her eyes were so wide, Gloriae could see white all around her irises.

I will kill you, Dies Irae, Gloriae swore again. *This is not the empire I fought for. This is not the vision you taught me. I will break free and I will kill you.*

When he had finished reviewing the prisoners, Dies Irae walked toward Gloriae and Agnus Dei. His boots, made from the golden scales of a young dragon, stood a finger's length from Gloriae's face.

"And now... these two."

His voice was soft, almost loving. He knelt and caressed Gloriae's cheek. She glared at him. His face was so different now. She remembered his face being strong, cold, and tanned gold. Now his face was gaunt, deeply lined, and ghostly white. A patch covered his left eye, and his right eye seemed paler too, a watery blue. He smiled at her, his lips like squirming worms, and touched her hair.

"This one... this one is strong. This one is steel. But she is treacherous, yes. A betrayer. Use what parts of her that you will, but leave me her head."

Next he knelt by Agnus Dei. She floundered in her bounds and her eyes shot daggers. Dies Irae leaned down and kissed her cheek, leaving a line of saliva on her skin.

"And this one... this one too is strong. Stupid, yes. Beastly and cursed, certainly. But *strong*. Use her body for your warriors, Warts and Bladehand. Leave me her head too. I will take their heads back with me to Confutatis."

Bladehand, the mimic who had carried Gloriae, nodded. "Yes, master. We will be building a new batch today, master. Their bodies will make good warriors." He knelt on all fours, leaned in, and licked Gloriae's cheek with a bloated tongue.

"Excellent," Dies Irae said. "Toss them in with the others for now." He smacked his lips. "Right now, it's time for breakfast."

Bladehand lifted Gloriae, and Warts lifted Agnus Dei. Grunting and licking their chops, the mimics carried the twins to a hut, opened the door, and tossed them in. The lock snapped shut behind them.

Gloriae rolled across the floor, and her head hit somebody's leg. Agnus Dei rolled too, cursing behind her gag, and came to a stop beside her. At once, hands covered the two, feeling and grabbing. One hand held a rusty shiv near her head. Gloriae began to struggle, but these hands did not hurt her, and the knife did not cut her.

"Hush, girls, we'll remove your gags."

The shiv worked at the rope around her face, and her gag came free. Gloriae coughed, sucked in breath, and coughed again. Prisoners crowded over her, wearing rags. They shivered in the cold, gaunt and sickly. Their skin draped over their bones, and their faces were skeletal. Their eyes were sallow, their hair wispy.

"Thank you," Gloriae whispered hoarsely, finding that she could speak no louder.

The prisoner with the shiv began cutting the ropes around her ankles and wrists. Gloriae moved her limbs only an inch, and pain blazed. She gritted her teeth. Every movement shot bolts through her. She massaged her wrists; they were chaffed and bleeding.

"Drink," said a prisoner, a young woman with large grey eyes. She held melted snow in her palms, and Gloriae drank. Another prisoner was busy freeing Agnus Dei.

"Gloriae!" her twin said once her gag was removed.

Gloriae crawled toward her--she felt too weak to walk--and the two embraced. Agnus Dei had tears in her eyes, and Gloriae felt her own eyes sting.

"Oh, sister," she whispered. "It's horrible, isn't it?"

Agnus Dei trembled. "Do you think Mother and the pup are here? I... I tried to look for them as they carried us through the camp, but I couldn't see them. I'm worried."

Gloriae looked around her, and for the first time, she got a close look at the hut. Its walls were frosty, splashed with blood, and lined with bunks like shelves. A single slop bucket stood in one corner, a pile of frozen bread in another. It was a small hut, smaller than her old bedroom at Flammis Palace. And yet hundreds of prisoners filled it. They covered the floor, shoulder to shoulder, or lay in the bunks. Many were missing limbs. Their eyes were glassy, their skin sweaty, and bloody bandages covered their stumps. Some lay mumbling, feverish, their wounds green with infection. A few were dead already. *Their limbs are now attached to mimics,* Gloriae knew.

The prisoner with the grey eyes, who had given Gloriae water, gestured around her. She smiled a sad, crooked smile.

"Welcome," she said, "to Dies Irae's imagination."

KYRIE ELEISON

It began to snow, and Kyrie cursed.

The trail had been easy to follow until now. A hundred mimics had marched from the mine, cutting a path through the snow. Kyrie and Lacrimosa had been following their trail for several hours now. It led them through lands of dead trees, frozen streams, and rocky hills. Kyrie remembered walking here last summer, fleeing griffins and seeking King Benedictus. Trees had rustled here then, and hope still filled the world. Dies Irae had burned these trees, and little hope filled Kyrie now.

"Damn it," he muttered. The snow swirled around him. He could barely see through it. Worse, the snow was covering the mimics' footprints.

Lacrimosa shivered and tightened her cloak around her. "Let's move faster. We can still see the trail. Hurry, Kyrie."

They ran through the snow, their torches crackling. Around them among the burned trees, creatures howled. *Mimics,* Kyrie thought. This time, if they attacked, he didn't know if he'd survive. They had no statues left; they lay smashed and buried in the mines. They had no Gloriae and Agnus Dei with their swords and arrows.

Gloriae. Agnus Dei. Kyrie's heart twisted, and ice seemed to fill his belly. He had never felt such anguish. It churned inside him, spun his head, and tightened his throat. They had been alive in the mines. He had seen them thrashing in their bonds as the mimics carried them off. But were they alive now? Kyrie shivered, cursed, and ran as fast as he could. Lacrimosa ran at his side, eyes narrowed.

Please, stars, Kyrie prayed silently. *Please protect Agnus Dei. Please.*

He loved her so much, that he felt his insides could crumble, his heart stop beating, and his lungs collapse. He wanted to hold her, protect her, kill anyone who harmed her. If she died, he thought he would die too.

"Be strong, kitten," he whispered into the snow. "I'll be there soon."

If the stars heard his prayers, they ignored them. The snow only fell harder, a blizzard that stung his face and buried the mimics' trail. Kyrie cursed and stumbled forward, but soon stopped, backtracked, and realized he was lost.

He cursed and looked from side to side. Screeches rose in the blizzard around him, moving closer. Kyrie raised his torch, eyes narrowing. Lacrimosa did the same.

"Kyrie," she said, "I don't like this."

"Me ne--"

A dozen shadows flew toward them from the trees.

Kyrie couldn't help it. He cried in fear. They were mimics, but more hideous than any he'd seen. They looked like oversized bats. They had human heads and outstretched human arms. But below the shoulders, their bodies tapered into nothing but a spine. Skin stretched from their wrists to their tailbones, forming wings. They flapped toward Kyrie, shrieking.

He screamed and swung his torch.

How can such terrors exist? The creatures' eyes blazed red. Their teeth snapped at him, and one bit his arm. Kyrie's head spun. He screamed again and lashed his blade and his fire. Lacrimosa screamed and fought beside him. The world was crackling fire, swirling snow, and everywhere those terrors, those bats, those things that had once been human.

No, he found himself praying feverishly. *No, please, stars, it can't be. They can't have been human. No mind can be sick enough to create these things. Please, stars, let me wake up from this nightmare. Let this all be a dream. How can this be real?*

"Kyrie, look!" Lacrimosa cried. She pointed, and Kyrie saw a tatter of green cloth hanging on a tree. Agnus Dei had worn a green cloak when captured.

"I see it!" he shouted and clubbed at the flying bats.

"The mimics carried the girls that way," Lacrimosa shouted back. "Let's go."

They ran through the snow, clubbing the mimic bats. One flew onto Kyrie's arm, flapping its wings against him. He tore it off and grimaced when he saw its face, the face of an old woman. He kept running, swinging his torch and sword. The bats were everywhere, screeching, swooping, crying.

146

"Broken ice, over there!" he shouted. A frozen stream lay ahead, its surface cracked and splintered in one place. Kyrie ran over it, and he saw a path of broken branches through the forest. "The mimics took the twins this way."

Lacrimosa swung her sword and cut a bat. Its blood sprayed the falling snow. "Keep going!"

They ran, the broken branches scratching them. Kyrie raced between two trees, and suddenly the ground sloped. He found himself tumbling down a ravine, snow cascading around him.

"Lacrimosa!"

She fell beside him, covered in snow. The bats screeched above, but did not follow. Kyrie tried to grab something, but found no purchase. He seemed to fall forever, before he finally hit a mound of snow, and was still. Lacrimosa rolled to a stop beside him, shivering, her torch extinguished.

Kyrie leaped to his feet and helped Lacrimosa up.

"Where's the path?" she demanded.

Kyrie looked up the slope they had crashed down. They had fallen a long way. The bats fluttered above between the trees, but dared not leave their cover.

"I don't know," he said, and suddenly his eyes stung, and his throat swelled. "I don't know, Lacrimosa. I'm... I'm scared. I don't know if... if...."

If Agnus Dei will become one of those bat things. Or if she is one already. If I will become one too. I don't know if this is real, or some nightmare. I don't know what to do.

But he could say none of these things. How could he? Benedictus had died, and he--Kyrie Eleison--was the last man of Requiem. It was his task to be strong, his duty to protect the others. Only... it seemed impossible. Even Benedictus, always strong and brave, had never dealt with humans twisted and cut and sewn into these horrors. How could Kyrie face them?

He lowered his head, and his body shook. "I'm not strong enough, Lacrimosa. I'm trying to be like him. Like Benedictus. But...."

She grabbed his shoulders. She stared into his eyes.

"Kyrie," she said. Her face was so stern, her eyes so angry. He was sure she'd yell at him. But then her face softened, and her eyes watered, and she embraced him. They stood in the snow, shivering together, holding each other.

"I'm sorry, Lacrimosa. I feel weak."

She touched his hair and kissed his cheek. "You were never weak, Kyrie. You are good, you are scared, you are in love with Agnus Dei. If you were cold and heartless, well, you wouldn't be a man I wanted fighting by my side. And you are a man now, Kyrie."

He took a deep, shaky breath and squared his shoulders. The snow fell around them. "Let's find them, Lacrimosa. Let's find the twins. The path was leading south. We'll move south along this ravine, at least until those flying creatures are gone, then pick up the trail."

Lacrimosa wiped away tears and took his hand. They ran together through the snow, the wind whipping their faces.

AGNUS DEI

She nibbled on her bread. It was stale and frozen, but she forced herself to chew it into mush, then swallow. *I'll need my strength to kill Irae,* she thought. *And I will kill him today.*

Her eye kept wandering to the prisoners around her, especially those missing limbs. One was a young woman, no older than her own nineteen years. She was missing an arm. The bandage around her stump was bloody, and her face was sweaty, even in the cold. *She will die,* Agnus Dei knew. *And then the rest of her will become a mimic.*

"There is a rebellion brewing," whispered a frail man, clutching Agnus Dei's arm. "The Earthen, they're called. Silva the Elder leads them, a great Earth God priest. They'll save us, child. They'll save us."

The man's eyes spun wildly. He was mad, she realized. Soon he retreated into a corner, where he hugged his knees and rocked.

It seemed forever that Agnus Dei huddled among the prisoners--some of them mad, most of them dying. Gloriae huddled by her, her eyes closed, her lips mumbling. Agnus Dei leaned against her, embraced her, and laid her head on her shoulder. She felt a little safer this way, but not much. There was no safe place here. The prisoners wept, moaned, and prayed around them. Agnus Dei did not know if prayers could be heard from a place like this.

Soon she had to make water. She was no pampered princess--she did not mind going in the bushes--but how could she truly go here, in a bucket, before everyone? And yet she lined up. And she did. And then she returned to Gloriae's side, and embraced her again, and closed her eyes lest her sister saw her tears.

"Sometimes... sometimes I think they're dead," she whispered to Gloriae. "Mother and Kyrie."

Gloriae opened her eyes and touched Agnus Dei's cheek. "Don't say that. This is no time to despair."

"When else is time for despair then? I'm so scared, Gloriae. I want to be strong. But I'm scared."

Gloriae smiled wanly. "That's why you're strong. Strength is conquering your fear. Dies Irae taught me that."

Agnus Dei shuddered. She huddled closer to her sister. "I don't know how you could have lived with him. He's a monster."

Gloriae sighed. "He was not always like this. He was always cruel, yes. And violent. Not toward me, but toward his enemies. And he was always so strong, so stern, so sure of his ways. But this? No, he was never like this. He followed the Sun God. He fought for light. For order. For his own brand of justice. Most of all, he fought for glory. But that was before the nightshades infested his mind. Before a shard of metal drove into his eye. He's insane now, Agnus Dei, which he had never been when he raised me. If we can kill him, it will be a mercy to him. He's trapped in his own insanity, helpless to stop it. The mimics he creates are reflections of his madness and nightmares."

"We *will* kill him." Agnus Dei clenched her fists. "We have to. Not only for Requiem, but for the entire world."

The door swung open.

The prisoners whimpered and screamed.

Dies Irae stood at the doorway, armored in steel, gold, and jewels. Umbra stood beside him, clad in her black leggings and black bodice, her eyes blazing. Four burly mimics stood behind them, carrying chains.

Agnus Dei snarled and leaped to her feet. "You die now, Irae."

She leaped toward him.

Dies Irae didn't move. Umbra did, however. Fast as a falcon's shadow, she crouched, slid forward, and reached out her leg. Agnus Dei tripped over it. She pitched forward. Umbra grabbed her hair, pulled her head back, and knocked her onto her back. Agnus Dei screamed and punched. She hit Umbra's face, but the woman only snarled, and a dagger gleamed in her hand. The blade pressed against Agnus Dei's throat, and she froze.

"Good girl," Umbra whispered. She licked blood off her lips. "Stay nice and still or I'll gut you like a fish."

A shadow leaped, and Gloriae crashed against Umbra, shoving her off. Agnus Dei leaped up and kicked. Her leg hit Umbra's side. The dagger slashed the air. *If I can only grab the blade....* She reached, caught Umbra's wrist, and twisted. Umbra screamed and punched. The blow slammed into Agnus Dei's cheek. White light flooded her. She kicked blindly. Gloriae screamed.

"Stop this!"

Dies Irae's voice filled the hut. Agnus Dei blinked and saw him standing above the fray, glaring.

"Mimics," he said, "grab the twins."

Agnus Dei tried to fight them. She kicked and punched and even bit a mimic's maggoty flesh, but only fire could hurt them. Soon she kicked and squirmed in one's grasp. A second mimic held onto Gloriae, its hand covering her mouth.

"Face me like a man, Irae!" Agnus Dei screamed. "You and me. Or are you a coward?"

He laughed, though there was no joy to it; it was a cold laughter, a cruel laughter that made Agnus Dei shiver.

"Dear Agnus Dei," he said. "Feisty as ever. Beastly as ever. You will go first. Mimics, bring her to the block."

Gloriae screamed into the hand that gagged her. Agnus Dei growled and kicked, but could not free herself. The mimic holding her began carrying her to the doorway. She screamed, struggled, and kicked the air. The mimic's grip was iron.

"Gloriae!" she cried, eyes burning. "Gloriae!"

Her chin bloody, Umbra laughed. "Your sister can't save you now. She'll go next." She spat onto Agnus Dei. "Scream louder. I want to hear it."

Dies Irae left the hut, and the mimic carried Agnus Dei after him. Umbra followed, laughing, spinning her dagger in her hand.

Stay strong, Agnus Dei told herself. *Stay strong. Stars, whatever happens, stay strong. For Kyrie. For Mother. For Gloriae.*

She saw the block ahead.

She felt the blood leave her face. Ice seemed to wash her belly, and she trembled.

"Stars, no...."

It was made of wood. Oak, she thought. Blood stained it. The block rose from the snow between the huts, iron rings embedded into it.

"Chain her down."

Agnus Dei kicked. For an instant, she thought she could break free. But two more mimics grabbed her. They forced her to her knees before the block.

"Irae!" she screamed. "I'll kill you! Fight me! Fight me, I dare you."

Umbra laughed again, grabbed Agnus Dei's hair, and pulled her head down. The block was cold and smooth against her cheek.

"Oh yes, you are a loud one," Umbra whispered, her cold lips brushing against Agnus Dei's ear. "I'm going to enjoy watching this. I bet you'll squeal like a pig."

The mimics surrounded her. Manacles were placed around her wrists. More chains bound her legs.

"Gloriae!" Agnus Dei screamed, eyes burning, throat aching, belly roiling. Tears sprang into her eyes.

Umbra grabbed her wrist. She pulled Agnus Dei's arm across the block and chained it down. *Stars, no, please,* Agnus Dei prayed. *Please. Stars, no....*

She heard the hiss of a sword being drawn.

"Mother," Agnus Dei whispered. "Mother, please...."

Through burning eyes, she saw Dies Irae walk toward her, holding a drawn sword. His face was blank. His eye looked dead. His face was pale, a white mask. *There is no humanity left.*

He raised his sword.

"Mother!" Agnus Dei cried, tears in her eyes.

The blade swung down.

Pain.

Blood.

She screamed.

Stars. It's gone. It's gone. My hand is gone. How could it be gone? Mother, please....

Umbra laughed.

Agnus Dei wept.

Dies Irae turned and walked away. Blood stained the snow, and distant trees creaked under a mournful wind.

KYRIE ELEISON

He crawled up the snowy hill, teeth chattering, clothes icy. Snow filled his mouth and clung to his stubble. At the hilltop, he lay on his belly behind a fallen tree. He parted the tree's branches and gazed into the valley below. He felt the blood leave his face. He turned his head.

"Lacrimosa!" he whispered down the hillside. "Come quick."

She nodded and crawled up beside him. She stared into the valley too, and her lips trembled.

"Stars," she whispered.

The camp sprawled across the valley below. A ditch and a wall of sharpened logs defended it. Beyond the palisade, blood stained crude huts. Every few moments, mimics would drag a prisoner from a hut, chain him against a butcher's block, and swing a sword. The severed body parts were sorted into bloody hills. Kyrie saw one pile of legs, another of arms and hands, a third of heads. The hills rose twenty feet tall. Some body parts--those deemed too frail, it seemed--were burned in ditches.

Kyrie had seen enough.

"We have to save them," he said, voice strained. "We can't wait a moment longer."

What if Dies Irae dismembered Agnus Dei and Gloriae while he hid here, watching helplessly? Kyrie stood up and made to run downhill.

"Wait, Kyrie!" Lacrimosa said. She grabbed his tunic, pulling him back. "Hide."

He spun to glare at her. She stared up from the cover of burned branches, her face pale but her eyes determined. He shook himself free.

"Lacrimosa," he said, "they're building mimics down there. And not just from old bodies now. He's *killing* people and sewing mimics out of them." He drew his sword. "We have to save the twins before it's too late. Stars, we have to save *all* these people."

He couldn't help but imagine Agnus Dei turned into a mimic, stitched together with foreign body parts, drooling, rotting, hunting him. He shuddered.

Lacrimosa pulled him down behind the fallen logs. "Kyrie, if you run down there brandishing a sword and torch, they will kill you, and they will turn you into a mimic, along with my daughters." Her voice was strained but steady, her eyes red but dry. "If the girls are alive, we'll save them. But not by rushing to our own deaths."

Kyrie raised his chin. His heart thrashed. "I'm willing to die for Agnus Dei."

"And some good that would do her." Lacrimosa opened her pack, revealing a hundred Animating Stones. "I didn't grab these from the mine because I think they're pretty. We'll build new warriors."

"From what?" Kyrie gestured around him. "I see no statues here, Lacrimosa. I see nothing but snow, ice, and burned trees."

Lacrimosa gave him a small, mirthless smile. "Dies Irae burned these trees and killed the Earthen who worshipped them. I believe that today, these trees will fight for us."

Kyrie stared at her in silence. She stared back. Finally Kyrie sighed and nodded. *If it can save the girls, it's worth a try.*

They crawled back downhill and began to move among the trees: old oaks, twisted and blackened, but still strong; thin birches, their bark burned off; charred pines, their roots still deep. *These trees are dead, but we will give them new life.* Kyrie and Lacrimosa moved silently, placing Animating Stones into holes that had once held birds, squirrels, and insects. Trees creaked. Icicles snapped and fell. Branches rose. A mournful cry like wind passed through the charred forest, a rustling of twigs, a shifting of roots, a sadness and rage.

Kyrie thought of Fort Sanctus, where Lady Mirum had raised him on fish, bread, and tales of the ancient days. In several of those tales, the trees would rise to fight the wars of men. Those trees always rustled with green leaves, and could talk and sing. There was nothing as beautiful here, but Kyrie still felt like a hero from one of Mirum's old stories.

As the trees creaked and moved, he whispered, quoting from one of her tales. "We are the children of the earth; our hosts are the rocks of the field, the trees of the forest, and the song in the wind...."

Lacrimosa came to stand beside him. She drew her sword and raised her torch. The trees crowded around them, raining ash and snow, their icicles snapping, their boles creaking. Their roots spread around them like the legs of spiders, twisting and seeking purchase.

"Stay near me, Kyrie," Lacrimosa said softly. "We'll find the girls."

They began to march.

The trees' roots groaned, dug into the snow, and dragged the boles forward. Their branches kept snapping, falling black and broken. They were frail things, burned and mournful, moaning in pain. But they marched. A hundred charred, twisted trees raised their howl, and gained speed, and soon began to charge downhill. Hostias Forest rose in rage.

Kyrie snarled. He waved his sword and cried with them. He ran among the trees, boots kicking up snow. Lacrimosa ran beside him, Stella Lumen raised in her hands. Snow flurried. The hillside shook. At the camp below, mimics squealed and rushed to the walls.

Kyrie shouted. The trees roared. They crashed into the palisade under rain of blood, steel, and fire.

GLORIAE

When she heard Agnus Dei screaming outside, Gloriae snarled, clenched her fists, and trembled. Prisoners pushed against her on every side; she could barely move between them. Elbowing and shoving them, Gloriae managed to reach the hut's door.

"Agnus Dei!" she shouted, eyes stinging. She slammed her shoulder against the door. It wouldn't budge. She slammed again, and her shoulder throbbed with pain.

"Dies Irae, let her go!" Gloriae shouted. She slammed against the door again and again, and kicked it, but couldn't break it.

"Fight me, you coward!" she shouted.

She heard Umbra laughing outside. The mimics howled. Agnus Dei's screams faded. *Is she dead? Stars, did he kill her?*

"Dies Irae!" she screamed and slammed against the door again. Her shoulder ached, but she didn't care. She needed to get out, to save her sister, to kill Dies Irae. She spun toward the other prisoners.

"Help me," she demanded. She panted and her hair covered her face. "Come on, help me break down the door."

The prisoners only watched her sadly. They were all too frail. They shivered in their rags, feverish, nearly dead with disease. *They cannot help me,* Gloriae realized, her chest rising and falling.

The door's lock clinked behind her.

Gloriae spun back toward it, growling, ready to kill whoever stood there.

The door opened, and Gloriae was about to leap... then froze.

"Oh stars," she whispered, and her knees shook. "Oh stars, no, please no...."

Dies Irae stood at the doorway, holding Agnus Dei before him. His face was icy, his eye dead, his mouth like a slit in leather. Blood stained his armor. Agnus Dei was unconscious, her chin against her chest. Her left arm ended with a bloody, smoking stump.

"Stars, Agnus Dei...," Gloriae whispered.

Dies Irae stared at her. He smiled a small, thin smile.

"The weredragon king took my left hand," he said. "So I will take the left hands of his followers. Yours will be next, Gloriae. But first, make sure this one lives. I want her alive and screaming when I cut the rest of her."

He tossed Agnus Dei forward. Gloriae caught her, held her, and lowered her onto the floor.

"I'm here, Agnus Dei," she whispered and touched her sister's cheek. "I'm here with you, I'll look after you."

Agnus Dei did not wake. Her breath was shallow, her forehead hot.

Rage blazed inside Gloriae. Her teeth clenched, and she spun around to leap at Dies Irae... but he slammed the door shut. Gloriae crashed against the door, but it was locked again. She could not break it. Outside, she heard Umbra's voice.

"Let's build a nice new mimic with her hand," the woman said and laughed.

"Very well, come with me," Dies Irae answered. Gloriae heard their footfalls leave the hut, and their voices faded in the distance.

"Glor... Gloriae...."

Agnus Dei was whispering, voice hoarse. Gloriae rushed to her side, knelt by her, and touched her hair.

"I'm here, Agnus Dei."

Her sister's eyes fluttered. She struggled to raise her head. A tear streamed down her cheek. Her lips moved, struggling to speak, but then her head fell back, and her eyes closed.

Wincing, Gloriae examined her wound. Dies Irae had cauterized it, burning the stump to staunch the blood flow. Gloriae had seen this done in battle before. The fire could close the arteries and kill infection, but it left a messy wound of sizzling, raw flesh. Gloriae gritted her teeth.

"I need bandages!" she called out.

A prisoner hobbled toward her, holding a rag. Gloriae grabbed it and wrapped Agnus Dei's stump.

"This isn't enough," she whispered. "I've seen such wounds before. It will fester. Blood will keep trickling. It will not heal this way." She looked around the hut, panting. "We need to file down the bone, so it doesn't cut the wound. We need to remove the burned flesh, and sew the arteries shut, and seal the stump with a flap of skin. We... we need medicine, and tools, and healers." Gloriae's eyes stung, and she rubbed them. "Bring me some tools! She'll die if we don't treat her. Why don't you move?"

The prisoners only stared at her. Gloriae trembled. She looked at them; so many others suffered the same amputations. So many others were already infected, bleeding, dying. The same would happen to Agnus Dei, she realized. *And the same will happen to me.*

Gloriae lowered her head, jaw clenched. *So this is how it ends,* she thought. *He'll cut us piece by piece, and turn us into a dozen mimics.*

She cradled Agnus Dei's head in her arms and kissed her forehead.

"I'm so sorry, sister," she whispered. "I'm so sorry we only had this short time together. I love you, Agnus Dei. I'm with you now. I'll be with you always."

Her twin's lips moved, and her brow furrowed, but she wouldn't wake. Snow and sweat drenched her tunic. Blood stained her bandage. Gloriae wished she had a blanket for her, a roaring fire, and water for her to drink. *Will she die today in my arms? If she does... that will be a kindness to her. If she lives, Irae will drag her out again, and cut off more.* Gloriae shuddered. *And soon he will cut me.*

Roars sounded outside. Feet thumped through the snow. A mimic squealed.

"Man the palisade!" Dies Irae shouted. "Man your posts, mimics."

Gloriae crouched, cocked her head, and listened. Further away, she heard another sound. She couldn't recognize it. It sounded like moaning wind and creaking wood, but almost human, a cry of sadness and rage.

"Agnus Dei!" shouted a voice in the distance. "Gloriae!"

Gloriae jumped, shouting. Tears filled her eyes.

"Kyrie!" she cried, jumping up and down, jostling the prisoners around her. She laughed and wept. "Kyrie, Kyrie!"

Eyes blurry, Gloriae knelt by her sister. She wept over her and cupped her cheek.

"Kyrie is alive!" she said, her tears splashing Agnus Dei's face.

Agnus Dei's eyes fluttered opened. She smiled wanly. "I knew he would be," she whispered.

Gloriae leaped back onto her feet. She shoved her way between the prisoners toward a window. It was a small window, only several inches tall and wide. Gloriae stared outside and gasped. Charred trees were moving through the camp, swinging their branches against mimics. The mimics hacked at them, but the trees kept charging, breaking through them.

"They animated the bloody forest!" Gloriae shouted and jumped up and down. "Agnus Dei, they brought a hundred trees!"

Gloriae looked back at Agnus Dei, and saw her twin smiling weakly from the floor. She turned back toward the window, stuck her face against it, and shouted.

"Kyrie! Kyrie, we're in here! Break open the door."

Where was he? Gloriae couldn't see him. She saw only dozens of trees crash against the mimics. Blood flew. Branches snapped and fell. She glimpsed Umbra racing between the trees, torching them.

"Kyrie!" she shouted.

A voice answered her. "Gloriae! Gloriae, is that you?"

Mother! It was Mother's voice!

"I'm here, Mother!" Gloriae shouted. "In the hut by the ditch. Get the trees to break the door down."

Across the hut, Agnus Dei cried out: "Mother!"

The lock creaked. The door swung open.

Gloriae rushed toward it, prepared to see Kyrie or Mother. Instead, she found herself facing Dies Irae and a group of mimics.

"Kill the prisoners," Dies Irae told his mimics. "Kill them all."

The mimics rushed into the hut.

Gloriae growled and leaped toward them.

One mimic swung an axe down toward Agnus Dei, who lay at its feet. Gloriae growled and slammed into the mimic, knocking it back.

The mimic Warts swung a sword at her. *Per Ignem! My own sword!* Gloriae ducked, and the blade whistled over her head. She grabbed Warts's arm and pulled it down. Per Ignem's blade hit the ground. Three more mimics rushed toward her. Dies Irae stood behind them, watching with a hard face.

Warts bit Gloriae's shoulder. She screamed. A spear lashed toward her. She dodged it and twisted Warts's wrist. Per Ignem fell. Warts's teeth pushed deeper into her flesh. Gloriae knelt, grabbed Per Ignem, and slammed its crossguard against Warts's head.

The mimic opened its mouth, screamed, and Gloriae's cut off its head. She swung the blade, and mimic blood sprayed.

"Pull her back!" Gloriae shouted to the other prisoners. "Get my sister back against the wall."

A dozen mimics faced her at the doorway, drooling and hissing. She slashed at them, spinning her blade, eyes narrowed, lips tight. Gloriae lived for this. She was a decent archer. She knew how to fight as a dragon. But swordplay... she had been born for swordplay. Per Ignem moved like a part of her. She snarled as she hacked and maimed. Mimics piled up at her feet, their arms and legs crawling and grabbing at her. She kicked them aside, shouted, and barrelled between mimics and through the doorway.

"Irae!" she shouted. She glimpsed him marching away, disappearing into a crowd of mimics. "Irae, you coward! Come fight me."

A shadow flew, and Gloriae raised her sword. Her blade hit a flying dagger, knocking it aside. The blades sparked.

"Hello, sweetheart," said Umbra. She came walking toward Gloriae, a dagger in each hand. Her black, chin-length hair swayed in the wind, and a crooked smile played across her lips. A second dagger flew.

Gloriae leaped sideways. The dagger glanced off her helmet, then hit the hut behind her. She snarled and ran forward.

A third dagger flew. Gloriae leaped, waving her sword and growling. The dagger hit her breastplate and fell. She swung her sword down.

Impossibly fast, Umbra drew two new daggers from her belt, crossed and raised them, and blocked her sword. Gloriae pulled her blade back, and a dagger slashed. She leaped aside, but the dagger sliced her arm. She growled and lashed her blade. Umbra parried. The woman was smiling, her eyes flashing.

"Do you know who I am, girl?" she asked.

Gloriae swung her blade. Umbra parried again. Sparks flew.

"One of Irae's pets," Gloriae said. She bared her teeth and lunged with the blade.

Umbra parried, sliced, and drove Gloriae a step back.

"I was a sister. I was a wife. You burned my husband and my brothers."

The sword and two daggers slammed together, showering sparks.

"Good," Gloriae said. "I hope they screamed loudly when my fire rained upon them."

Umbra snarled. Her eyes blazed. She leaped forward, daggers flashing.

"My husband and brothers never harmed you," she said, teeth bared. "They were Blood Wolves, warriors of the alleys. You burned the city with your dragonfire. You killed innocent people, Gloriae the Gilded."

Gloriae snickered. "I don't care." She lashed her sword, slamming it against a dagger. The dagger fell from Umbra's hand.

Umbra snarled and leaped carelessly, driving down her remaining dagger. Gloriae raised her arm, blocking the blow on her vambrace. The two women fell into the snow, Umbra atop Gloriae.

"You will suffer now, Gloriae," she hissed. She raised her dagger and brought it down.

Gloriae swung the hilt of her sword, hitting Umbra's wrist. The dagger drove into the snow, an inch from Gloriae's face. Umbra screamed and tried to bite, but Gloriae kicked her stomach, knocking her off. She leaped to her feet and swung her sword down, but Umbra rolled. The sword hit the snow.

Umbra crouched, eyes blazing, snarling like a wild animal. She tossed her last dagger. Gloriae rolled aside, and the blade sliced her thigh. She screamed and ran toward Umbra, sword waving. Umbra snarled. Her daggers gone, she leaped back and disappeared into a crowd of mimics.

Gloriae tried to chase her, but the mimics blocked her way, howling and slamming their blades against Per Ignem.

"I will burn you like I burned your husband!" Gloriae shouted after her, voice hoarse. "Run, Umbra. Run from me and cower. I will find you, and I will burn you."

The mimics shouted and waved their blades. Gloriae narrowed her eyes and parried left and right. *I will kill these mimics.*

And I will kill Umbra. And I will kill Dies Irae. Her blade spun, raining blood.

"Gloriae!" Lacrimosa cried, leaping into battle beside her. "Mother!"

Mother and daughter fought side by side, hacking at mimics.

"Where's Agnus Dei?" Lacrimosa shouted.

"She's in the hut! She's hurt. Go to her, Mother. I'll hold back the mimics."

Lacrimosa nodded and ran to the hut, hacking her way between mimics. When Gloriae looked around, she saw animated trees crashing into the huts, freeing the prisoners, and knocking mimics aside. The prisoners were limping toward the breached palisade that surrounded the camp; some were already fleeing into the forest.

"Hullo, Gloriae," Kyrie said, leaping into the battle beside her. Snow, ash, and blood covered him. He swung a sword and torch at the mimics.

"Hullo, Kyrie," she answered. She stabbed a mimic and kicked it down. "About time you showed up."

Kyrie torched a mimic who leaped at him. "Thought I'd drop by and save your backside."

Gloriae sliced off a mimic's leg, then drove her sword into its neck. "You haven't saved it yet. There are hundreds of these damn mimics around."

Kyrie nodded. "It was fun, but I think it's time to leave this party."

"Agreed."

Swinging their weapons, they pulled back toward the hut. As she fought, Gloriae stared around, seeking Dies Irae. When she saw him, she growled. He stood across the camp upon a hilltop, Umbra at his side. They were watching the battle from safety. Gloriae snarled, wishing she had her bow or crossbow.

"Oh stars," Kyrie said beside her. His voice was choked. "Stars, Agnus Dei. Oh stars...."

Gloriae gritted her teeth and kept fighting, her back to the hut. Her eyes stung. She heard Lacrimosa cry in mourning. Gloriae snarled. Rage bloomed through her. She looked up at Dies Irae, the man who had maimed Agnus Dei, who had killed her father, who had brought her family this pain. More than anything, Gloriae wanted to rush through the army of mimics, reach Dies Irae, and kill him.

But no, she thought. *My family needs me now. They need me to lead them to safety.*

"Come on!" she shouted over her shoulder at them. Kyrie and Lacrimosa were huddling over Agnus Dei. "Help her up. Follow me. We're leaving."

More mimics kept pouring toward her. She saw no end to them. Their teeth snapped, their claws slashed, and Gloriae's arms ached. She couldn't hold them back much longer, and few trees remained standing to help her.

"Let's go!" Kyrie shouted. He and Lacrimosa held Agnus Dei between them. She was conscious, but sweat matted her hair, and pain filled her eyes.

Gloriae gestured with her chin. "The palisade is breached over there. Let's get her out of here."

Five trees crashed into the crowd of mimics, kicking their roots, lashing their branches. Mimics fell and rolled. Gloriae used the diversion to drive between them, clearing a path with her blade. Mimic limbs and blood flew. The other Vir Requis followed her.

She reached the breached palisade. Other prisoners were limping through it. Mimics were leaping onto them, killing those who were too slow.

"Come on, hurry!" Gloriae shouted. She stabbed and kicked a mimic. It crashed against a pile of amputated legs. The bloodied limbs rolled, tripping the other mimics.

"Put me down," Agnus Dei said. "I can run. I can fight!"

"Kitten, come on," Kyrie said. "We're leaving."

Agnus Dei growled. She managed to walk on her own, then run. She leaped out of the breach, holding the stump where her hand had been. Kyrie and Lacrimosa leaped after her, swinging their torches at mimics. Gloriae stayed a moment longer, fighting inside the camp. She saw no other prisoners; they had all fled or died.

She looked up and stared at Dies Irae. He stood atop the hill across the camp, arms crossed--the real arm, and the steel one. He stood three hundred yards away, but it seemed to Gloriae like their eyes met.

She growled. "We'll meet again, Irae. This isn't over."

Then she turned and leaped out of the camp. She ran with the other Vir Requis through the snow, mimics howling and chasing them.

They ran fast, even Agnus Dei. They ran until they lost the mimics between the trees and boulders. They ran until the curse of the Animating Stones faded in the distance.

Gloriae roared and shifted into a dragon. Her wings thudded. Her maw roared fire. She leaped up and flew. Her tail whipped and her fire bathed the world. It had been so long since she had flown. She sounded her roar.

Three more dragons flew up from the forest: Lacrimosa, silver and slim, blowing blue flames; Kyrie, blue and fast, roaring fire; Agnus Dei, a red dragon missing her front foot.

Gloriae dived toward her sister, held her, and helped her fly. The four dragons roared, blew fire, and flew into the clouds. They streamed over burned forests and fallow fields, heading west, heading to Requiem.

Gloriae shut her eyes. *We should never have left*, she thought. *We should never have attacked the mines. Now Agnus Dei is hurt, and we've lost our Animating Stones. What will we do now?*

She swallowed, opened her eyes, and looked at her sister. Agnus Dei stared back, wincing, jaw tight with pain. Her wings roiled the falling snow.

"I'm so glad you're alive," Gloriae said to her. That was what mattered, she knew.

Agnus Dei blinked back tears. "I never thought we'd make it out in one piece. I guess I was right."

Gloriae laughed and sobbed. The sun began to set. The dragons flew into its dying beams.

MEMORIA

She flew over plains of ice, bloodied and bruised. The giants had chipped her scales, pummelled her body, and nearly killed her... but she kept flying. For Requiem. For Kyrie.

"Terra, we're almost there," she said.

He flew beside her, grunting. He was hurt, but still he flew, eyes narrowed.

They each wore one of Adoria's Hands around their necks. They had split the Giant King's chain and hung the segments around their own necks. As Memoria flew, she looked at the hands. They were so small, pale, folded into fragile fists. They swayed on the chains like worms on a fishing line. *Could such dainty things truly hold back the mimics' curse?*

The Ice City was never where she left it. It forever floated on its iceberg, moving with the currents. Finally she saw it ahead, its hundred palaces glistening like crystal shards.

Home, she thought, and the thought surprised her. On the eve of her return to Requiem, did her place of exile become her home? She would miss the icelings, she realized. Old Amberus, with his long beard and wise eyes. Small and silly Gif, only five years old, who would carve ice sculptures with her. Her friends, Illa and Oona, who were shy around Terra and giggly around her. *Yes, this too has become a home to me,* she thought, and she smiled sadly. The Ice City was cold, lonely, and far from Requiem, but it had been a good home.

"Amberus will heal our wounds," she said to Terra. "And then we'll fly to Requiem. We'll fly to Kyrie. He's alive. I know it."

Terra only grunted, eyes wincing with pain. They dived toward the iceberg, snow gusting around them, and flew between its palaces. All but one were abandoned now, their towers still, silent, and glistening. The two dragons, one green and one bronze, flew between the steeples of ice, kissed with snow. They glided toward the tallest palace, the place Amberus ruled, the place where they'd hidden for eleven years.

They landed outside its gateway, and Memoria's breath died.

Blood stained the ice at her feet.

Memoria growled.

Grunts sounded inside the Ice Palace. A screech echoed. Wind blew, carrying the stench of bodies.

"Mimics," she said.

Terra grumbled and fire crackled between his teeth. "Looks like we're still in for some fighting today."

Memoria kindled flame in her maw and ran into the palace.

The front hall, a towering chamber that dwarfed even two dragons, was splashed with blood. Bodies of icelings lay strewn across its floor, torn apart. Mimics leaned over them, feasting.

Memoria screamed and ran forward.

"Get off them!" she cried.

They raised their bloody faces from their feast, glared, and hissed. Their curse hit her with a thud, like air from a bellows. Memoria gasped and faltered. She felt their magic crash into her own, wrestle it, shove it, try to claim it.

"No!" she cried and gritted her teeth. If she became human now, she could not defeat them all. Not with only her sword. Her scales began to melt off. Her wings began to fold into her body. Her fangs retracted into her gums.

Around her neck, Adoria's fist began to uncurl.

Memoria shook her head wildly, struggling to cling to her magic. The mimics began racing toward her, drooling and hissing, brandishing swords.

Adoria's Hand opened.

It felt like a wave crashing forward. The power shoved back the mimics' curse, and Memoria's magic refilled her. She was fully dragon. She was fang and claw and fire.

Her jet of flames blazed across the hall, spinning and crackling, and crashed into the mimics. They burned and squealed and fell. Terra shot flames beside her. A few mimics reached them. The dragons lashed their tails and claws, sending them flying. Adoria's Hands rose on the chains, holding back the mimics' curse. The flames filled the chamber, and the walls wept.

It only took moments, and the mimics across the hall lay burned. Memoria ran from iceling to iceling, but they were all dead, their innards eaten.

Screeches rose from other chambers across the palace. Memoria raced between the rooms, shooting flames, burning mimics, lashing them with her tail, clawing them open. Iceling bodies filled every chamber.

"They're all dead," she whispered. "All dead."

Kyrie! she had called. *Kyrie, do you hear!*

Lanburg Fields stretched around her, drenched in blood, piled with bodies. She was rummaging through them again, searching for her brother, weeping over his body.

Kyrie!

Terra ran up behind her, flames dancing between his teeth.

"A hundred mimics are streaming into Whale Hall. Come, Memoria."

They ran across the ice, flapping their wings to steady themselves, and burst into Whale Hall. Mimics ran toward them, bloated and rotten, hideous creations that were part men, part beasts. Terra and Memoria blew their fire. The hall blazed. Water streamed down the walls. Mimics screamed.

Finally the flames died. The mimics lay twitching and burned. And among them....

Memoria ran forward, tears on her cheeks.

No.... Stars, no.

But it was him. Amberus, kindly old Amberus with the long white beard, the elder iceling who had become a father to her. He lay in the corner, his belly split open, his entrails consumed. Mimic drool covered him. He had tried to shield his followers; the bodies of iceling children lay in the corner behind Amberus. Young Gif, whom Memoria would sculpt with. His sisters. So many others.

"All dead," she whispered.

She turned to Terra. Her throat was so tight, she could barely speak.

"They came here searching for us," she said. "It's our fault."

Terra stared at the bodies with dark eyes. His claws shook, and he dug them into the ice floor. "We will avenge them. We will kill the man who sent them here." He looked up at her. "We will kill Dies Irae."

She shook her head. "I don't care about Irae." Tears welled up in her eyes. "I just want to save whoever I still can. Agnus Dei. And Kyrie. My Kyrie."

They pulled the bodies outside, and placed them on the ice, and prayed for them, and wept for them, and let the sun and moon shine upon them.

"The last of the icelings," Memoria whispered. "The end of a race. A people extinguished, but forever in my memory, forever in my soul."

She had never prayed to the northern gods, but she prayed to them now. She whispered to Father Walrus to bless the memory of the ice people. She sang to the Wind Goddess, to Sky Eagle, to Sister Moon. She prayed to Mother Turtle who glowed green and purple upon the horizons. She wept as she lowered the icelings into the water, one by one, until they sank into the embrace of Old Whale, their guardian of afterlife.

They bound their wounds. They mourned for days. And they flew. Terra and Memoria, soldiers of Requiem. Exiles. They flew over icebergs, over oceans, over plains of snow and lifeless rock. They flew over forests of pines, the first trees they had seen in eleven years. They flew over fields of grass, over herds of deer, over fields and villages of men.

They flew home.

DIES IRAE

"They are beautiful," Umbra said.

She stood beside him on the walls of Confutatis, staring down into the field. The wind swayed her black hair. Her eyes were narrowed. A small smile twisted the corners of her mouth. She placed one hand on her hip, the other on his shoulder, and licked her lips.

"They are beautiful," Dies Irae agreed, "they are strong, and they will kill the weredragons."

The army roared below in the field, the greatest army he had ever mustered.

"Come," he said to Umbra, "let us walk between the troops. Let us inspect them."

They descended the city wall and walked into the field. Umbra slung her arm through his, a wolf's grin across her face. They approached the army's vanguard--thousands of howling mimics--and walked between their formations.

"Fifty thousand mimics scream here," Dies Irae said. "The world's greatest soldiers."

The mimics bared teeth, screeched, and banged their blades against their shields. Stench rose from them, and their eyes blazed. Some had the heads, legs, or claws of animals. Others sprouted many arms. A few towered twenty feet tall, giants stitched from gobbets of leftover flesh.

Dies Irae stopped by a burly mimic with a bull's head and four arms. Its hands held an axe, a spear, a sword, and a warhammer.

"Look at this one, Umbra. Look at the hand holding the axe. Do you recognize this hand?"

Umbra gasped. Her grin widened. "It's *her* hand. The hand we cut."

Dies Irae nodded, smiling silently.

Umbra laughed. "Brilliant, my lord! I hope that hand cuts the rest of Agnus Dei."

"Come, I will show you more."

For long moments, they walked by the lines of howling mimics, until they emerged from the vanguard and approached the left flank. Thousands of snowbeasts drooled here, towering creatures of white, loose skin hanging over knobby bones. Seven feet tall, they looked to Dies Irae like great white spiders, or perhaps furless cats with six legs.

"Their legs are fast, and their jaws will tear into weredragon flesh," he said.

Umbra caressed one. "They are beautiful."

They continued walking. Past the snowbeasts, they reached a battalion of skeletons. Wispy beards, flakes of old skin, and rusty armor clung to them. They held spears and their eye sockets glowed.

"The skeletons of Fidelium," Dies Irae said. "I have freed them from two thousand years of underground shame. They will fight for me now."

Umbra's own eyes seemed to glow. Her breath grew heavy. "I love them, my lord. Show me more."

They walked between the skeletons, passing row after row of them. Finally they reached an army of great reptiles, the size of dragons, who growled and snapped their teeth. A thousand of them roared as Dies Irae and Umbra walked between them.

Umbra's cheeks flushed, and her lips parted. "What are they?" she breathed.

"Swamp reptiles," Dies Irae answered. "Terrors from Gilnor. They are as large as dragons, and with larger teeth."

"Show me more," Umbra begged. "I want more, my lord."

He nodded. They kept walking. They reached a field where twisted, scaly creatures stood. They looked like men, but fish scales covered them. Their eyes bulged. Some had eyeballs that hung on stalks. Their fingers were webbed, their arms long and twisted. Blood dripped from sores on their faces.

Umbra bit her lip in delight. "What are these things, my lord?"

"They are the Poisoned," he answered. "Years ago, with green smoke from my dungeons, I turned many weredragons into these things. Today I found peasants, prisoners, soldiers who were once men; they are the new Poisoned, and they will fight for us with tooth and claw."

Umbra trembled in delight. "Show me more."

He took her past the Poisoned, and to a field where
thousands of nightshades coiled. They shrieked, took flight, and
roiled above them. They looked like storm clouds, creatures of
black smoke, thunder, and lightning. Their eyes blazed like stars.
Their mouths snapped, showing and hiding smoky white teeth.

"They hunger for weredragon souls," Dies Irae said. "The
weredragons will not have a chance to use their Beams this time.
The nightshades will swoop from the clouds and break them."

Umbra panted. Her cheeks were red. Her eyes closed.
"More, my lord."

He led her past the nightshades into a field drenched with
blood.

"Here, Umbra. My proudest creations."

She screamed in delight. "Sun God!"

Five thousand mimic dragons roared before them. They
took flight and circled above, showering droplets of blood. Their
wings were made of human skin. Their bones and flesh were sewn
together from thousands of bodies. Fifty Animating Stones pulsed
inside each one's breast. When they screamed, the sound shook
the earth.

He looked at Umbra. She held her hands to her chest,
gasping.

"This army will descend upon Requiem," he told her. "The
weredragons have defeated scattered enemies before. Now they
will face an army such as the world has never seen. Soon we will
have their heads."

She stared at him, eyes blazing, lips parted. She panted. *Such
cruelty in this one,* he thought. *Such strength, such hatred, such fire.*

When Gloriae had served him, she had never shown fire,
only ice. Gloriae had always been so cold, so calculating. But
Umbra... this one was a demon's daughter, a creature of shadow
and malice. Dies Irae pulled her toward him, clutched her throat,
and squeezed her body. She gasped and her eyes shone.

"You will bear me sons," he said.

She bared her teeth. "Sons who will lead. Sons who will
bring fear to the world." She clenched her fists. "Sons who will
rule a land with no weredragons."

He pushed her to the ground. She lay in the dust and mimic
blood, looking up at him. He tore her bodice open, exposing her
goose-bumped flesh, and she growled. He took her violently, until

171

she screamed, and the mimic dragons screamed above. When he was done, he dragged her through the mud, and returned with her to the city walls. They climbed atop the tallest guard tower. They stood above this grand army, this sea of dark wonders, this glory and power and lust and blood. He raised his arms, and they howled. The mimics brandished blades, the snowbeasts snapped their teeth, the skeletons clanked, the swamp lizards growled, the Poisoned screamed, the nightshades screeched, the dragons roared.

Dies Irae smiled.

He put his arm around Umbra's waist.

"We march now," he said. "We march to victory and glory. You will march by my side."

She drew her daggers and snarled. "I will kill by your side."

"We march to Requiem!" he called to his army. Their howls shook the city. The sun itself seemed to tremble.   With dust and noise and fury, they marched.

LACRIMOSA

She wiped Agnus Dei's forehead, kissed it, and lifted the bowl of soup.

"You must eat, Agnus Dei. Kyrie made soup."

She held the bowl up to her daughter's lips. Lying on a pile of furs, Agnus Dei sipped, winced, and spat it out. She coughed.

"The pup... he's flying too slow. We must reach Salvandos. We have to keep flying."

She coughed again and trembled. Her face was pale, and her eyelids fluttered. More sweat beaded on her brow. Lacrimosa had lit a fire at the cave's entrance, but it was still cold here, so cold that she was always shivering. She rearranged the furs covering Agnus Dei.

"Salvandos is far away, sweetheart. You flew there already with Kyrie, do you remember? It was in the summer. Drink the soup, Agnus Dei. It'll help you."

She held the bowl up again, but Agnus Dei only coughed when she sipped and shivered. Her forehead was so hot. Lacrimosa kept the bowl up, and sip by sip, Agnus Dei managed to drink half the bowl.

The campfire cast flickering light against the cave walls. This place lay far north in the ruins of Requiem, in the mountains where few dragons had ever flown. It was a hidden place, but Lacrimosa did not feel safe here. *We hide, but he'll find us,* she thought. *Dies Irae's armies will scour this land, and they will find us anywhere we hide.*

She touched her daughter's cheek. "It's time," she whispered.

Agnus Dei shut her eyes, mumbled, and nodded.

Lacrimosa pulled back the furs, revealing Agnus Dei's left arm. It ended with a wet bandage, one of only two bandages they owned. Blood and pus painted the bandage red and yellow. It smelled of infection.

Wincing, Lacrimosa unpeeled the bandage. Agnus Dei grimaced and clenched her fist. Sweat poured down her face.

"This will hurt," Lacrimosa whispered.

But Agnus Dei did not hear. She had lost consciousness again. Her eyes moved under her lids, and her lips mumbled.

Lacrimosa had only one bottle of spirits left; Gloriae had found it in an abandoned inn ten leagues east. Lacrimosa took a deep breath and splashed the wound. In her sleep, Agnus Dei winced, trembled, and mumbled.

"Dada," she said. "Dada, please, they'll hurt you. You have to fly. You have to fly, Dada."

Struggling to keep her fingers steady, Lacrimosa replaced the old bandage with the new one, then wiped the sweat off Agnus Dei's brow. They had done all they could. They had filed down the bone's sharp edges, removed the burned flesh, and sewn it over with skin. And yet the stump still festered. For the past two days, Agnus Dei only woke briefly from unconsciousness. Lacrimosa worried that soon she would not wake at all.

She shut her eyes. *Please, stars. Please. I lost my husband; don't let me lose my daughter too.*

Wings flapped, and Lacrimosa looked outside the cave. She saw two dragons block the stars. Soon Kyrie and Gloriae landed at the cave, shifted into humans, and walked in.

"More spirits," Gloriae said. She held out a bottle. "We flew for hours, and finally found the bottle in a town two leagues east of the border."

"And another blanket," Kyrie said, holding it out. "Warm fur. We also found flour, a jar of honey, and three jars of apple preserves; they're in my pack."

They walked to Agnus Dei and knelt by her. Kyrie kissed her lips, and Gloriae wiped her forehead.

"Watch over her," Lacrimosa said. "Call me if she wakes up."

Before they could answer, she stood up and stepped outside the cave. Her eyes stung and she shivered. The night was cold, and her breath frosted before her. She stood on the mountain and looked at the stars. The Draco constellation shone there.

"Winter has come," she whispered. "It has covered Requiem in snow, and it has covered my heart in ice. I'm scared, Ben."

She looked at the Draco stars. They seemed so cold, so far from her.

"He's coming here to kill our family," she whispered. "He'll have armies, greater than any we've seen. And... I don't know how to face them, Ben. I don't know how I can protect our children." Her eyes dampened. "Agnus Dei is hurt, and her fever won't break. I'm scared." She tightened her cloak around her. "Are you up there, Ben? Are you watching over me? If so, give me strength. Guide me, Ben, for I'm afraid and lost."

The stars glistened, casting rays of light, blurring behind her tears. Lacrimosa rubbed her eyes, but the stars still seemed misty. Strands of starlight spread out from them like cobwebs. Lacrimosa gasped. The strands moved through the night and connected the stars in her constellation, forming the shape of a dragon. In the star maps she'd read in childhood, scribes would connect the stars with lines, accentuating the shape of each constellation. *Does some scribe now paint these lines in the sky? Ben, are you up there, pulling a great brush between our starlit halls?* As she watched the starry dragon, Lacrimosa felt peace spread through her like those strands of starlight.

She stepped back into the cave.

"Children!" she called. "Come outside. Come see."

Gloriae and Kyrie leaped to their feet and drew their swords.

"What is it?" Kyrie said.

Gloriae snarled. "Mimics."

Lacrimosa shook her head. "No mimics. Come look. Let's carry Agnus Dei outside. I want her to see this."

Gloriae and Kyrie exchanged uneasy glances, and cautioned that Agnus Dei could not be moved, but Lacrimosa insisted. Alcohol and bandages had not staved off infection; if anything could save Agnus Dei, maybe it was this miracle.

Agnus Dei moaned when they carried her outside, and her skin burned, but once the starlight hit her, her face seemed calmer to Lacrimosa, her skin cooler. They lay her on a fur blanket in the night air.

"Look, Agnus Dei," Lacrimosa whispered, holding her daughter's hand. "Your father is up there. He's watching us."

Agnus Dei's eyes fluttered open. She looked at the dragon in the stars. A smile touched her lips.

"Hi, Father," she whispered. "I'd wave, but... Mother's holding one of my hands, and I think Dies Irae is holding the other."

Gloriae gaped at the sky. The starlight glinted in her eyes, painted her hair silver, and kissed her cheeks.   "What does it mean?" she said, voice awed.

Lacrimosa pulled her close and kissed her cheek. "Hope," she whispered.

DIES IRAE

They marched through the empire, feet shaking the earth, howls splitting the sky.

Dies Irae rode before his army upon a black mimic horse, its fur matted and its mouth foaming. When he looked over his shoulder, he snarled and grinned. A hundred thousand warriors marched behind him, covering the countryside like spilling oil, swallowing the empire beneath them. Thousands of nightshades and mimic dragons circled above, shrieking.

"We draw near Requiem, my lord," Umbra said, riding her mimic horse up beside him. She wore no armor and bore no sword. She was a Blood Wolf, and she rode to war as one, garbed in black. Her leather boots rose to her knees over her leggings, and six daggers hung from her belt.

Dies Irae nodded. "The ruins of Requiem lie beyond the mountains ahead." He scanned the horizon and saw a town below those mountains. Chimney smoke rose in fifty columns; there would be survivors there. His grin widened. "We will stop before crossing the mountains, and we will dine."

Umbra licked her lips.

They rode toward the town, the army roaring and drooling behind. When they got closer, Dies Irae saw a hundred cottages, a temple, and several fields. Soon he rode through the streets, Umbra at his side. His army surrounded the town like ants around a fallen piece of fruit. The streets were empty.

"The peasants are hiding," Dies Irae said.

Umbra looked around, eyes narrowed. "Like rats."

"Burn them out, Umbra. Burn these rats' nests."

Soon she held two torches, and ran from house to house, setting their thatch roofs afire. The rats began to flee. They ran out of their houses, haggard peasants, their clothes tattered, their faces gaunt. Some began to run to the mountain, wailing.

"Dine, my lovelies!" Dies Irae called. "Dine upon them."

The mimic dragons swooped. The nightshades flowed between them. The mimics and monsters stormed from house to

177

house, grabbing whoever they could. It only took moments, and the lucky ones feasted. The unlucky creatures, those who could not catch a peasant, growled and screamed. Some began to eat one another. Blood splattered the town.

Umbra emerged from the smoke, manhandling a peasant girl. She held a dagger to the girl's neck.

"I found one for us to dine on," she said.

Dies Irae smiled. The girl was thin but comely, about the same age as his daughters. She had red hair, white skin, and teary eyes.

"We too will dine," he agreed.

He dragged the wench to the town square, backhanded her, and shoved her against the well. Umbra sat on the well's edge, smirking, and held the girl down as Dies Irae lifted her skirts. The girl struggled as he took her, and Umbra laughed. When he was done, he tossed the weeping girl toward a group of mimics.

"Enjoy," he told them.

They leaped upon her, drooling and howling, and she screamed.

Soon his army moved again, marching, shuffling, crawling, flying. They howled, they drooled, they screeched and moaned and growled and hissed. They oozed into the mountains, leaving the light of Osanna behind, spilling into the mountains of Requiem's ruin.

"Soon I will have you, Lacrimosa," Dies Irae whispered as he rode at the van. "Soon I will hurt you, Agnus Dei and Gloriae. Soon I will break you, Kyrie Eleison. You will be my basest mimics, pathetic slaves to my warriors' lusts."

Umbra fingered her daggers. "Your glory will soon cover the world."

The ruined town faded in the distance. Requiem rolled ahead.

AGNUS DEI

Strange dreams filled her world.

She saw strands of starlight form a dragon in the stars. She saw mimics bearing her face, fifty thousand strong, marching through snow and ash. She saw her father, clad in dark green and silver, ruling in a marble palace, his eye sockets empty and bleeding. They smiled at her, this dragon, these mimics, her father, smiles that flowed around her head. When she reached for them, they vanished and laughed, flowing into the sound of sad pipes and wind through tunnels.

"Mother," she whispered. "Mother, the Poisoned... I have to burn them. I have to. I have to save the scrolls."

Mother held her hand. "They're gone, sweetness. The Poisoned are gone."

Agnus Dei blinked. "But we need to find the Beams, Mother. They're in a swamp, I think. The pup said something about a swamp."

He touched her cheek, that pup, his face blurry. Was he truly there? She heard him.

"Rest, kitten. Don't worry about the Beams."

She tried to see him, to blink, to clear her eyes. But she saw only tunnels stretching before her, diving under mountain and ruins. Skeletons surrounded her. Was Father one of these skeletons? She tried to find him.

"Father! Father, don't worry. You can be a skeleton. I'll be one soon too. I don't care, but Mother will say I'm too thin."

Her left hand hurt. She could feel the fingers twisting. Someone was burning it.

"No, Umbra, please," she begged and wept. "Let me go."

But the woman only chained her down, and *stars, no, please, no....*

She heard the hiss. A sword being drawn. *His* sword.

"Please, Irae... Mother, help me!"

Stars, it's gone. My hand is gone. How could it be gone? Where is it?

She had to find it. She had to. *The pup will hate me without a hand. He'll leave me. He'll go be with Gloriae.* She had beautiful hands.

Tears streamed down Agnus Dei's face, so hot. *I'm like him now. I'm like Dies Irae.*

"He'll take my other hand," she whispered, trembling. "Please, Mother, he'll take my leg. Please don't let him."

Arms embraced her. "I won't let him, sweetheart. I promise."

Where was she? Who was holding her?

"Mother!"

She fell into tunnels. She wanted to stay with her mother, with her sister, with her pup. But the tunnels pulled her down. Pain! Fire on her hand. The fingers moved.

I am mimic. My hand is cruel. My hand will hurt me. Stars, it's gone. How could it be gone? Please, Irae, please.

She saw her hand before her. It rose from the shadows, speckled in blood. It wielded an axe toward her. *Please, don't cut my other hand....*

The hand grew from a mimic with four arms and a bull's head. Its hair was long, black, curly, rustling with bugs. Its eyes mocked her. It smiled, showing pointed teeth and a slobbering tongue.

"Agnus Dei," it hissed. "He will cut your head. He will make you a mimic like me." It tightened her hand around the axe. Worms crawled over the knuckles.

She trembled. She tried to kick, to fight it, but was too weak. The darkness pulled her. The heat! Fire burned her hand, her forehead, her lungs. Sweat drenched her.

"The nightshades broke me," she whispered. "They're pulling me into their worlds, into the shadows."

The darkness shattered her, tugged her into pieces, drowned her. Fire everywhere. Pain and fire. Her eyes rolled back. *I'm sorry, Mother. I'm sorry, Gloriae. I'm sorry, Kyrie. I don't want to leave you. I love you all so much.*

Golden light rolled across her, like the hint of dawn over a swaying field.

"Mother?"

The heat left her.

The pain vanished.

When she opened her eyes, she saw light like feathers. It tickled her face. Blue wisps floated above them; bits of sky. She heard rustling leaves, and saw rolling hills, rays of light between birches, and columns of white marble. Figures robed in white floated before her, harps in hand.

"Requiem?" she whispered.

Snowy mountains and valleys of pines spread before her. A great mountain soared ahead, all in gold, dragons flying around it, bugling, sunlight on their scales. They were true dragons, wingless, limbless, flying serpents of brilliant colors, of fluttering white beards, of crystal eyes.

"Salvanae!" she said. She smiled softly under their light. "I am here again, in Salvandos. I remember flying here with Kyrie."

Tears flowed down her cheeks. Was this the afterlife--to spend eternity with the salvanae? Hope welled within her and she wept. This was a good place to die.

I'll wait here for you, she swore to her family. *One day we'll fly here together.*

A golden salvana flew toward her, coiling and uncoiling. His white moustache and beard fluttered in the wind. His eyes were the size of melons, spinning and glowing.

"Nehushtan!" Agnus Dei cried. "It's me. Agnus Dei. Do you remember?"

She found herself lying in grass in human form. Nehushtan floated above her. He lowered his head, so that his beard brushed against her. His head was larger than her human body. His eyes blinked, his long white lashes fanning her.

"Wake, daughter of stars," he said, his voice like harps. "The song of Requiem calls you."

Stars floated around her, spun, streamed. *But I am awake,* she thought. *I live among the stars.*

Somebody squeezed her hand, and she heard Mother's voice.

"Wake up, Agnus Dei. Open your eyes. It's not yet your time to leave me."

But my eyes are open, she thought. *I can see beauty and light.*

Yet she managed to open them again. New light shone. She gasped, and cold air filled her lungs, scented of mountains. Nehushtan seemed to smile at her, teeth glinting, moustache fluttering. His golden scales chinked and glimmered as he floated.

Behind him, thousands of other salvanae hovered in the sky, their long bodies undulating like snakes in water.

"Mother?" she whispered. She looked to her right and saw Mother sitting there, the salvanae's light against her face. Kyrie and Gloriae sat there too, their eyes soft.

"Agnus Dei." Mother kissed her forehead and caressed her cheek. "How do you feel?"

She blinked. "I feel better. I... am I dreaming? I see the true dragons, Mother. Thousands of them. Are we in Salvandos?"

"You are in Requiem still," said Nehushtan, his voice like crinkling old paper and the wind in pines. "We saw the strands in our stars, and sang to them, and heard your prayers sing with ours. So we flew here, daughter of Draco, and we will help you again. We sang too for your healing."

Agnus Dei gasped and raised her left arm. For an instant, she hoped to see her hand regrown. That hope crashed. Her arm still ended with a stump, though the wound was healed. Instead of infected stitches, she saw pale, smooth skin.

"Thank you," she said softly, though she could not feel joy. She felt, instead, only shame. Her wound was healed, but her arm looked strange to her, deformed. Tears stung her eyes. She was still crippled. Impure. Ugly.

Agnus Dei looked at Kyrie, her pup. *Does he think I'm a freak now? A gruesome cripple? Will he still love me? Or will he leave me for Gloriae, who is whole and still beautiful?* Suddenly she wished he'd look away. She wanted to hide her arm, to never show it to anyone again. She lowered her eyes.

"Oh, pup," she whispered. "I'm sorry."

He shifted closer. "Sorry for what?"

That I'm like this, she wanted to say. *That I'll be forever different.* But she could not bring those words to her lips. Instead, she looked up at him, her pup, her love, her best friend, and she said, "I love you."

His eyes softened, and he scooped her into his arms, and kissed her. His hands held her head, and she placed her good hand on his back. They kissed in the light of the true dragons, and tears flowed down her face.

"I love you too," he said, holding her. "I'll always love you, Agnus Dei."

Laughter burst from her lips, surprising her. She pinched his cheek. "You really are a pup, do you know that?"

She looked over his shoulder at the mountains and valleys of Requiem. The snow was melting. Winter would soon end. Beams of dawn fell between the thousands of salvanae. War would come here, Agnus Dei knew. Dies Irae would march into these lands with all his might and malice. *But that is tomorrow*, she thought. *Today... today life is beautiful.*

Gloriae leaned down, kissed her cheek, and smiled. Mother held her good hand. They sat on the mountainside, embracing one another, watching the sunrise.

TERRA

When he saw the army in the distance, he felt the blood leave his face.

"Stars," he whispered. "Down, Memoria!"

They dived, landed on a snowy mountainside, and shifted into humans. Wind moaned, flurrying snow around them, sneaking under his armor like the fingers of ghosts.

"There are thousands," Memoria said, gasping. "A *hundred* thousand."

Terra narrowed his eyes. It was hard to see from here. The army moved leagues away, a black stain upon the ruins of Requiem, oozing forward. He could hear faded roars and battle cries, a sound like an angry sea. Creatures flew over the army, thousands of them, like murders of crows. They were too distant to see clearly, but they had to be massive, the size of dragons.

He scowled. "This army was mustered to kill the last Vir Requis."

Memoria clutched the hilt of her sword, as if that sword could defeat such an army. "To kill Agnus Dei, and to kill Kyrie," she said.

Terra stared at this spreading black puddle, his stomach twisting. He was no stranger to war. He was a bellator, a knight of Requiem. He had fought griffins at Draco Murus, the Poisoned in Requiem's tunnels, the giants of the north. But this.... Terra had never seen forces that chilled him so. Strange things moved there. He saw the shapes of great beasts towering over smaller troops, and he saw stars and lightning crackle between the creatures that flew. This army marched with dark magic.

"They move slowly," he said. "We fly fast. Let's find Kyrie."

Memoria nodded. "The ruins of Requiem's palace. King's Column. So long as Vir Requis live, that column will stand." Her eyes dampened. "I know Kyrie. He's there."

If he's alive, Terra thought, but said nothing. Memoria believed. *Let her cling to hope while she can. Hope might be all we've got.*

"Let's fly," Memoria said. "I remember the way. Follow m--"

Before she could finish her sentence, a distant shriek rose. Terra cursed. A dozen flying beasts, the size of specks from here, disengaged from the army and came flying toward them.

"They saw us," he said. "Damn it. Let's fly!"

He shifted into a dragon, roared fire, and soared. Memoria flew beside him, snow flurrying around her green scales. They flew west, the clouds streaming around them, the snow slapping their faces. The mountaintops rose around them. When Terra looked over his shoulder, he saw his pursuers gaining on them.

"Those things are fast," he said.

"So are we. Fly, Terra!"

He narrowed his body, flapped his wings mightily, and shot forward through the wind and snow. He growled and fire filled his mouth. He looked behind him again and cursed.

"Damn it! They're gaining on us. What *are* they?"

Jaw clenched, Memoria looked over her shoulder, and her eyes narrowed.

"They look... they look like dragons," she said.

Terra shook his head. "No. Not dragons. But whatever they are, there are six of them, and two of us. Fly higher. We'll lose them in the clouds."

They soared and crashed into the snow clouds. Wind, ice, and snow stung Terra's eyes. He lowered his head and narrowed his eyes to slits, pushing himself forward. He couldn't see ten feet around him.

"Memoria, are you with me?" he shouted.

Her voice came from the clouds to his left. "Right beside you. Fly against the wind; it'll take us to the ruins of the palace."

And maybe slow down those creatures following us, he thought. He kept flying, driving through the clouds, and heard the screeches behind him. They were closer.

"They're fast bastards," he said.

Green scales flashed beside him between strands of clouds. "What the stars *are* those things? They were leagues away only moments ago."

Terra grunted. "Friends of Dies Irae."

The siblings kept flying, driving through the storm until the clouds parted. They found themselves over valleys of toppled ruins and fallen trees. Marble columns, each a hundred feet long, lay fallen like so many sticks below them. Snow dappled the ruins like patches of leprosy. The cries sounded again behind them, like the sound of butchered elephant seals. When Terra turned his head, he saw the creatures emerge from the clouds, only five hundred yards away.

"Bloody stars," he muttered. Beside him, Memoria gasped.

They were dragons, or at least, shaped as such. They were sewn together from the dead. Men's bodies, trussed up like hams, formed their necks. Their wings seemed made of human bones and skin. Their tails, their bodies, their limbs, their heads; all were patched from body parts, sewn together, rotting and wormy. They opened their maws and squealed.

Mimic dragons. Lovely.

He felt the Animating Stones; their curse slammed against him, tugging at his magic. Memoria grimaced; she felt it too.

Around their necks, Adoria's Hands opened.

The mimic dragons shrieked and flew at them, claws extended.

Terra and Memoria blew their fire.

The streams of flame roared, crackled, and hit two mimic dragons. They screamed and burned, their skin peeling, their flesh blistering. The four others flew around them, lightning fast, and blazed toward Terra and Memoria.

Terra had no time to muster more fire. The things moved so fast, he could barely see them. Two crashed into him, their claws--they seemed made of sharpened femurs--lashing at him.

Those claws scratched his side. He growled and bit. His teeth sank into soft, rotten flesh. It tore free easily, filling his mouth with juices and dead flies. The taste made him gag. He spat and clawed, hitting the beast's head.

It growled and bit, and its teeth broke several of Terra's scales. Roaring, Terra flapped his wings, kicked, and pushed himself back. He swiped his tail, hit the creature's head, and blew fire.

The mimic dragon burned. Its skin peeled back as it screamed. Its stitches melted. The bodies composing it came loose and began falling from the sky--men, women, children, pale and rubbery.

"Terra!" his sister cried.

He growled and flew toward her. Three mimic dragons surrounded her, scratching. Terra roasted one and swung his tail at another. Before it could recover, he swiped his claws, bit, and tore its head off. Memoria burned the last mimic dragon, and it fell to the ruins below, coming apart into two dozen bodies.

"That was easy," Terra muttered, rubbing a wound at his side.

Memoria growled. "I hear more."

Terra heard them too. It sounded like hundreds were flying in the clouds, moving closer. *Once they emerge from the clouds, they'll see us.*

"To the ground," Terra said and began to dive. "We continue on foot, as humans."

They dived, the air whistling around them, the snow stinging them. The clouds growled and the mimics screamed in the distance. They landed by a fallen tower, shifted into humans, and crawled under the ruins.

"Damn," Memoria whispered, peeking through the ruins to the sky. Snow filled her hair and kissed her cheeks pink.

Terra grumbled. A hundred mimic dragons emerged from the clouds above, squealing. Their wings creaked and roiled the snow. *How are we to defeat so many, even with Adoria's Hands?*

Memoria clasped his hand. "Do you think... do you think these things found Kyrie?"

Terra shook his head. "If Kyrie survived this long, he's good at hiding, at fighting, at *living*. If he's alive, we'll find him." *Terra... I found him.* He grabbed his sword. "We'll look in the west. We'll look at King's Column."

The mimics above shrieked and flew over them, soon disappearing into the distance. Terra and Memoria hid for long moments, shivering in the cold. Finally they crawled out of hiding and began to walk. Their feet ached, their teeth chattered, and their limbs were weak with hunger and wounds.

When Terra looked behind him, he saw that black puddle oozing over the horizon. He cursed and quickened his step.

KYRIE ELEISON

He walked through King's Forest, holding Agnus Dei's hand. The snow glided around them.

"Oh, pup," Agnus Dei said, head lowered. "This place feels so sad, doesn't it?"

The trees were fallen now, burned and toppled years ago. It seemed to Kyrie like all the horrors of the world had been born here.

Twenty years ago, Dies Irae raped Lacrimosa here. Four years later, he stole the griffins here, and toppled these columns. Five years after that, Requiem's survivors gathered in this place, and marched to Lanburg Fields. Kyrie sighed. *And now... does Requiem fall here now?*

Kyrie raised his eyes and looked at King's Column. It rose in the distance from the ruins, two hundred feet tall, its marble bright. Salvanae coiled above and around it, bugling their song.

"It is sad," he said, "but look, Agnus Dei. New dragons fly here now. And we're still here. We still fight. We can win this war."

Agnus Dei raised her head and looked at him. Her eyes seemed so large to Kyrie, pools of sadness.

"I'm so afraid," she said. "I lost Father. And... at the camp, when...." She swallowed and hid her left arm. "It feels like somebody else died. I grieve for my hand, the same way I grieve for Father. Is that strange, Kyrie?"

He shook his head, touched her cheek, and kissed her forehead. "It's not strange."

She lowered her eyes, her eyelashes brushing his cheek. "I'm so scared of more loss. Of you dying, or Gloriae, or Mother. Kyrie, I... I want to be brave again. I want to growl and shout for battle. But I can't feel that way anymore."

He nodded. "You're growing older and wiser." He tapped her head. "Maybe soon you'll be as wise as me."

Normally she would punch him, wrestle him, and pull his hair for such a taunt. Today she did not even smile. She sighed and he held her, his arms around her. She held him with her good hand, but kept her left arm hidden behind her back.

"Oh, pup, I can't even hug you properly now."

"You can."

She shook her head, and Kyrie felt her tears on his cheek. She trembled.

"Kyrie, I'm ashamed. I'm sorry. I don't even like holding you now. I don't like when you hold me." Her voice shook. "I used to like you looking at me. It made me feel funny and good. I wanted to be beautiful for you, as beautiful as Gloriae. But I can't now. Not without my hand, with this arm that... that just ends with a stump. It looks so ugly to me. I hate it. I'm ugly now, and I'm so embarrassed whenever you look at me. I'm so sorry that I'm like this for you."

He laughed softly, and she stiffened. She pulled back an inch, looking at him with narrowed eyes.

"Why do you laugh at me?" she asked.

He caressed her cheek. "Agnus Dei. You have the largest, most beautiful eyes I've seen, with the longest lashes. You have the softest, bounciest, curliest hair I've seen, like lamb's fleece. And most importantly, you are good, and brave, and kind. You are beautiful, Agnus Dei. You are the most beautiful woman I know, inside and out, and you will always be beautiful to me. No matter what. I will always think this, and I will always love you." He held her hand tight. "If you ever doubt it, I'll beat you up."

She sighed again, lowered her head, then raised her eyes. A soft smile touched her lips. "Oh pup, you're such a poet, do you know? Not a very good one, but an earnest one." She touched his cheek. "And you know that you can't beat me up. I can still beat you in a fight, even with one hand."

She kissed his lips. They held each other, kissing deeply, the salvanae coiling and singing above.

"Come with me," he said. They walked through the forest, and found a hollow between three fallen columns. He lay down his cloak, and they sat upon it, holding each other. They pulled her cloak above them and huddled for warmth. He kissed her lips, her ear, her neck. She moaned and dug her fingers into his back.

They undressed each other, trembling with cold, goose bumps rising across them. His lips moved down her neck, and he kissed her breasts, then pulled her atop him. She sat in his lap, and tossed back her head, so that her mane of curls cascaded to his knees. She wrapped both arms around him, her eyes closed.

Soon Kyrie was no longer cold. He remembered the first time he made love to Agnus Dei, in the summer on the border with Salvandos. It seemed so long ago. Back then, Agnus Dei had confused him, taunted him, teased him, seemed so much older and mysterious and intoxicating. Today she was more to him: a kind, brave, sensitive woman he loved, a woman he wanted to be with forever. They kissed and swayed in the cold, their furs draped over them.

They were walking back to King's Column, hand in hand, when they heard shrieks and thudding wings above.

Agnus Dei's eyes widened. "Griffins! The griffins are here!"

Kyrie looked up, shielding his eyes with his hand. He gasped. Thousands of griffins flew above, snow clinging to their fur, their eyes bright. Volucris flew at their lead, King of Leonis, Dies Irae's old mount. Rays of sun fell between them, and their shrieks seemed to shake the world.

"They too have seen our stars," Kyrie whispered. "They too have come to fight." He squeezed Agnus Dei's hand.

She nodded. "The great battle of our generation will be fought here, I think. All the nations of the world gather. To fight Dies Irae. To fight darkness." She swallowed, tears in her eyes. "Salvandos, Leonis, Requiem... we join together to fight for life. This war is not only about us anymore, Kyrie. Irae's evil has crawled to all corners of the world, I think... and the world is fighting back."

The griffins began to land in the forest. They stood atop the fallen columns, the smashed walls, the shattered mosaics that lay buried in snow. Kyrie passed by one, a golden female with yellow eyes, and placed his hand against her fur. She cawed and tilted her head at him.

He kept walking with Agnus Dei and approached King's Column. It rose before him, its capital glimmering in the sun like a beacon. Lacrimosa and Gloriae stood below the column, wrapped in cloaks, talking in hushed tones.

A man and woman stood by them, speaking with them. Kyrie frowned. Something about these strangers made him freeze.

The two strangers had not seen him yet. The woman was short, slim, and fair-haired. She wore furs and bore a sword in the style of Requiem blades. Tall and broad, the man bore a similar sword, and wore plate armor and a horned helm. His face was haggard, sporting a walrus moustache like Kyrie remembered his father wearing.

"Who are they?" Agnus Dei whispered, eyes narrowed.

"I... I don't know," Kyrie said, but somehow he did know, or used to. He knew these people. He knew that the man had a deep laugh. He knew that the woman had brown doe eyes, though he could not see them.

"Kyrie!" Agnus Dei said. "Your hand is trembling."

He wanted to walk forward, but could not. His insides roiled. He saw a vineyard, not far from here, kissed with sunlight and humming with dragonflies. He saw a mosaic floor, dragons and dolphins and griffins all twinkling with thousands of stones. He saw a balcony, and tasted wine, and he saw these people; he knew them, he loved them.

Lacrimosa saw him first. She looked toward him from King's Column, and her eyes softened. Gloriae looked at him too, and then--slowly, almost hesitantly--the two strangers turned to face him.

Their eyes. I know their eyes. Brown eyes like his own, the woman's kind and round, the man's weary and haunted. Both pairs stared at him, piercing him.

The two walked toward him. Kyrie stood frozen, half of him wanting to disappear, the other half burning for answers. He held Agnus Dei's hand tight.

When the strangers reached him, their eyes turned soft and damp.

"Kyrie?" the woman whispered. Her voice shook, and a tear streamed down her cheek. "Kyrie, is that you?"

Kyrie! she called. *Kyrie, the geese are flying outside, come see them. Kyrie, I wrote you a story, come hear. Kyrie, I love you.*

He breathed heavily, staring at her through narrowed eyes. He turned to stare at the man, the tall man with the walrus moustache and the plate armor, a man who looked so weary, so haunted... and Kyrie saw him younger, happier.

Go on, Kyrie! Pull the line, you've got him. It's a trout, and a big one. You caught him, Kyrie. He saw the sunlight on the water, smelled frying fish, heard his brother laugh as they wrestled.

My... brother?

"Kyrie?" the man said. He stepped forward and held Kyrie's shoulder, examining him, his mouth opening, his eyes widening.

Yes, I had a brother once. And I had a sister. But they died. They died years ago, along with my parents, with my friends, with everyone I've ever known.

"Who are you?" he whispered.

The woman smiled--a warm, teary, loving smile. "It's Memoria, Kyrie. I've come to you again. Do you remember me?"

He shook his head, mouth hanging open, eyes still narrowed. "I... no. I'm sorry, but I don't."

"She's your sister," said the tall man. "And I'm Terra, your brother."

And suddenly they were embracing him, and crying over him, and saying so many words he did not understand. They spoke of a tunnel trapping them, and of seeking him in Lanburg Fields, and fleeing into an Ice City, and something about a sorceress and a giant, and a palace built all of ice, and mimic dragons.... Kyrie understood none of it.

"Don't you remember us, Kyrie?" Memoria asked, tears spiking her lashes. "Do you remember our home?" She touched his cheek. "You were so young. You were only six years old when we lost you. Do you remember?"

"I... I remember having a family. I remember my parents. I remember having many cousins, and friends, and older siblings. But... I've always only remembered blurry images, sounds, smells. I...."

Suddenly his knees felt weak, and he had to sit down on a column. Everything spun around him. Memoria and Terra kept holding him, and laughing, and crying over him. Lacrimosa laughed and cried with them, and Agnus Dei still held his hand, and Gloriae moved silently around them. They all blurred around him, becoming smudges of color and sound like his memories.

"I have a sister?" he whispered. "I have a brother?"

It was impossible! *I'm the last Eleison. I've always been the last. Dies Irae murdered my family. He....*

Terra.

Memoria.

He remembered those names. He remembered! They pounded through him. He remembered the mosaic floor, the balcony, the vineyard, the stream where Terra would take him fishing.

"I have a sister. I have a brother."

He shook and his eyes dampened. Terra patted him on the back and laughed again, that old laughter Kyrie still remembered, and Memoria hugged him, and he was confused, so confused, and he could barely tell memory from reality.

Memoria kissed his cheek, trembling, sobbing now. "I'm so sorry, Kyrie. I'm so sorry we left you. I'm so sorry you had to survive without us for so long. But we're back for you now. You'll never be alone again."

I have a sister. I have a brother.

He looked toward Agnus Dei. She looked into his eyes, her smile trembling.

"Is this real?" he whispered. "Am I dreaming?"

She laughed and mussed his hair. Her eyes sparkled. "It's real, pup. They look just like you."

Kyrie looked at them. Terra. Memoria. With the same sandy hair, the same brown eyes, survivors, fighters, siblings. He lowered his eyes.

"I'm sorry," he said. "I want to remember more. I... I didn't know your names until you told me. I didn't even remember your names. I thought you had died so long ago. I'm sorry that I never found you, that I never.... You know who I am. You have all these memories of me. I wish I could say the same." He lowered his head, ashamed.

But they only laughed, and hugged him again, and they cried together.

"We found him, Memoria," Terra whispered. "We found him."

Kyrie held them. The dragonflies hummed in his mind, and the vineyard rustled, and the stream splashed with fish.

It's real, pup. They look just like you.

"It's real," he whispered. *I have a sister. I have a brother.*

The griffins cawed around them, and the salvanae bugled, a song of reunion and joy, of light and hope and love... before the fall of night.

DIES IRAE

His black horse grunted beneath him, rot seeping through its stitches, foam dripping from its mouth. Dies Irae dug his spurs deep.

"Weredragons were here," he said. He tossed back his head, and his nostrils flared. "I smell them."

Umbra rode beside him, scanning the ruins with narrowed eyes. Night had fallen, and only a glimmer of red light remained in the west. She sniffed too.

"I smell nothing but rot," she said.

Dies Irae pointed up the mountainside that loomed before them. An orphaned, crumbling archway crowned the mountain, the remnants of a weredragon fort. *Draco Murus, they called it,* he remembered and snickered. The greatest of Requiem's fortresses-- smashed upon the mountain.

"This is where my pets found them. Let us seek them there."

He kneed his horse, leading it up the mountainside. Umbra rode at his side. Behind them, his army marched, crawled, and flew, a hundred thousand creatures all howling and drooling. Stones tumbled, but the undead horses plowed on, stronger in death, faster and needing no food or rest.

"The place is an utter ruin," Umbra said, disgust and glee mixing in her voice. "It's worse than Confutatis."

Dies Irae nodded. "Confutatis will rise again, stronger and more glorious than before. This place, this Requiem, will sink further into ruin and pain."

Soon his forces covered the mountainside, like worms covering a body. The snowbeasts smashed down the archway, squealing. Its stones cascaded, hitting several mimics, incurring laughter from their comrades. Dies Irae dismounted on the mountaintop, his boots scattering snow from the cobblestones of an old courtyard. Umbra dismounted beside him, drew her daggers, and hissed.

"The air is rank with the stench of reptile," Dies Irae said. He spat. Mimics howled around him, waving their blades.

"A hole," Umbra said, pointing her dagger.

Dies Irae nodded. "A rat hole. Light a torch and follow me."

He climbed into the darkness, Umbra behind him, torch crackling in her hand. A stairway led him into a network of cellars. *Do you hide here, weredragons? Do you cower from me?* He couldn't wait to find Lacrimosa, to tear off her clothes, hurt her, take her, crush her, to pull her hair and see her tears. He licked his lips.

"Where are you, my lovely?" he whispered. "Where do you cower, my lizard whore?"

Tree bark, broken branches, and sap filled some chambers; wood had been stored here. A second chamber held a bear rug, a table, and four clay bowls.

"Where are they?" Umbra demanded.

A tattered dress hung on a peg in the wall. Dies Irae lifted it, held it to his face, and inhaled deeply. *Lacrimosa's dress. Yes.* She had worn this the night he caught her in the field. He savored the scent of it.

He turned and began walking back upstairs, the dress in his hand.

"They went to King's Column," he said. "They retreated to the only place their light still shines." He clenched his fist around the dress, gritted his teeth, and smiled. "That's where we'll find them."

Umbra snarled. "They will be our mimics soon. Slaves for our warriors to torment. I will hurt them too."

Dies Irae nodded. He stepped out into the courtyard and stood on the mountaintop. His army spread around him, line after line of mimics, snowbeasts, the Poisoned, swamp lizards, skeletons, rotting dragons, and coiling nightshades. Their cries shook the earth.

"We will smash King's Column!" he shouted. "We will destroy the weredragon curse forever. Their bodies will be yours!"

They howled. The clouds roiled. Dies Irae mounted his horse, spurred it, and galloped down the mountain.

LACRIMOSA

Lacrimosa flapped her wings, circling above the burned trees and shattered halls of King's Forest.

It felt good to fly. She had barely flown all winter, and she needed to feel the clouds around her wings, the wind in her nostrils, the fire in her belly.

"Requiem!" she said. "May our wings forever find your sky."

The words of her fathers, of her priests, of her life. She still flew for her fathers, for her priests, and for life--her life, the life of her children, the life that still flickered in Requiem.

"I still find your sky. And I will fight for you. Give me strength, stars of Requiem. Give me strength, Ben. The great battle of our time comes to us. I pray that I can withstand its tide."

She circled above King's Column, the last pillar of their halls. She remembered a hundred griffins slamming against it, trying to topple it, but the Draco light still blessed it; so long as Vir Requis lived, it would stand. *I will not let it fall.*

The griffins now flew around her, her allies. The salvanae flew here too, coiling and uncoiling, their eyes spinning, their scales glimmering. Volucris flew at her right, shrieking, wings churning the clouds--King of Griffins. Nehushtan flew to her left, a hundred feet long, his moustache fluttering and his scales like molten gold--King of Salvandos.

"Thank you, my friends," she said to them. "Thank you for flying with me, with Requiem."

Nehushtan bowed his head to her. "The evil of the tyrant spreads across earth and heaven. The stench of it has carried to our land. It poisons the glow of stars. We have come to fight. For Requiem. For Salvandos our home. For Leonis, realm griffins. We fight for all lands of civilization."

Lacrimosa remembered travelling across the ruins of Osanna, the empire of men. She had crossed it by foot, and taken ship from Altus Mare on the sea. She had seen ruin, death, desolation. Cities lay crumbled, farms burned, forests wilted, bodies rotting. *And who will fight for Osanna?* she wondered. *Who will fight for the realm Dies Irae rules, enslaves, and burns?*

The griffins shrieked, and the salvanae bugled.

Drums and trumpets sounded in the north, answering her.

Lacrimosa stared and gasped. She blew fire, and her eyes stung.

They marched from the burned forest, thousands of them, bearing banners of green and brown. They flowed forward like a snake emerging from a basket. A hundred horsemen rode at their lead, clad in armor, bearing lances and standards. Behind them walked thousands of women, children, and old men, all wrapped in cloaks, huddling together for warmth. Thousands of men surrounded their grandparents, mothers, wives, and children. Some wore armor and bore swords. Others wore peasant tunics and carried pitchforks and torches.

"The Earthen," Lacrimosa whispered. Children of Osanna. Followers of the Earth God. *Friends.*

She flew down and landed on a snowy, fallen column. She stood, wings folded against her back, and watched the Earthen approach.

An old man led them, she saw. He rode a brown horse and wore a green cloak over chain mail. His hair and beard were long, and more white than brown, but his back was still straight, his eyes still bright, his hand still steady on the hilt of his sword. He rode up to her, two armored riders flanking him.

Lacrimosa bowed her head to him. "Silva the Elder," she said. "Welcome to Requiem. May our stars, and your Earth God, bless you."

The priest nodded to her. His face was deeply lined, his voice hoarse. "Queen Lacrimosa of Requiem. A great host approaches. Our scouts have seen them. They cover a league, and they march fast. It's an army of beasts and demons, abominations to the Earth God and to your stars. They'll be here soon."

"Our own scouts have seen them," she replied, remembering what Terra and Memoria had reported. She swallowed. "An army of mimics, snowbeasts, nightshades, and all other creatures of darkness. We stand ready to fight them."

Silva gestured to the riders beside him. "These are my sons. At my right is Silva the Younger. And here is Silas, my second son, a great priest like his brother."

The two men drew their swords.

"We stand ready to fight with Requiem," said Silva the Young.

"We fight for the Earth God," said Silas, snow in his hair.

Lacrimosa looked over their heads at the people they led. Horsemen. Footmen. Peasants. Women and children. *Dies Irae has hunted them for years. Here is their final stand. Will this be their Lanburg Fields? Will this be death to us all?* A few of the children began to cry, and Lacrimosa looked back to Silva.

"Lead the mothers and children into the trees west of King's Column. They are burned and many have fallen, but they will give some shelter. Place armed men around them. Take the fallen logs, and build what palisades you can. Then take what men you can spare, and what women can wield a weapon, and rejoin me here at the pillar. We will hold council."

She took flight, soaring as high as she could, until the air thinned, her lungs hurt, and her head spun. In the east, she saw them approach, a league away, a shadow falling over Requiem. Fear coiled in her belly. There were so many, a vast host like she had never seen. Countless nightshades and mimic dragons flew there. Fifty thousand mimics marched below, howling and banging war drums. Behind them moved endless skeletons, reptiles the size of dragons, herds of snowbeasts on gangly legs, and mobs of oozing Poisoned.

And one man I must kill. One man who has haunted my life. The man who raped me, murdered my husband, murdered my parents, murdered my people. One man I must face today. Lacrimosa tightened her jaw. *Be strong, daughter of Requiem,* she told herself. *Now is your hour.*

She looked below her, surveying her forces. Five thousand salvanae, the true dragons, creatures of fang and lightning. Five thousand griffins, their talons bright, their beaks sharp. Ten thousand soldiers, followers of the Earth god, protecting ten thousand women and children.

"And us," she whispered. "Six Vir Requis."

She saw the others below, huddling together by King's Column. Her daughters, the lights of her life. Kyrie Eleison, who was like a son to her. Terra and Memoria, new hope for their race.

That was all. A small force, she thought. A sparrow against the swooping vulture of Dies Irae's wrath. *But we will meet them still.*

She dived toward King's Column.

"Nehushtan!" she called. "Volucris!"

They flew to her, and landed with her in the shattered hall of Requiem's kings. Silva joined them, tall upon his horse, his sword in hand. King's Column rose above them into the rays of setting sun. Darkness was spreading fast, the stars emerging.

Lacrimosa shifted into human form. She placed a hand upon Stella Lumen, her father's sword.

"Daughters," she said, turning toward the twins. "Kyrie. Do you have the Beams?"

They nodded. Gloriae opened a sack and spilled out three golden skulls, each twice the size of a man's skull. Their orbits glowed and their jaws grinned.

"You have wielded Beams before," she told them. "Today you will wield them on griffinback. Choose your griffins and ride them against the nightshades. Burn them with the Beams and scatter them."

Gloriae nodded and lifted one skull. Snow filled her hair, scratches ran down her arms and cheek, and most of the gold had peeled from her breastplate. And yet her eyes were still strong, ice and fire. Once she had worn samite and jewels, Lacrimosa remembered. Once Gloriae the Gilded had hunted for Osanna, had killed and maimed for the glory of the Sun God. Today Lacrimosa saw a woman of justice, of honor, and of starlight.

"We will kill them," Gloriae said

Agnus Dei lifted the second skull. At first she held it awkwardly with one hand. Then she steadied it with her left arm, tightened her lips, and stared solemnly at Lacrimosa. Her leggings were tattered, her bodice was torn, and her cloak was shaggy. She wore only rusty pieces of armor: a pauldron on her left shoulder, vambraces on her forearms, dented greaves, no breastplate or helmet. Her sword hung on her hip. Lacrimosa remembered Agnus Dei not a year ago, full of rage and sadness, a beast trapped in a cage. Today she saw not an angry youth, but a strong woman.

"We will kill them all," Agnus Dei said, standing by her sister.

Kyrie lifted the third Beam. He too wore rags and dented armor, but his eyes were solemn, his face hard. Lacrimosa remembered meeting a boy in the summer, a boy who ran and hid from those who would kill him. Here in the winter snow, a man stood before her, a man who had fought and killed for those he loved.

"We will wield them for you, and for Requiem," he said.

Lacrimosa turned to face Nehushtan, ruler of the salvanae. The true dragon hovered several feet in the air, his serpentine body undulating. He blinked, his eyelashes fanning the snow. His moustache swayed in the breeze, and his crystal eyes glowed.

"Nehushtan," she said and placed a hand against his cheek. His scales were cold and smooth like mother-of-pearl. "I ask you to lead your salvanae against the flying mimic dragons. They are fast demons and do not die easily. Burn them with your bolts of lightning, and tear them apart with your fangs."

He nodded, his beard dipping into the snow. "They have woken the wrath of Salvandos. The Draco stars call us to war. We will fight them, Queen of Requiem. We will fell them from the sky, or die defending our stars."

She turned to Volucris next. The great griffin knelt in the snow before her, head lowered. Lacrimosa walked toward him, placed her hand against his beak, and rested her head against his.

"Volucris, my old friend," she whispered. "I'm proud to fight by you again. I ask of you this. Lead your griffins against the crawling beasts of Dies Irae. Fall upon his skeletons, his reptiles, his Poisoned, his snowbeasts, and all his horrors. Tear into them with your beaks and your talons, and kill them all."

He nodded, his eyes narrowing. They seemed to tell her: *We will kill them all.*

Lacrimosa nodded and turned toward Terra and Memoria. She wanted to be stern, but when she saw them, she couldn't help it. She felt her face soften, and she smiled.

"Terra," she said. "Memoria." She took their hands, and her eyes stung. "You have blessed us today. You have brought us new life, new love, new hope. Thank you."

They bowed their heads to her.

"My queen," Terra said, voice deep and gruff. He was only thirty, Lacrimosa knew--five years her junior--but she saw that white already invaded his temples, and lines already marred his brow.

"How should we serve you?" Memoria asked, fear and determination in her eyes. *She's so small,* Lacrimosa thought. *So delicate. But she was a soldier of Requiem. She will be a soldier again.*

Lacrimosa stared at the siblings. New Vir Requis. New survivors. *Will they die today, leaving us so soon?*

"You two wear Adoria's Hands," she said, nodding at the hands they carried on chains. "You two can shift around mimics, which we cannot." She squared her shoulders. "Tonight, fly as dragons, and swoop, and blow fire. Shower the battlefield with flame. Burn all mimics who march upon the ground of Requiem."

"We have burned them before," Memoria said.

"And we will burn them again," Terra finished.

Finally Lacrimosa turned to face Silva, priest of the Earth God. He stood by his horse, his hand resting on the pommel of his sword. The wind blew his long beard and green cloak, and his eyes stared at her steadily.

"Silva," she said. "For many years, Dies Irae hunted your priests, and burned your temples, and now he has murdered your people and turned them into his mimics. He murdered many of my people too. I'm proud to fight with you against him. Tonight let us fight side by side. We will lead the ground forces of our camp. The others will fight from above; we will face Dies Irae on the field."

His sword's grip and crossguards were made of twisting roots, like the old roots that had formed Requiem's throne. He drew the sword. Lacrimosa drew Stella Lumen, and they touched their blades.

"We will face him on the field," Silva agreed.

The sun disappeared behind the horizon. The Earthen lit torches, and the salvanae blew lightning above. War drums thudded in the east. Howls rose, a hundred thousand voices. The earth trembled. The squeals and grunts of beasts echoed among the ruins.

"It has come to us," Lacrimosa said. She took a deep breath, fighting to steady her fingers and the thrashing of her heart. "The great battle of our war is here. May we fight it well."

And if we must, may we die well.

She looked them over one last time. Her daughters. Kyrie and his siblings. The true dragons, the griffins, the children of Osanna. They stared back, eyes solemn, lightning crackling above them.

"It begins," she whispered.

She looked to the east and saw countless red eyes and shadows.

The battle of King's Forest began.

GLORIAE

She ran, boots kicking snow, as the howls and shadows descended upon King's Forest. Men were running and griffins taking flight around her.

"We need griffins!" she shouted. "Griffins, hear us."

But they were soaring from the ground, shrieking, flying into battle. Gloriae cursed and tried to shift, but could not. Mimics were near.

"Volucris, give us griffins!" Kyrie shouted, running beside her. Snow flurried around him.

Great wings thudded, billowing Gloriae's hair. Volucris landed before them, talons digging into the earth. *Dies Irae's old mount.* He towered over her and lay down his wing.

"Agnus Dei, ride him!" Gloriae shouted. "He's strong and swift."

Agnus Dei nodded. Clutching her Beam, she ran up Volucris's wing and sat bareback upon him.

"Fly, Volucris!" Agnus Dei cried. The golden skull glowed and hummed in her grasp. His wings blowing snow, his talons digging, Volucris took flight. The griffin king soared into the night, screeching, and drove into a storm of mimic dragons and nightshades. Already Agnus Dei's Beam blazed, shooting a ray that seared the storming nightshades.

Standing beside Gloriae, Kyrie pointed. "There's another griffin."

They ran through the snow. Men ran around them, shouting, swords drawn. Mimics crashed into the battlefield, roaring, their teeth and eyes red in the torchlight. Lightning blazed above them as the salvanae roared and fought the mimic dragons.

"Kyrie, you fly this one," Gloriae said when they reached the griffin. "His name is Malathor; he was one of Lord Molok's griffins. Fly, Kyrie! Fly now!"

Kyrie nodded and leaped onto Malathor. With shrieks and thudding wings, they soared into battle. Fire and light blazed around them. Kyrie's Beam seared through the night, and nightshades screamed and burned.

Gloriae scanned the battlefield, but the griffins had all taken flight. She saw them above--crashing into mimic dragons, swooping down to cut swamp reptiles, slashing at nightshades. On the ground around her, men and mimics still fought.

"Griffins!" Gloriae shouted. "I need a mount!"

"I'll mount you, girl," hissed a mimic, lunging toward her. She recognized the hunchbacked, warty form and matted red hair. *Lashdig, the chief miner.* It swiped its claws at her. Gloriae growled, leaped back, and swung her sword. Lashdig's arm flew, then came crawling through the snow toward her. She kicked it aside, spun, and cut Lashdig's legs at the stitches. The mimic fell and began crawling forward on its arms.

Gloriae raised her eyes. The nightshades were everywhere. They swarmed between the salvanae and griffins, wrapping around them, sucking their souls like a glutton sucking marrow from bones. Salvanae and griffins rained from the sky, helpless to hurt the nightshades. Agnus Dei and Kyrie shot the Beams in all directions, slicing through the demons of smoke, but they were overwhelmed.

Lashdig grabbed her leg and cackled. "You will be our slave, Gloriae." Spiders spilled from its mouth.

Gloriae kicked the creature, swung her sword, and cut off its head. She ran through the snow, hacking at mimics.

"Griffins!" she shouted.

A golden figure swooped.

Tears sprang into Gloriae's eyes.

Feathers flurried, talons glinted, and she saw her griffin.

"Aquila?" Her voice was small, hesitant. The griffin looked at her and lowered her wing.

"Aquila!" Gloriae shouted. She ran and embraced the griffin's head. "You've returned to me, girl. I thought you were dead."

The griffin cawed and tilted her head, anxious.

"Yes, Aquila, there's no time. We fly." She looked around her, ran forward, and grabbed a fallen branch the length of a lance. She leaped with the branch onto Aquila, her Beam held tight in her other hand.

"Now fly, Aquila!" she shouted over the roar of battle. Fire, blood, and lightning filled the night. "Fly like in the old days. To battle. To war. To glory. Fly!"

They soared.

The snow and blood dwindled below them, and they crashed through swarms of mimic dragons, swooping nightshades, roaring salvanae, and shrieking griffins. Blood, feathers, scales, and smoke blazed around her. Flaming arrows flew; mimics were firing them from below. Lightning flashed. Gloriae glimpsed Terra and Memoria flying to her north, raining fire upon the battle. Agnus Dei flew to the south, and Kyrie to the west, their beams rending the night. The roars, shrieks, and howls nearly deafened her.

"There, Aquila!" she shouted. "To the east. To those nightshades."

The demons of smoke and shadow were wrapping around salvanae, and the true dragons were falling fast. Gloriae snarled and dug her knees into Aquila. They shot through smoke, fire, and darkness. Gloriae nearly fell off, and she tightened her legs around Aquila as hard as she could.

She raised her Beam.

Lights shot from the skull's orbits, searing the night, slamming into nightshades.

They howled. The light turned them grey, and they shrivelled up, smoking, curling, falling. Gloriae spun the skull from side to side. Nightshades flew at her, maws opening, eyes blazing. She cut them down.

"I am Gloriae!" she shouted. "I fight for Requiem. I am her daughter. You will die before me."

Her armor was dented and dulled, its gilt chipped away, its jewels fallen. Her clothes, once priceless and embroidered with golden thread, were tattered and muddy, revealing more skin than they hid. Her lance was but a charred stick. Her griffin no longer wore gilded armor or a saddle; she rode bareback and wild. And yet Gloriae felt more powerful than ever. This was true power, she knew; this was justice and righteousness. This was the war she had always craved.

"I am Gloriae," she cried, "daughter of King Benedictus and Queen Lacrimosa, heir to Requiem. I kill for her tonight."

Flaming arrows blazed around her. One slammed into Aquila, and the griffin screeched but kept flying. As she swung the Beams, slicing through mimics, Gloriae scanned the night.

"Where are you, Irae?" she hissed. Where was the man she had called Father? Where was the man who had kidnapped her, who had murdered her friend May, who had murdered her true father?

Salvanae roared around her, scales flashing, lightning shooting from their mouths. Mimic dragons screamed and darted and bit. Flaming arrows flew, and smoke filled the air. The battle for Requiem raged, but Gloriae cared for only one man.

"I will kill you, Irae," she swore. "You die tonight."

MEMORIA

Fire, lightning, and beams of light shot around her, a storm of war. Arrows whistled, mimics roared, wings flapped, dragons swooped. The night spun around her, darkness and light, fire and blood.

"Terra!" she cried. Three mimic dragons mobbed him, slashing and biting. She flew, eyes narrowed, and slashed at one. Its flank opened, spilling snakes and cockroaches. When it turned to bite her, she blew her fire.

Terra shook off the others, growled, and torched them. A gash ran down his side, bloody. Salvanae, griffins, nightshades, and more mimic dragons spun around them, battling in the air.

"They need us down there," Terra said. "With me, Memoria! Let's burn the battlefield."

They growled, pulled their wings close, and swooped. The ground rushed up to meet Memoria, bristly with mimics. Their lines stretched into the night, endless formations of rot. She righted herself several feet above them and blew fire, raining the flames upon their ranks. They howled and fell, blazing. Javelins and arrows flew. One arrow shot through her wing, and she screamed. For a moment, the pain blinded her. A javelin grazed her leg.

"Memoria, fly! Higher!"

Terra flicked his tail, guiding her. She growled and flapped her wings, soaring into the clouds. Flaming arrows flew around her. She crashed into a nightshade, and it began to suck at her soul. She screamed. She felt the creature ripping pieces of her, laughing, lapping them up. And then Kyrie swooped forward on his griffin, his Beam blazing, washing her with light. The nightshades screeched and scattered.

"Terra, let's dive!"

She swooped again, Terra at her side. They broke apart near the ground and raced over the lines of mimics. They rained more fire, and more mimics burned. They soared, arrows snapping against their scales, and Memoria surveyed the battle. She cursed.

The mimics were tearing into the lines of Earthen, slashing their limbs off, digging into their bellies to feast. The Earthen lines were crumbling, and more mimics kept flowing forward. Lacrimosa fought there, swinging Stella Lumen, hacking at mimics. Blood splattered her.

"They need us!" Memoria shouted. "Down there, by the column."

Terra heard and nodded. Memoria steeled herself, drew flames into her mouth, and dived toward King's Column.

Ten mimic dragons soared toward her, claws outstretched.

Memoria blew her flames, hitting one dragon. It screamed and fell. The others crashed into her, lashing their claws and biting. She whipped her tail around her, and bit into their maggoty flesh, and cut and burned them. But they kept swarming. When she glanced below her, she saw more Earthen dying.

"The mimics are getting near the women and children!" she shouted.

Terra was battling a mob of mimic dragons. He roared and blew fire in a ring, scattering them, and dived. Memoria joined them. She drew fire and torched the line of mimics. Another arrow hit her, and she roared and flew higher, only to crash into a biting mimic dragon. She tried to dive for another round of fire, but could not. The mimic dragons filled the sky around her, protecting their comrades below

"Nehushtan!" she cried. "Cover us."

She stared above and saw the salvanae blazing all around, shooting lightning and biting into mimics and nightshades. They too were overrun.

A dozen mimic dragons flew at her from all sides. She blew fire in a ring, cursing. She could not shoot fire forever. Soon her reserves would dwindle, and she'd need rest to rebuild them. Would Lacrimosa and the Earthen survive until then?

A mimic dragon bit her calf, and she screamed and beat it with her wing. It opened its mouth to roar, and she slammed her tail into it, breaking it into a dozen bodies that rained onto the field. More flew at her. Memoria lashed her claws and tail, cursing.

LACRIMOSA

Her sword was a beautiful thing, she thought, a work of art, its blade filigreed, its grip glimmering with diamonds in the shape of her constellation. *But today... today there is no beauty to Stella Lumen. Today my blade deals death and blood.*

She swung that blade, cutting into mimics, their pus and blood and rot spraying. She screamed as she fought--for her children, for all free people, and for all her fallen.

Silva fought at her side, his beard fluttering in the wind, his eyes blazing, his sword bloody. His men fought around them, eyes solemn, green cloaks covered in snow and gore.

"Fight, friends!" Silva called over the din of battle. "Fight for the Earth God. We will kill the tyrant."

The enemy kept coming at them. Lines of flayed mimics burst forward, their bared muscles glimmering with blood, their internal organs shiny and pulsing. They looked like men turned inside out, and they swung jagged blades. One slashed at her, its eyeballs bulging from its skinned face. Lacrimosa parried, shouted, and swung her blade into it. Blood sprayed her.

"Terra!" she shouted to the sky. "Memoria! Burn their lines. Scatter them!"

Yet when she glanced up, she saw the mimic dragons mobbing the siblings, biting and lashing at them. More mimics and nightshades filled the sky all around. Lacrimosa cursed and parried another mimic's blade. Three attacked her at once, flayed and dripping, their teeth sharpened. She parried left and right, stabbed, thrust, and suffered a wound to her arm. She screamed and kept fighting until they lay dead.

For only a moment, she could catch her breath. Then new horrors burst from the battlefield.

Snowbeasts.

They towered seven feet tall, lanky things with six legs, flaps of white skin draping over their bones. They snapped their teeth, spraying the field with drool, and shoved between the mimics, charging toward Lacrimosa.

She ducked, dodging a blow from one's leg, and swung her blade. She hit its other leg, it fell, she leaped, she stabbed. Black blood sprayed. Another rose behind her, jumped, and slammed into her. She fell and its teeth came down. She raised her sword, screaming, and stabbed it through the mouth.

Lacrimosa lay on her back, panting, bleeding, her head spinning. More snowbeasts scurried around her like spiders. Silva cried commands to his men. Swords swung, horses thundered, and arrows blazed overhead. Above in the night sky, rays of light, pillars of fire, and streams of scales and shadow flowed.

They're too many, she thought in a haze. *We can't defeat them. We have to run.*

Bodies lay around her. Men and women of Osanna, come to fight here and die. Dead salvanae, the light of their eyes extinguished. Dead griffins. Everywhere--death, darkness, despair. Her eyes stung, and she felt herself sinking into the snow and blood.

The nightshades, salvanae, and dragons parted briefly above, and between them, Lacrimosa saw one of her stars. Its light was soft. She could almost not see it beyond the battle. But its glow seemed to call to her. *Lacrimosa. Child of the woods. You are home, you are home.* The words of her fathers.

Lacrimosa tightened her lips. *Not yet. I still fight for you, Requiem.* She leaped to her feet, shouting, and swung her blade.

Poisoned charged across the battlefield, shrieking in high-pitched, tortured voices. They had been men once, Lacrimosa knew, men twisted by green smoke and dark magic. Fish scales covered them. Their arms had grown long and twisted, their fingers clammy and webbed. Their eyes hung from their sockets on bloody stalks, slapping against their cheeks as they ran.

Lacrimosa fought them. She fought with blade and torch. She fought for Requiem. For her dead parents. For her husband. For her children. She fought as griffins and salvanae rained from the sky, dead or dying. She fought as men fell around her. She fought because her stars still shone, and life still filled her, and Lacrimosa would fight so long as she could. *Until my last breath. Until my last drop of blood. I will die fighting for Requiem, and then I will be with you again, Ben, in our halls beyond the stars.*

The creatures howled before her, blood rained from the sky, and Lacrimosa swung her blade.

AGNUS DEI

Flaming arrows whistled around her. Nightshades swooped in every direction, eyes blazing, maws dripping smoke. The mimic dragons bit and clawed. Volucris spun between the enemies, three arrows in his breast, his wings roiling smoke and flame.

Agnus Dei wished she had a second hand to hold onto Volucris. Her good hand held the golden skull, pointing its beams at swarming nightshades. Her left arm hung uselessly.

"Careful, Volucris!" she cried when he swooped, soared, and swerved. She nearly fell, and she pressed her legs against him so hard, she thought they could break.

Flaming arrows blazed around them, and one hit Volucris's leg. He howled and bucked, and Agnus Dei screamed. She slid down his back, tightened her knees, but kept sliding. She had to push the Beam against her chest with her left arm, then grab Volucris's fur with her right hand.

"Damn it!" she shouted. Her Beam dimmed, then extinguished.

The nightshades howled with new vigor, cackled, and swooped toward her. Their eyes burned like collapsing stars. Their maws opened wide, revealing white teeth. She felt them tugging at her soul, tearing piece by piece from her body. She growled and screamed.

"Not again, you don't," she said and gritted her teeth. They had stolen her soul once, and the memory still flooded her with terror.

Damn my missing hand! If I had two hands, I could hold on with one, and fire the Beam with the other. She howled in rage. *I'm crippled now. I can't even fight any more.*

Arrows flew, mimic dragons bit, and Volucris swerved and soared and dipped and spun. Agnus Dei bounced atop him, flew into the air, and fell back onto him. The ground spun below her, distant, swarming with mimics and monsters. Rays of fire and smoke shot around her through the sky. The Beam began to slip from under her arm, but she dared not release her fistful of Volucris's fur. The nightshades howled and flowed around her, brushing her with their icy bodies, and she screamed. She felt her soul being ripped away, pulled from her like stuffing from a torn doll.

She shook her head wildly, struggling to cling to herself. *I need my hand.*

"Volucris!" she screamed. "Catch me."

She released his fur and leaped off his back.

She fell through fire and smoke and raining blood, the battle spinning around her. The nightshades yanked her soul, and she saw her body tumbling below her, shouting in the night.

Volucris's talons caught her, knocking the breath out of her, nearly knocking the Beam from her grasp.

Her soul slammed back into her body.

She grabbed the skull with her good hand.

Rays of light blazed out, spinning and crackling, bleaching the world. They seared nightshades, slicing them in half. More nightshades screamed to her left, and she spun the Beam, burning them.

Kyrie flew by her on his griffin, waving his own Beam. "The damn things keep coming," he shouted. "Agnus Dei, you all right?"

She nodded, held in Volucris's grip. "Take the north, Kyrie! I'll deal with the south. The nightshades are tearing into the salvanae. We've got to do better."

He nodded and flew off, firing rays of light.

"Fly into them, Volucris," she shouted. "The cluster of them in the south. Let's burn them."

The griffin shrieked and flew, crashing into hundreds of nightshades. Their screams nearly tore her eardrums. She held her Beam before her, cutting into them. White smoke rose from them, and they crumbled and rained like ash.

Agnus Dei glanced below her and cursed. Dies Irae's forces spread into the distance. She could see no end to them. Mimics and snowbeasts swarmed closer to King's Column, tearing into the lines of Earth God followers. She saw Mother fighting there, surrounded by mimics. Every second, another Earthen fell dead.

Lights blazed below. The mimics were lighting arrows. The flaming missiles shot into the sky. Hundreds blazed around her like comets. Three flew so close, she felt them stir the air. One arrow grazed her thigh, tearing her skin, and slammed into Volucris's belly.

The griffin shrieked and bucked, tossing Agnus Dei in his talons. More arrows flew. One whistled an inch from Agnus Dei's face, sliced through her hair, and slammed into Volucris's neck.

Three mimic dragons swooped upon them, and Agnus Dei gritted her teeth.

Fire, blood, and darkness exploded. Mimic claws of steel scratched. Eyes blazed. Feathers fell and blood streamed down Volucris.

"Fly, Volucris!" Agnus Dei cried. "Get out of here, fly south."

He tried to flap his wings, but the mimic dragons tore into them, biting, tearing off feathers. Flaming arrows flew. They slammed into his belly, his neck, and one into his head. The Griffin King roared, but still he held Agnus Dei in his talons.

Smoke and tears filled her eyes, and Agnus Dei screamed.

"Let me go," she shouted. "Let me fall. Use your talons!"

But still he held her in his left talons, fighting only with his right. The mimic dragons cackled and flew at his left side. Agnus Dei pointed the Beams at them, but they were not nightshades; it would not burn them. They bit into Volucris, tore off chunks of his flesh, and began to eat.

"Volucris!" Agnus Dei screamed. She dropped the Beam and caught it between her legs. She drew her sword and swung it, but could not reach the mimic dragons.

The nightshades howled and wrapped around Volucris's neck.

Arrows whistled, slammed into Volucris, and fire blazed across him.

"No!" Agnus Dei cried, horror pounding through her. Her eyes burned so badly, she could barely see. "Volucris!"

Flaming arrows peppered him... and Volucris, King of Griffins, fell from the sky.

The ground spun, racing up toward her. Agnus Dei cursed, freed herself from the talons, and scurried up Volucris's leg. She leaped onto his back, but he was still falling. She clung to his fur with her good hand. Her Beam tumbled, and the night swallowed it.

"Fly, Volucris!" she screamed and tugged his fur. The air roared around her. Fire and smoke churned everywhere. They spun. "Fly, damn you, *fly!*"

His eyes rolled back. He gave her a last stare. He cawed softly.

The ground rushed up, black and white and red, mimics racing across it.

Volucris's wings flapped once. He managed to steady himself, to slow his fall.

Mimic javelins flew.

They slammed into him. One tore through his neck, emerging bloody near Agnus Dei's cheek. She cried. Volucris slammed into the ground.

At once, mimics came rushing forward. They began to hack the griffin, climb upon him, and eat his flesh. Agnus Dei howled and leaped to her feet, standing atop Volucris, swinging her sword.

"You will not touch him, scavengers!" she cried. Tears in her eyes, she leaped off Volucris's body, slamming herself into the ranks of mimics.

She fought against hundreds of mimics, snowbeasts, and skeletons. They surrounded her, and she sprayed their blood upon the snow. She could not see her forces. Mother fought across the forest, hundreds of yards away. The others flew above between the flaming arrows and bolts of lightning. She stood alone.

"But I will not die alone," she said and growled. "I will take hundreds of you with me."

Her sword swung. For Requiem. For her parents. For her sister. For Kyrie. She fought. A mimic cut her leg with a blade, and she fell, screaming. She swung her sword, cutting it down. Salvanae lightning rained from the sky, white and purple, torching the dead trees. Fire and smoke filled the air, melting the snow, intolerably hot against her cheeks. She coughed and snarled and narrowed her eyes as she fought.

A howl rose above the din of battle.

A great shadow emerged from the flames, shoving mimics aside.

It came marching toward her, snarling and drooling blood. Mimics fled from it. It was a mimic too, but taller and burlier than the others. It had a bull's head and four arms. Its four hands held an axe, a spear, a sword, and a warhammer.

The bull's lips opened, and it spoke in a growl. "Agnus Dei...." It raised the hand holding the sword. "Do you recognize this hand, Agnus Dei? I thank you for it."

Agnus Dei stared, eyes narrowed. Its hand was long and slender, a woman's hand. *My hand.* Ice washed her belly.

"No," she whispered, shaking her head. *Stars, no.*

The bull mimic smirked. "I will kill you with your own hand, weredragon."

It lunged toward her, its four weapons swinging. Agnus Dei screamed, a howl of horror and rage. *My hand. It has my hand.* She ran through the blood, leaped, and swung her sword.

The mimic's sword clanged with her own. Sparks rained. Its axe swung over her head, narrowly missing it. Its warhammer glanced off her vambrace, and its spear grazed her shoulder.

She screamed, pulled back, and slashed her sword again. The mimic swung its blade, parrying, and thrust. Agnus Dei blocked the blow, but barely. It glanced off her shoulder, tearing her shirt. Its warhammer swung, and she ducked, dodging it. She lashed her blade and hit the mimic's chest. Blood spurted, but it only laughed and swung its axe and sword.

I can't beat it. Stars, I can't win this battle. We can't win this war.

The mimic growled and lashed its spear. She parried, driving it aside, but the axe swung too, and she leaped. It hit her pauldron, denting the steel, sending pain through her.

No! Don't give up. Never give up. Not until death. I will fight so long as I live. She screamed and thrust her blade. The mimic parried, laughing, blood and centipedes spilling from its wound. Hundreds of mimics formed a ring around them, howling, watching the fight.

Agnus Dei leaped sideways, and the axe clanged against her armor. The sword nicked her hip, drawing blood. She spun, swinging her blade, and slammed it into the mimic's leg. She cut deep into its flesh, and when she pulled it free, bugs spilled. The mimic laughed, spraying saliva, and advanced toward her. It lashed all four weapons.

She ducked and parried, and the spear ran down her thigh, scraping skin. The warhammer hit her blade, shattering it.

Agnus Dei fell onto her back, staring up in horror.

She clenched her jaw.

Goodbye, Mother, sister, Kyrie. I love you all. Goodbye.

Its axe came down.

Agnus Dei screamed and raised her arm.

The axe hit her vambrace, shattering it. The blade cut her skin, but the armor had blocked most of the blow. It did not reach bone. *I won't lose my second hand so easily.*

She tossed the hilt of her sword. The broken shards of blade slammed into the mimic's eyes.

It howled.

Agnus Dei leaped to her feet, grabbed its axe, and pulled it free.

The mimic pulled the shattered blade from its face. It had pierced its forehead and right eye. The creature grinned, worms and drool dripping from its maw.

Agnus Dei swung her axe and cut off its hand--*her* hand. It landed at her feet.

"How does it feel, bastard?" she screamed and swung her axe. The blade drove into its neck, tore through the stitches that held the bull's head to the torso, and emerged dripping from the other side.

For a second, the mimic stood still.

Then its head slid off its body and splashed against the ground.

Agnus Dei swung her axe, opening its skull. Snakes filled the skull instead of brains. They fled. The mimic's body tried to keep fighting, but was blind. Agnus Dei hacked at it, screaming hoarsely.

"How does it feel, you bastard?! You will feel this too, Irae. You will feel my blade."

She hacked at it until it fell, cut to pieces. She grabbed a burning branch and tossed it onto the body. Soon it blazed in a pyre, drying her tears.

Her hand burned with it.

Agnus Dei wiped her eyes and spat onto the burning body. She looked around her, panting. Countless mimics still surrounded her. They howled, brandished their blades, and attacked.

TERRA

The battle raged around him, a song of light and fire in the night. Salvanae and mimic dragons battled above. Griffins and nightshades streamed at his sides. Beasts crawled and grunted below him, slamming against Lacrimosa and her troops. Everywhere he looked, he saw flame, smoke, and lightning.

The battle is lost, he realized. *We are overrun.*

He growled, remembering the war that had killed his people, that had shattered his family. His growl turned into a roar.

I am the last bellator. I will defend Requiem to my last breath. If we die here tonight, I die with blood on my talons, and the flesh of my enemies in my jaws.

He howled and dived, knocking between the hordes of flying mimics, and blazed fire across the ruins of King's Forest. Skeletons withered in his flames. Poisoned ran like living torches. And yet more kept coming, wave after wave of them, their ranks stretching into the darkness. Mimic giants, each limb woven of dead bodies, charged through the ranks of Earthen, tossing men and women aside, roaring to the sky.

Terra swooped toward one giant, readying his fire. Before he could reach it, squeals rose in the night around him. A hundred creatures burst from the shadows, shooting toward him. They looked like great bats, but they were mimics. Terra grunted with disgust. Dies Irae had taken men and women, stripped their bodies away below their shoulders, and left them with only heads, outstretched arms, and spines. He had pulled skin between their wrists and tailbones, crafting them wings to flap. They flew at him, biting, their eyes blazing red.

Terra blew his fire, spraying it in all directions. He fought down nausea; he had never seen anything so hideous.

They were people once. Stars, they were people. He clenched his jaw. *But they are not people now. The only mercy I can give them is the mercy of fire.*

He roared, summoned more flame, but had no time to shoot it. More bats emerged from the darkness, smoking and screeching, and flew onto him. They covered his back and crawled along his wings, biting and scratching.

Terra roared and flapped his wings, but the creatures clung to him. Their teeth bit, and he howled in pain. He shook and flapped his tail against them. They scurried across him, screeching. When he knocked one off, three more swooped from the darkness onto him.

"Terra!" a voice cried above.

"Kyrie!" Terra shouted. "Get out of here. You fight the nightshades."

Kyrie swooped down on his griffin, his sword drawn. Ash painted his face and hair. Blood trickled down his cheek. *I remember him a boy,* Terra thought through the haze of pain. *He is a warrior now.* As the mimics bit him, and as the fires burned, Terra felt pride well inside him. *My brother is a warrior of Requiem.*

"You've got something on you," Kyrie said, hovering over him. His griffin leaned sideways, and Kyrie swung his sword, hacking off the bats. They shouted and fell into darkness.

Terra shook himself and turned around, and Kyrie hacked at the other bats, slicing them and knocking them off. Terra's wings blazed in pain. He could barely flap them. He felt the wind rushing through holes the bats had left.

"How are those nightshades?" he called over the roar of battle.

Kyrie ducked, dodging a salvanae that roared above him, flying at a mimic dragon.

"We're handling the nightshades," he shouted back. "It's the ground I'm worried about. The Earthen are being butchered down there."

Terra nodded. "Going to swoop again. I--"

A great dragon of rot and stitch burst from the clouds, tumbling toward them, blazing. It crashed into Terra with smoke and heat and howls, and he saw nothing but fire and darkness.

"Kyrie!" he shouted. He tried to flap his wings, but they burned, and he grimaced. The mimic dragon blazed, but still lived, snapping its teeth and clawing at Terra. He growled and bit into its neck, tearing out a chunk of arms and legs, but could not shake the beast loose. Its weight shoved him down, and he tumbled. He crashed against a salvanae who flew below, and then more mimic bats were on him, biting his tail and legs.

Terra roared, tumbled upside down, and crashed into the ground.

The mimic dragon rolled off him, and Terra shoved himself up. He swung his tail, knocking the mimic's head aside, then spun to face a horde of skeletons racing toward him.

He lashed his tail, knocking them over, and slashed his claws, hitting leaping wolf mimics.

"Kyrie!" he shouted. He looked up, but saw only smoke, coiling salvanae, and flaming arrows. He tried to flap his wings, but the mimic bats were covering them again, biting and weighing them down.

Roars pierced the night, and footfalls shook the ground. Terra turned to face the sounds. From the smoke and fire, three towering reptiles charged forward, each the size of a dragon.

"Perfect," Terra muttered, howled, and roared fire.

He had been blowing flames for hours, and could muster only a weak spray. It barely fazed the reptiles. They crashed forward, stepping onto mimics, and leaned in to bite.

Terra lashed his claws and lacerated one's head. He swiped his tail, hitting another's flank. The third bit his arm and tugged him down.

Growling, Terra kicked and hit one. It fell back, and he blew whatever fire he still had, hitting a second reptile. Each was his size, with claws and fangs like swords. Claws scratched along Terra's back, and he rolled over, kicking and biting.

A reptile crashed down onto him, knocking his breath out. Terra clawed at its face. He pushed it off and tried to fly, but could not. The bats tugged on his wings, pulling them to the ground.

"Here goes nothing," Terra said... and shifted into a human.

The bats fell off him. The reptiles crashed around him. Terra ran between one's legs. He drew his sword as he ran and swung it, slicing the creature's hamstrings. It fell behind him, and Terra ran through the snow. He jumped into the air, shifted, and flew.

The reptiles howled. Terra spun, swooped, and rained his last reserves of fire. The creatures blazed and fell, burning.

Terra soared into the aerial battle, flying through smoke and fire and battling creatures. He gazed over the battle and his heart sank. Thousands of salvanae and griffins lay dead upon the ground, mimics tearing into them. Dozens were falling around him from the sky, bitten, bristly with arrows, crackling with fire. Terra searched the air for the other Vir Requis, but couldn't see them through the smoke and lightning.

When he looked below him, Terra's spirits sank deeper. Dies Irae's ground forces still covered King's Forest, stretching as far as he could see. Lacrimosa and Silva still stood by King's Column, swinging their swords, but their forces had been decimated. Hills of dead Earthen rose around them.

Terra swooped. He had no fire left, but he clawed at skeletons, at mimics, at the dark forces that kept charging. He roared in the night.

KYRIE

His griffin plummeted, blazing. The smoke flew over Kyrie, stinging his eyes, entering his nostrils, choking him. He coughed and clung to the griffin. He wanted to shift, and tried to summon his magic, but too many Animating Stones pulsed around him.

"Gloriae!" he shouted. "Agnus Dei!"

Where *were* the twins? He could see nothing, nothing but smoke, darkness, and the ground rushing up toward him.

"Oh stars," he said, tightened his jaw, and winced.

His griffin crashed into the field, landing atop mimics and skeletons. Bones snapped beneath it. The griffin slid over bodies, snow, and blood, and finally crashed into a fallen log, dead.

Arrows flew.

Kyrie cursed, leaped off the griffin, and crouched behind it. He clutched his sword and gritted his teeth.

"Oh bloody stars, this is bad."

The ground shook. Mimics galloped toward him, centaurs sewn from dead horses and dead women. Their hair was woven of snakes. Their arms ended with bloody blades. They swung those blades at Kyrie.

He crouched, slid through the snow, and hacked at one's legs. He rose and ran, shoving his way between skeletons, bashing them with his blade.

"Lacrimosa!" he cried. "Where are you?"

He saw King's Column rising ahead from smoke and flames. He ran toward it. Hooves galloped behind him, and he turned to see the mimic centaurs chasing him. He cursed, grabbed a spear from a dead man, and tossed it. The spear pierced one centaur's chest. Kyrie ran at the other and clanged swords with it. He ducked, sliced at its legs, and ran.

"Lacrimosa!"

Was she alive? Mimics surrounded him--starfish, centaurs, giants, dogs, bats. He saw no end to them. Dead salvanae, griffins, and Earthen covered the ground. The mimics were feasting upon them, or leaping over them to kill more.

Ten mimic centaurs came galloping toward him from the smoke, bearing lances. Kyrie cursed. He gritted his teeth and raised his blade.

A horn blared. A hundred Earthen leaped from the flames and swung swords.

"For the Earth God!" cried Silva, their High Priest. "Kill the abominations."

Kyrie swung swords with them. Blood spilled and mimic limbs burned. Lightning fell from the sky, hitting more mimics. The salvanae swooped, biting, clawing, killing. Mimic dragons flew around them, tearing them apart with their claws. Blood splattered.

Kyrie glimpsed Lacrimosa ahead, only a hundred yards away. She seemed to glow in the battlefield, her blade bright, her hair sparkling, her face like glimmering marble. King's Column rose above her.

"Lacrimosa!" Kyrie cried again and ran toward her, hacking his way through skeletons. He had to step over the bodies of men, his boot even stepping on one's head. He winced but kept running. Enemies surrounded his queen; he had to protect her.

The skeletons parted before him.

A woman emerged from the shadows.

Kyrie growled. "Umbra."

She gave him a mocking smile and placed her hands on her hips. "Weredragon."

Kyrie knew this one. He had seen her capture the twins in the mine. He had seen her battle Gloriae at the camp. He knew about her chaining down Agnus Dei's hand so that Dies Irae could sever it.

"You might have escaped Gloriae's sword," he told her, "but you won't escape mine."

He raised his dripping blade. Umbra drew her daggers. The skeletons and mimics formed a ring around them, like spectators eager to watch the fight.

Umbra tossed a dagger.

Kyrie parried with his blade, knocking it aside.

Snarling, Umbra tossed two daggers.

Kyrie knelt and raised his blade. He knocked one dagger aside, and the other glanced off his helmet. He ran forward, swinging his sword.

The mimics howled. Umbra slid through the snow, drew two daggers, and crossed them. Kyrie's sword slammed into them, and Umbra twisted her daggers, yanking the sword from his hand. The mimics cheered and Kyrie's heart leaped with horror.

He jumped back, defenseless, as Umbra lashed her daggers. One bit under his arm, grazing him, drawing a line along his ribs. The second dagger hit his raised arm, glancing off the vambrace.

"Are you ready, boy?" Umbra said, smirking.

Kyrie leaped back, dodging her daggers. "I'm not dying yet."

Umbra laughed and winked. "I didn't ask if you're ready to die. I asked if you're ready to become my mimic." She lashed her dagger, nicking his shoulder, and Kyrie cursed. "I will carve you like a pig, and sew you back together into my slave."

Kyrie fell to one knee, grabbed snow, and tossed it at her face. Umbra shook her head, snow in her eyes, and Kyrie jumped forward. He barrelled into her, knocking his shoulder hard into her chest. She grunted, and Kyrie grabbed her wrists and twisted them.

Umbra snarled and clenched her fists around her daggers, pointing their blades toward him. Kyrie grunted, struggling to push her arms away, shocked at her strength. She was as strong as he was--maybe stronger--moving the daggers closer and closer.

Kyrie kicked her shin. She grunted and he headbutted her.

Umbra screamed and fell back. She thrust a dagger. Kyrie ducked and the dagger hit his helmet. He grabbed his sword and swung it, but Umbra parried. The blade hit the snow. A dagger lashed. Kyrie blocked it with his vambrace and pulled his sword up. It sliced Umbra's thigh; she screamed and stabbed her blade.

The dagger scratched Kyrie's neck, and ice flooded him. For an instant, he was sure he was dead. Umbra's eyes widened, and a smile found her lips.

No. It only cut skin, Kyrie thought. He could still breathe, still shout, and he swung his blade.

Umbra parried with both daggers. She tried twisting the sword between them again, but Kyrie pulled his blade back. Umbra lunged at him, leaping through the air, howling, daggers gleaming.

Kyrie thrust his sword forward.

Umbra twisted, parried with one dagger, and brought the other down hard.

Turning sideways, Kyrie dodged it and punched Umbra's shoulder. He knocked her down and stepped on her wrist. She screamed and tossed her second dagger. Kyrie ducked. It flew over his head.

The skeletons and mimics howled. Kyrie placed his sword against Umbra's neck.

"You will be the mimic, Umbra," he said. "Once I cut you, Dies Irae will have no other use for you."

She kicked hard, hitting his knee. The pain suffused him. He fell, cursing, and Umbra leaped up. She drew another dagger, and the blade flashed down.

Kyrie raised his sword.

The blade pierced Umbra's stomach.

The mimics and skeletons roared. Kyrie sucked in his breath, stars floating before him, his blood dripping. Pain spun his head. He pushed himself up, Umbra impaled on the sword, and shoved her down.

She fell and curled up, clutching her stomach. She glared up at him, snarling, a wild animal.

"Weredragon!" she screamed and spat at him. "I curse you. I curse your kind. I curse you all to the abyss, and to pain, and to eternal slavery. You are monsters. You killed my family." Blood filled her mouth and her eyes blazed. "I curse you, weredragon! My lord will destroy you!"

Her clothes soaked with blood, she leaped to her feet and jumped at him. Her daggers lashed. Kyrie parried, thrust his blade, and pierced her chest.

She fell to her knees.

Blood poured down her clothes.

She stared up at him. Kyrie stared back, panting. He expected her to rage, to curse, to spit... but tears filled her eyes. She whimpered.

"Why?" she whispered. "Why do you do this? I miss my husband. I miss my brothers. I'm sorry I couldn't avenge you. I'm sorry."

She fell to her knees, then fell forward, and her face hit the snow. She lay still.

Kyrie knelt by her, surprised to find pity fill him. He placed a hand on her head.

"You fought well," he said softly. "Whatever your pain was, I'm sorry if we caused it. May you find some peace in the world beyond... with your husband and brothers."

He rose to his feet and looked around him. The mimics and skeletons were screeching and fighting the Earthen. Blood and fire filled the night. He looked above him. The nightshades had scattered, but many mimic dragons and bats still flew. Salvanae kept falling; they covered the battlefield, sliced and battered and burned.

"Pup!"

He turned, and his heart leaped to see Agnus Dei running toward him. Snow, blood, and ash covered her. She hacked at a skeleton, jumped over a dead salvanae, and came to fight beside him. They swung their blades, holding back attacking mimics.

"Agnus Dei, what do you know?" he shouted over the din.

"It's bad, pup. Silva's troops are falling fast. Most are dead already. Half of the salvanae have fallen, and most of the griffins."

Kyrie cursed. "Lovely. How's our friend Irae?"

Agnus Dei pierced one of the Poisoned with her blade. "I can't find the bastard. But his troops keep coming at us. There's no end to them. Pup... what do we do?"

A snowbeast leaped at them. They hacked at it, chopping off its legs, and stabbed its mouth until it died.

"I don't know," Kyrie said and cursed again. The monsters kept slamming against them, endless in the night. He looked at Agnus Dei. Blood filled her hair and smeared her face. Her armor was dented and her clothes were mere tatters.

"I love you, Agnus Dei," he said.

She looked at him, fear in her eyes. "I love you too, Kyrie. In this life and in our starlit halls."

They fought back to back as the shadows and horrors of the night surged toward them.

DIES IRAE

He swung his mace, crushing an Earthen's head. The man's
helmet was weak. The spikes in Dies Irae's mace punched through
it. When he yanked his mace back, it came free with a spurt of
blood.

A swordsman attacked at his right--a mere peasant garbed
in Earth God green. The man's chipped blade slammed against
Dies Irae's plate armor, glancing off with sparks. Dies Irae swung
his mace. The man tried to parry, and the mace shattered the
blade. Dies Irae smiled and clubbed his head. When the man fell,
he swung his mace down, finishing the job.

Pathetic, he thought. These were no warriors. This Silva had
brought farmers to fight, their armor weak, their weapons
chipped, their bodies fragile. He swung his mace side to side,
shattering bones. Their blades could not pierce his armor. Their
bodies piled up at his feet.

"Where are you, Lacrimosa?" he said softly. "Where are you,
my lizard harlot? You will be mine, Lacrimosa. I will burn your
body, and sew your head onto one of my women, and you will
warm my bed every night."

He scanned the battlefield, seeking her. *She will try to defend
King's Column.* He turned northward and saw the column rising
from smoke and flame and lightning. Yes, she would be there.

Smirking, Dies Irae began cleaving a path through the
enemy, clubbing them, tossing them left and right. His mimics
fought by him, burly beasts, each with four human heads sewn
together at the napes, so they could see in every direction. They
swung bloody war hammers, shattering their foes' bones.

They drove through the lines of Earthen, and Dies Irae saw
a sight that made him grin. A ring of Earthen surrounded a hill,
guarding a makeshift palisade. Behind the palisade, thousands of
women and children huddled atop the hill.

"Look at them," Dies Irae said to his mimics, laughing.
"Once more, the weredragons bring women and children to fight
their wars."

His mimics laughed, spraying blood and drool from their maws.

Dies Irae clenched his fist. "We smashed their women and children at Lanburg Fields. We will crush these Earth God peasants too."

I will join you soon, Lacrimosa. First I will whet my appetite.

He began driving a path toward the hill, grinning savagely. The Earthen seemed desperate. They crashed against him, shouting, thrusting their spears like madmen. They fell fast. For every mimic they slew, they lost three men. Dies Irae grinned as he clubbed at them, breaking knees, ribs, arms, heads.

He reached the palisade, a frail wall of thin logs, and clubbed it with his mace.

"Tear it down!" he shouted. "Tear down the wall."

His mimics attacked the logs with their war hammers. Within moments, they had breached the palisade. Earthen soldiers crashed against them, howling, torching and cutting them. Mimics fell blazing. The women and children on the hilltop screamed, sobbed, and held one another.

Mimic bodies piled up at the breach in the palisade, smoking. *Weaklings,* Dies Irae thought in disgust. He stepped over their bodies, the smoke rising around him, stinging his eye and filling his lungs. Laughing, he swung his mace at the Earthen who attacked him. Their blades sparked against his armor. He drove forward, mace swinging, and crossed the palisade.

"Mimics, after me!" he bellowed and pointed his mace at the hilltop. "Kill them all."

The women and children screamed.

Roaring, his mimics stormed through the palisade behind him, clashing against the Earthen soldiers. Dies Irae drove forward. The women and children were trying to flee, but the hill was too crowded, and the palisade locked them in. They fell and cried and shouted. Dies Irae laughed. *They doomed themselves.*

He tore through the last line of soldiers, and saw the women and children fleeing. He ran forward, grabbed a child by the hair, and pulled it around. The young girl stared at him with huge, teary eyes. Dies Irae clubbed her head and kicked her body aside.

Her mother knelt and wept over her, and Dies Irae slammed his mace into her skull. The others fled, trampling over one another, a mad rout. Dies Irae grinned and moved between them, swinging his mace. They didn't even fight back. They died around him; it was like slaughtering lambs.

Dies Irae laughed. He had not enjoyed himself so much in many days. He grabbed a baby from its mother, and was about to club it, when a shout rose behind him.

"Let the child go, Irae. Face me instead."

Dies Irae's smile widened.

He turned around slowly.

"Lacrimosa!" he said in delight and tossed the baby aside.

She stood before him, covered in blood and ash. Her armor was dented and nearly falling off. Her clothes were mere tatters. Her hair was singed. She stared with blazing eyes from a blackened face. When she raised her sword, it caught the light and glowed like the stars of Requiem.

"Dies Irae," she said. "Your crusade of death ends here."

He licked his lips. "It's only beginning."

She leaped toward him, swinging her sword.

LACRIMOSA

Stella Lumen hit his breastplate. It sparked and glanced off the steel, shooting pain up Lacrimosa's arm. Dies Irae swung his mace. She leaped back, and the steel arm of Dies Irae swung before her.

Do not parry, she told herself. *He will shatter your blade. Jump. Dance. Attack where his armor is weak.*

His mace swung again. She leaped back, hitting a fleeing child, and bounded forward. She swung her blade toward his helmet, its visor shaped as a monstrous beak. He parried with his arm, and her sword scratched along the steel, showering sparks. He thrust his mace again, and she ducked, dodging it.

Do not parry. Jump. Dance. He is slow and you are fast.

She sprang up, swinging her sword. She aimed for the chain mail under his arm; it was weaker than his plates of steel. But he twisted, and her blade hit his breastplate, not even chipping it.

"You are feisty, lizard whore," he said, eyes blazing behind the slits in his visor. "Will you be feisty in my bed too?"

She growled and thrust her blade. *Do not waste words on him. Jump. Dance. Kill him.* She aimed again for his armpit, but he moved, and the blade slammed against his pauldron. He swung the mace again, and this time Lacrimosa did have to parry. The mace glanced off the base of Stella Lumen, and she caught her breath, sure it would shatter. But her father's blade was strong, stronger than most blades of steel; it glowed and rang. She swung it and hit Dies Irae's helmet. He grunted but did not fall.

"Did you hear the sound your husband made when I butchered him?" Dies Irae said, swinging his mace. "He sounded like a pig in heat. You will make the same sound every night when I thrust into you."

Lacrimosa's eyes stung with smoke. Her limbs shook with weakness. The mimics had cut her, and blood stained her left leg and trickled under her ribs. She did not know how bad the wounds were, but she could still stand, still breathe, still kill.

Leap. Jump. Dance.

And they danced. It was the dance of her life--against death, against evil, against blood and darkness. She danced for life, for the light of her stars, for the love of her family--because she could not stop dancing, she could not give up, not when her children needed her, not when her people cried to her from the earth. She was Queen of Requiem. She was a widow. She was a mother. So she swung her sword, and cried to her stars, and lashed her blade at the man who'd raped her, who'd killed her family, who'd shattered the halls of her home. She danced and cried and pierced his armor below the arm, so that he screamed and his blood spilled.

"It's over, Irae," she said, face drenched in sweat. He clutched his wound, glaring at her. "It's over. I end your reign this night."

She swung her sword.

Snarling, he raised his mace and slammed it against her wrist.

Lacrimosa screamed. She felt the bones in her wrist snap. The blade fell from her hand. Dies Irae swung the mace again, and she could not breathe. Pain filled her, white and blinding. Her shoulder shattered. She fell to her knees, gasping for breath. She tried to leap, to run, but he kicked her, and she fell.

Stars of Requiem... give me strength. Help me rise.

He stepped onto her neck, his boot bloody, made from the golden scales of a Vir Requis child. She could not breathe or speak. He lifted her sword with bloody fingers.

"My my," he said. "You still struggle beneath me?"

She tried to speak, but his foot constricted her, nearly snapping her neck. *I'm sorry, Ben. I'm sorry, Gloriae, Agnus Dei, Kyrie. I love you all so much. I love you.*

Blackness was spreading before her eyes. Through blurry tears, she could see that the women and children had fled the hill. She smiled softly. *I saved them. He will kill me now, but I saved them.*

He lifted Stella Lumen above her. The Draco Stars shone above between the smoke and flames, glittering across the sword.

"I'll kill you like I killed your husband, whore," he said. "I'll butcher you with your own sword."

Stars floated around her. Stars glowed on the hilt of her sword, and in the sky beyond the fire and shadow--the stars of her life. The light of Requiem fell upon her, waiting for her. *I will join you soon, Ben. I will join you soon, Mother and Father.*

Dies Irae lifted his foot off her neck.

"Will you plead for your life now, weredragon?" he asked. "Beg for it."

His boot crushed her shattered wrist, pinning her down. She saw her husband again, her love, her eternal companion. They danced in the halls of Requiem among marble columns. They raised their daughters in the light of stars and the song of harps. They fled together, hid together, fought together. She sat with him again by the stream outside Confutatis, the night they had summoned the griffins. *The young ones went seeking supplies, and we kissed, and he loved me by the water.*

She smiled softly. It began to snow. The snowflakes glided, so beautiful to her, and coated her.

"I do not fear death," she whispered, staring up with blurred eyes. "I do not fear my father's blade. But yes, I beg you, Dies Irae. If you still remember Requiem... if you still have any pity in you... spare me. Spare me for the child that I carry within me."

His eyes widened.

"Pregnant," he whispered. "With his child."

Her lips parted. The blade slammed down, a streak of starlight.

She gasped.

Blood bloomed across her breast, poppies in the snow.

She tried to speak, but no words left her lips. He stood above her, boots crushing her. He twisted the blade, his eyes alight. But Lacrimosa felt no pain, only love and warmth. She smiled softly and her fingers uncurled.

Harps played, and the stars seemed so close, their light no longer cold and distant, but warm against her. She looked at King's Column, which rose from the fire, and it seemed to her like the halls of Requiem stood again, all in white, awash with light. The birches rustled around her, their leaves silver.

"I return to you, Ben," she whispered, tears in her eyes. "I love you."

She held his hand as starlight flooded her.

KYRIE ELEISON

He was running uphill when he saw her fall.

His heart froze.

He gasped.

Lacrimosa. Stars, no.

"Mother!" Agnus Dei shouted beside him, voice torn.

Stars, no, Kyrie prayed. *She lost a father already, don't let her lose her mother too.*

"Lacrimosa!" he shouted and ran uphill, his eyes burning. Smoke flowed around him. Fire licked at his boots. He ran, shouting, horror pulsing through him. *Stars, no, please.* He shoved his way between battling Earthen and mimics.

He reached the hilltop and saw Dies Irae laughing, Stella Lumen bloody in his hand. Lacrimosa lay at his feet, eyes glassy and staring. Kyrie shouted, eyes blurred, and leaped at him. He swung his sword.

The blade slammed against Dies Irae's breastplate. Rubies flew from it. Dies Irae laughed and swung his mace, and Kyrie leaped back, dodging it.

"Murderer!" Agnus Dei screamed, swinging her blade at Dies Irae. Her hair was wild, her eyes blazing. "I'll kill you, bastard! I'll kill you!"

Her blade slammed against his helmet, knocking his head sideways, but he stayed standing. He swung down his mace. Agnus Dei leaped back, and the mace grazed her thigh. She screamed and thrust her blade.

Shouting, Kyrie swung his sword too. He wanted to go to Lacrimosa. *Is she dead? Oh stars, is she dead?* But he dared not. He leaped onto Dies Irae, screaming, the world turned red. He slammed the pommel of his sword against Dies Irae's visor, a monstrous beak of steel. It dented, but Dies Irae only laughed.

Agnus Dei whipped around him and slammed her sword behind his knees, where his plates of armor joined. Dies Irae shouted. Agnus Dei swung the blade again, tears on her cheeks, shouting hoarsely. Blood splashed down his armor.

Dies Irae fell.

"You killed her!" Agnus Dei screamed, weeping. "You killed my parents, bastard."

Dies Irae was on his knees, blood seeping from his legs. More blood poured from his armpit, trickling over his armor.

"Knock him down!" Agnus Dei screamed and swung her sword into his helmet.

Dies Irae swung his mace at Kyrie, but missed. Kyrie hacked at his helmet too, and kicked, and Dies Irae fell onto his back. His blood darkened the snow.

Wet, gurgling laughter came from his helmet. "Yes, weredragons, fight me. I like it when you fight me."

Kyrie placed his foot against Dies Irae's chest, holding him down. He slammed his sword against the beak visor, knocking it open.

Bloody stars.

Kyrie froze, nausea filling him. For a moment, he could not move.

Moons ago, Benedictus had taken Dies Irae's left eye in battle. Today Dies Irae wore a new eye, sewn into his face with bloody stitches. It was the eye of a horse, three times the size of his right eye. It spun madly. Blood poured down his forehead, seeping into it.

"Stars," Kyrie whispered. "What have you done to yourself?"

Dies Irae opened his mouth and cackled. His human teeth were gone. Instead, wolf teeth were screwed into his rotting, bleeding gums.

"I am strong now," Dies Irae said, blood bubbling in his mouth. "I am mimic. I will live forever. I am too strong for you to kill."

He struggled to rise, but Kyrie kept his boot pressed against his breastplate. Agnus Dei stepped on his mace, pinning it down. Roaring, she ripped off his helmet and tossed it aside. Kyrie placed the tip of his sword against Dies Irae's neck.

"Call off your troops," he said.

He laughed, spraying blood. "Weredragon, you—"

"Call off your troops!" Kyrie shouted, pushing down his blade enough to tear the skin. A bead of blood trickled down Dies Irae's neck.

Dies Irae laughed and coughed. His chest rose and fell. "Mimics!" he shouted. "You heard the weredragon. Place down your arms. This is between the weredragons and me now."

The mimics grunted, howled, but obeyed. They tossed their weapons into the snow. The blades clanked against one another. The Earthen paused too from battle, panting, their cloaks red and black with blood.

Kyrie stared down at this man, this beast, this wretched creature who bled and cackled. *He's no longer a man,* he thought. *He stopped being a man moons ago, maybe years ago.*

"Agnus Dei, go to Lacrimosa," he said, never removing his eyes from Dies Irae.

Agnus Dei ran to her mother, knelt, and cradled her in her arms. She cried to the sky, a wail so heartbroken, that Kyrie knew that Lacrimosa was dead.

He tightened his fingers around the hilt of his sword, keeping the blade pressed against Dies Irae's throat.

"You killed her," he said. "You killed so many. Why, Irae? Why?"

The creature cackled, his horse eye spinning wildly. Blood dripped down his teeth. "You...," he said, coughed, and laughed. "You are weredragon. You infested this world. You will die. You will be my mimics. You will be my slaves."

He tried to rise, but Kyrie held him down, his boot against the creature's breastplate. Agnus Dei cried and howled behind him. Kyrie realized that the entire battle had paused; the armies watched from a distance, smoke rising between them. From the corner of his eye, he saw that Terra and Memoria had joined the hill. They knelt by Agnus Dei in human forms, watching him.

"No, Irae," Kyrie said softly to the creature below him. "No. You failed. You murdered so many. You destroyed so much. But you failed. It has already ended for you."

The creature laughed, spitting blood. Maggots squirmed in his mouth. "Try to kill me, weredragon. You cannot. You are a lizard. You are weak." He coughed.

Kyrie shook his head, and suddenly his eyes stung, and he could see Benedictus again, hear the man's voice, feel his spirit with him.

"No, I will not kill you," he said. "King Benedictus wanted to put you on trial. He wanted the world to know your sins. I will not give you the honor of dying in battle." His took a deep breath. "I will honor his wishes. Dies Irae, you will live today, and you will watch Requiem be reborn, and you will stand trial in her halls. If you are found guilty of your crimes, you will spend your life as our prisoner, and rot in a cell as our nation blooms."

Agnus Dei raised her head, her eyes red.

"Yes," she whispered, holding her mother's body. "He will stand trial."

Terra and Memoria held each other, covered in blood and ash, their eyes huge and haunted. Fires burned behind them, and they both nodded. *Yes*, their eyes told him. *He will stand trial.*

Fire crackled. Smoke unfurled. Mimics and Earthen whispered and bustled.

A long shadow fell upon the battlefield. Covered in ash and blood, Gloriae emerged from the smoke and fire.

She walked forward, her eyes green ice, her face blank, her sword drawn in her hand. Her hair flew in the wind, black with smoke.

"Gloriae," Dies Irae whispered, choking on his blood.

Gloriae the Gilded, the Light of Osanna, Heir to Requiem, walked toward the man she had once called Father. She said nothing. Her face was a dead mask

"Gloriae," Kyrie said softly, and she shoved him.

He fell off Dies Irae and stumbled two steps. Before he could leap back, Gloriae pointed her sword at Dies Irae's neck.

"Stand back, Kyrie," she said quietly. "This is between me and him."

"Gloriae, he--"

"Stand back, Kyrie!" she shouted, and her eyes blazed. Kyrie froze.

For sixteen years, Gloriae lived captive to this man, he reminded himself. *Let her say what she will.* He stood watching.

"You murdered May," she whispered.

Dies Irae nodded. "I raped her too. What is your point?"

She bared her teeth. Her knuckles were white around the hilt of her sword. "You murdered my parents."

He shook his head. "But I am your parent, child. I created you when I took the lizard queen. You are mine, child. You are mine."

Her voice shook, and her eyes burned. "I am not your child."

He raised a bloody hand to her. "Gloriae. Leave these weredragons. Join me. We will rule again. You are forgiven, child. You are still beautiful and pure. Leave these creatures who corrupted you. Let us rule together like we used to. Look at you. You wear rags now. You hide in mud and grime. Join me, and I will forge you new armor of gold, and you will rule a great empire again, not these piles of ruin."

Gloriae stared down at him, her lips tight, and her eyes dampened. She shook her head. Her voice trembled.

"I believed you once," she said. "I loved you once. I fought for your ideals. For glory, light, order and justice." She gestured at the battlefield. "Look around you, Irae. Look at the creatures you created, that you brought to war. There is no light and justice here. You always told me that you fought monsters. But you have become the monster, leading a host of them. I still believe in light and justice and glory. But I found it among the mud and ruins. You will pay for what you've done. But you will not stand trial; I will not allow it."

Dies Irae stared up at her, eyes widening. "Gloriae. Please. Gloriae, I--"

Gloriae screamed.

Smoke unfurled and fire crackled.

"You will die on the blade that you forged me." She drove Per Ignem into his neck.

Blood painted the snow.

The stars glowed.

Dawn rose in the east, and Kyrie fell to his knees, and held the body of his queen, and wept. His siblings held him. His beloved cried with him. Sunrise flowed over King's Forest, a dawn of blood, tears, and light.

Kyrie lowered his head. *All victory is vanished; all joy is forever lost.* His queen had fallen.

GLORIAE

She stood apart from the others. With dry eyes, she stared at the grave, and at the last survivors of Requiem who huddled together with tears and whispers.

Another funeral, she thought. *Another sacrifice for our nation, our life, our sky.*

The wind blew, ruffled her hair, and stung her cheeks. It sneaked under her breastplate to kiss her skin. The wind too seemed to cry, but Gloriae could not. She could shed no tears, could whisper no whispers, could not embrace the others and share their pain. Her mourning was her own. *They will think me cold,* she knew. *Gloriae the Gilded, the warrior of ice.*

Her pain was a private thing; it always had been. The pain of her exile. The pain of losing May. The pain of finding her true parents, only to lose them like this, so quickly, a flash of stars soon overcome with clouds.

Gloriae rested her hand on the hilt of her sword. Her mother's sword. Stella Lumen, diamonds upon its grip, shaped like the Draco constellation.

"I will carry this sword, Mother," she whispered.

Crows flew above, circling the sky. *The crows have returned. Winter is ending.* Gloriae took slow steps toward the grave. The others saw her approach and pulled apart silently, tears in their eyes. She saw the tombstone behind them. It rose beside the grave of Benedictus--twin stones.

It was tall and white, taller than Gloriae, carved of marble from Requiem's fallen columns. Kyrie had carved text upon it.

Queen Lacrimosa
and her sleeping child
lights of Requiem
our guiding stars

Now tears did sting Gloriae's eyes. She thought of this unborn child, the sister or brother she would never know.

"He would have been a great son of Requiem," she whispered. "I would have taught him. But he would not have been a warrior. He would not kill like I have killed. He would have been a ruler of peace. I would have loved him."

Agnus Dei approached her, and placed her arms around her, and leaned her head against Gloriae's shoulder. Gloriae held her sister, lowered her eyes, and found tears streaming down to her lips.

"I'm glad I have you, sister," Agnus Dei whispered. "I love you."

Gloriae's tears fell, and she held her sister tight. "I love you too," she whispered.

The others joined their embrace. Terra, Memoria, and Kyrie. Young, brave, foolish Kyrie, the boy who had grown up in fire, the warrior whose promise whispered within her. She looked at him over Agnus Dei's shoulder, and he met her eyes.

They flew over Requiem. Five dragons, streaming over ruins and snow. The last of their kind, diving through the clouds, roaring their fire. The wind filled Gloriae's nostrils, streamed under her wings, and stung her eyes. She blew flame and flew, like she would fly on Aquila, and she roared for her new home.

This is my home now, Gloriae thought. She who had lived in palaces, who wore gold and samite, who killed for light and glory... she lived now among ruins and whispers, but this was her home. *This is who I am. This is where I find my strength.*

No bones remained here. They had buried and burned the slain mimics and Earthen. The living beasts had fled with the death of their master; Silva and his men still hunted them. For this day, peace had come to Requiem. Only ruins. Graves. Wind rustling the last snow. Gloriae roared her fire.

She found herself flying to King's Forest. Memories would always haunt this place, but Gloriae would not avoid them. She had seen horror there, and anguish like she'd never known... but there too pulsed the heart of Requiem, and she flew toward it through her fire and the icy wind. The others flew around her. *We are a new herd, like the herds of old.*

She landed by King's Column. Even in dragon form, she felt dwarfed by this column; it towered above her. The other dragons landed around her, their claws silent in the snow.

Gloriae shifted into human form, drew her sword, and place its tip on the earth. She knelt before the column, and she prayed.

"Draco stars," she whispered. "I have never prayed to you before. But I beg that you hear my words now. I am Gloriae, daughter of Benedictus and Lacrimosa, a warrior of Requiem. Let me serve you now. Let me defend you with sword, claw, fang, and fire."

The others knelt around her and whispered their own prayers. For Requiem. For their constellation. For the memory of the dead and their souls in starlit halls.

Gloriae closed her eyes and lowered her head. "And for you, Father and Mother. For you, the brother or sister I never knew. I will restore this land for your memory. I swear this to you. I love you always."

When she rose to her feet, she found the others looking at her strangely, their eyes soft.

"It is time," Memoria whispered and smiled sadly.

Kyrie nodded. "It is time," he agreed.

Gloriae frowned. She looked from them to Terra and to her sister. They stared back, solemn.

"It is time," Agnus Dei whispered.

"For what, sister?" Gloriae asked, sword still drawn. "Tell me."

Agnus Dei approached her, smiling sadly, her eyes soft. She placed her hand on Gloriae's shoulder.

"It is time that we crown a new queen of Requiem."

Gloriae couldn't help it. She laughed. "Sister, I... do you mean to crown me?"

She nodded. "You were born before me, Gloriae. Only a few minutes before me, but you are still the rightful heir."

Gloriae laughed again, though her eyes stung. She looked at the others, one by one, but they all stared back solemnly. She shook her head in bewilderment.

"My friends... the Oak Throne is burned. It burned years ago. Our halls are shattered."

Kyrie shook his head. "King's Column still stands. We stand in the hall of Requiem's kings, as many generations have stood before us."

Gloriae swept her arm around her. "I see ruins. Only five of us remain. Would I rule over a single column, a sister, and three friends? There is no more meaning to ceremony, to titles, to queens or kings."

Agnus Dei nodded. "Maybe, Gloriae. Ceremony and titles might be meaningless now. But not to me. Not in my heart. Not if we're to survive, and honor the memory of our fathers, and rebuild this land. For seventy-six generations, since King Aeternum, we have passed down the reign and ruled here. For our stars, and for those who died, let us continue their tradition." She looked at King's Column, and she took Gloriae's hand and squeezed it. "Maybe ceremony and titles are still worth clinging to."

Gloriae lowered her head, and her throat felt tight. She remembered her arrows, lance, and crossbow. She remembered leading her griffins on the hunt, killing and burning. She remembered the child she had killed, a young boy with teary eyes, and how her blade had pierced him.

"I... I cannot be queen," she whispered. "I do not have a good heart. I am not just, or righteous, or gentle. I am not like you, Agnus Dei, or like you, Kyrie. You two have kind souls. You feel love, you feel compassion. But I am cold. I am steel; all I know is war. My hands are stained with the blood of innocents, even children. I killed children when I myself was a child. How could I, who sinned, who killed, who did such evil... how could I rule Requiem?"

Kyrie approached her, eyes somber. A scar ran along his forehead, a lingering whisper from the Battle of King's Forest. A beard was growing over his cheeks, frosted white, and Gloriae found herself wondering at how he had grown. She had fought a boy once, and mocked him, and hurt him; the war had killed that boy.

"Many kings and queens of Requiem have sinned," he said. "They enslaved griffins. They cast out Dies Irae from their court, and scorned him, and drove him to his rage. From the fire, we are reborn, purer, stronger. This is true of Requiem herself. It is true of you too, Gloriae. You have been raised to destroy Requiem. Let your hands be those that rebuild it. This is just." He knelt before her and lowered his head. "My queen."

Agnus Dei knelt too, tears in her eyes. "My sister. My queen."

Terra and Memoria knelt next, their heads lowered, their drawn swords held with tips in the snow.

"My queen."

"My queen."

Gloriae looked at them kneeling around her, and looked up at King's Column, and looked at the sky strewn with winter's last clouds.

I am no longer Gloriae the Gilded, she thought. *Let that woman fade into the wind. I am Gloriae of Requiem, of starlight and fire.*

She whispered softly, and the others whispered along with her, echoing her words.

"As the leaves fall upon our marble tiles, as the breeze rustles the birches beyond our columns, as the sun gilds the mountains above our halls--know, young child of the woods, you are home, you are home. Requiem! May our wings forever find your sky."

KYRIE ELEISON

He stood alone in the snow, the burned trees icy around him. He wrapped his cloak around him and watched the sunrise. It spread pink and yellow fingers across the sky, rivers of dawn.

"I miss you, Mirum," he said softly. "We used to watch the sunrise together from Fort Sanctus above the sea."

He sighed, his shoulders heavy. Requiem was free now, beautiful under the snow, and they had defeated their enemies... but Kyrie couldn't stop thinking about all those he had lost in this war. His parents. The Lady Mirum, his foster sister and best friend. Benedictus, his king and mentor. Lacrimosa, his queen, his inspiration. So many had died. So much pain still filled him, even in this victory.

He looked over the valleys and hills and took a deep breath. *But I have Agnus Dei,* he thought. *I have my brother and sister. And I have Gloriae.*

He tightened his cloak around him. Gloriae. Who was she to him? He had hated her once. He had fought her. He had watched her laugh as Dies Irae murdered Mirum. And... he had lain with her in the ruins of Osanna. He had sworn to defend her with his sword. She was his queen, his friend, and....

"Kyrie."

He turned his head and saw her emerge from the ruins. Gloriae no longer wore her armor. Today she wore a green dress Silva had given her, a silver cloak lined with fur, and a pair of moleskin gloves. Her golden locks cascaded over her shoulders, and her eyes stared at him, solemn.

"Gloriae."

She approached him, stood behind him, and placed her hands on his shoulders. She laid her head against him.

"Kyrie," she said softly, "do you know what I want to tell you this morning?"

His throat itched and his fingers tingled. "Yes."

She walked around him, faced him, and held his hands. "It's been over three moons now, four I think. You remember that night, when autumn leaves covered the ground."

243

He nodded, and his heart thrashed against his ribs. His eyes stung. "I remember," he whispered.

She embraced him and kissed his cheek. "I told Agnus Dei," she said. "She's happy for us, Kyrie. She won't let this change what you two have. I won't either. This is a great blessing."

Her eyes were soft, and she smiled. He smiled too, his breath shook, and he held Gloriae as they watched the sunrise.

"Are you still ready, Kyrie?" she whispered.

He nodded. "I am. I've never wanted anything more."

They walked through the ruins and frosty trees, and saw King's Column before them. Terra and Memoria stood there, garbed in green and silver, their swords at their hips. They smiled at him, eyes damp.

When he saw Agnus Dei, Kyrie's breath caught.

She stood between his siblings, head lowered shyly, arms behind her back. When she looked up at him, her eyes were shy, questioning, trembling with tears. She was more beautiful than he'd ever seen her. She wore a green gown and flowers in her hair. She smiled through her tears, and reached out to him. On her left arm, she wore a giltwood hand Silva had carved her, its fingers moving on invisible joints.

Kyrie approached his bride and held her hands, one hand soft and warm, the other hard and smooth. They walked to stand before King's Column, and gazed over the shattered hall of Requiem's kings. Snowflakes fell around them, filling their hair.

Terra and Memoria stood at their sides. Gloriae stood before them, eyes solemn.

"This is a sad day," the Queen of Requiem whispered. "This is a day when we still mourn those we lost. But I know that Benedictus and Lacrimosa are watching over us. They stand now in our starlit halls, and they smile."

Agnus Dei nodded, biting her lip. Tears spiked her lashes.

Kyrie could never afterwards remember Gloriae's words. She spoke of love, and joy, and a future for Requiem. And he spoke too--spoke of meeting Agnus Dei, of loving her always, of growing old by her side. But words glided like snowflakes, and he thought only of her eyes, and her smile, and the light in her hair, and he marvelled at how much joy she gave him, and how the mere touch of her hand spread warmth through him.

He kissed her, arms around her. She mussed his hair and laughed.

"Pup," she said, and winked, and cried.

They walked through the forest, hand in hand.

The snowflakes fell, and melted, and the ice left the trees. They planted gardens, and for the first time in years, life grew in Requiem: sweet peas, and mint, and squash, and enough flowers for Memoria to pick every day, and place inside the cave where they lived. And they lived--like the wild dragons of old, nesting upon cliffs, sleeping in caves, roaring in the dawn and herding across the sky.

"It's a new spring," Kyrie said as they planted birches around the ruins of their temples. He brushed soil off his hands. "These trees will be saplings next year, and the year after that. But when our children pray here, tall trees will shade them, and countless leaves will rustle around them."

The twins smiled and placed their hands upon their bellies.

Under summer's blue skies, Gloriae lay in their cave and shouted and clutched Kyrie's hand. Memoria delivered their child, and held up the squalling, red creature that Kyrie thought looked so ugly, he couldn't help but laugh and cry.

"It's a girl," Memoria said. "A golden-haired girl."

Gloriae took the baby into her arms, and nursed her, and kissed her head. "Her name is Luna."

Autumn winds blew, and Kyrie found himself in the cave again, holding Agnus Dei's hand as she shouted, and cursed him, and swore to beat him bloody. When Memoria held up the child, Kyrie thought this one ugly too, wrinkled and red and squealing. This babe had curly black hair, like lambs' wool.

"It's a son," Memoria said, smiling, and placed the baby in Agnus Dei's arms.

Agnus Dei nodded, her brow and hair sweaty, and kissed the child. "His name is Ben."

Once he had lain in blood, dying. Once he had hidden in a tower, trapped and frightened. Once he had fought wars, and killed, and seen those he loved die. Two years after he escaped Fort Sanctus, flying over the sea with Dies Irae in pursuit, Kyrie found himself waging a new war--battling soiled swaddling clothes, and cleaning baby sickness off his shoulders, and nursing sick and crying creatures that he loved deeply. *I am happy,* he often thought, even when bone-tired after hunting, farming, tending to the babes, and fleeing Agnus Dei when she chased him for breaking a plate or forgetting to weed the garden.   *I am happy.*

And yet... at nights, he often lay awake, and those memories returned to him. Lady Mirum, her skull shattered, falling upon the tower. Benedictus, dead in his arms. Lacrimosa, blood pouring down her chest, soaking the snow around her. When night fell, and the others slept around him in the cave, he stared into the darkness, and still saw the mimic bats, and the eyes of the nightshades, and the fire and blood of Lanburg Fields.

He would gently remove Agnus Dei's arm which draped over him, and tiptoe out of their cave, and stand in the darkness. He would stare into the horizon, and wait for sunlight, and he would miss them. Mirum. Benedictus. Lacrimosa. His friends. *I am happy. I've never been happier.* And he knew then that time did not heal all hurts. Not all memories faded. The scar on his forehead would remain; so would these terrors in the night, and this pain in his chest.

He'd return into the cave, and sneak back into their pile of furs, and kiss Agnus Dei's cheek as she mumbled and shifted. *I love you, Agnus Dei. Now. Forever. I am happy so long as I have you.*

When the first snow fell, they gathered in their cave. The twins, holding their babes. Kyrie and his siblings. Seven Vir Requis, the last of their kind. They ate the sweet peas, and the squash, and the turnips, and the other crops they grew in their garden. And they ate the game they hunted beyond Requiem's borders, in the forests of Osanna where Silva now reigned.

And for the first time, they spoke of it.

"What happens when they grow?" Kyrie said softly, watching his children.

The twins looked up at him, rocking their babes in their arms. Terra and Memoria looked at each other, then back at him.

Agnus Dei answered him. "I don't know," she said softly.

Kyrie touched Ben's cheek. The baby reached out and held his pinky finger.

"They... they have nobody but each other," he said. "Brother and sister. How will... well, I mean...." He tongue felt heavy. "Being related, how would...."

Agnus Dei groaned. "Pup, I think the babies are more eloquent than you. You want to ask how they'd *breed*. How our people will continue, if the entire next generation is brother and sister."

He bristled and felt his cheeks redden. "Well, I might have phrased it better than that, if you'd have given me a chance."

Agnus Dei rolled her eyes, but it was Gloriae who answered.

"He was terrified of it."

They all looked at her. She stared at them over her meal, face blank.

"Who, Gloriae?" Kyrie asked her. "Terrified of what?"

"Dies Irae," she answered, and Kyrie shuddered. He saw the others shudder too. They had not spoken his name since he had died.

"Terrified of what?" Kyrie asked softly.

She stared at him, eyes icy. "Of our magic. Of our curse. He claimed that weredragons would rape the women of his empire, and infect them with reptilian blood. That their disease could spread." She caressed Luna's hair and sighed. "Many men and women of Osanna died too; they too want to rebuild the world."

They all looked at one another, the words sinking in. Terra laughed softly. Memoria raised her eyebrows, then laughed too. Agnus Dei looked at them all in shock. Kyrie only sighed--a deep, contented sigh.

Yes, he thought. *I am happy.*

Gloriae--the Light of Osanna, the Maiden of Steel, the Queen of Requiem--smiled. She rocked her baby, and her voice was warm.

"It's time to mingle with the people who feared us, hated us, and hunted us... and give them a bit of our magic."

THE END

AFTERWORD

It was a long journey, and we've come to its end. The story that began in *Blood of Requiem*, at Fort Sanctus by the sea, is now complete. I hope you enjoyed reading about Requiem. I'm grateful and humbled that you've chosen to share this story with me.

The question now is... will there be more? Will I write a fourth *Song of Dragons* book?

The answer is... maybe. One story arc has ended, but there are more stories to explore. What will happen to Ben and Luna? Will we spend more time with Terra and Memoria? Will the Vir Requis rebuild their home, or will new enemies threaten it?

If you'd like me to write more *Song of Dragons* books, let me know. Email me at Daniel@DanielArenson.com or message me on Facebook. And please help spread the word—talk about *Song of Dragons* online or simply over your backyard fence.

If you'd like to read more of my work, I've also written the fantasy novels *Firefly Island*, *The Gods of Dream*, *Flaming Dove*, and *Eye of the Wizard*. That last one seems especially popular among *Song of Dragons* fans.

Thank you, dear reader, for reading this story. I hope we meet again between the pages of another book.

Daniel, 2011

NOVELS BY DANIEL ARENSON

Standalones:

Firefly Island (2007)
The Gods of Dream (2010)
Flaming Dove (2010)
Eye of the Wizard (2011)

Song of Dragons:

Blood of Requiem (2011)
Tears of Requiem (2011)
Light of Requiem (2011)

KEEP IN TOUCH

www.DanielArenson.com
Daniel@DanielArenson.com
Facebook.com/DanielArenson
Twitter.com/DanielArenson

Acknowledgements

I'd like to thank several people for their help with *Light of Requiem*.
Thank you beta readers Greg Baum and Janelle DeCelis.
Thank you Anne Victory for editing the manuscript.
Thank you authors Michael Crane, David Dalglish, Robert Duperre, Amanda Hocking, Jason Letts, David McAfee, Daniel Pyle, and Sean Sweeney.